Praise for t

You will be captivated by this beautifully written story and the characters come to life right from the start. *Shelley's Book Case on Deadly Wedding*

I love this series. The attention to detail, the well plotted mystery, and the burgeoning romance in the background provide a captivating look into a fascinating era. *Cozy Up with Kathy on Deadly Wedding*

If you're looking for an all-around good read, this one is for you. *Booklady's Booknotes on Deadly Wedding*

I loved Kate Parker's Victorian Mystery Series. She has a great writing style and her stories feature strong women. I knew I would enjoy this book before I even started reading, but she exceeded all of my expectations. *Escape with Dollycas into a Good Book on Deadly Scandal*

And I'm ever so glad to hear that this is part of a series. It's hard to get enough of our favorite characters, and Olivia definitely ranks on my list. I can't wait to see what she gets up to next! *Back Porchervations on Deadly Scandal*

Kate Parker has hit this one (out) of the park and I am eagerly awaiting the release date of the next. *Kimberlee in Girl Lost in a Book on Deadly Scandal*

Also by Kate Parker

The Victorian Bookshop Mysteries

The Vanishing Thief
The Counterfeit Lady
The Royal Assassin
The Conspiring Woman
The Detecting Duchess

The Deadly Series

Deadly Scandal
Deadly Wedding
Deadly Fashion
Deadly Deception
Deadly Travel

The Milliner Mysteries

The Killing at Kaldaire House
Murder at the Marlowe Club

Deadly Fashion

Kate Parker

JDP PRESS

Deadly Fashion copyright © 2017 by Kate Parker

ISBN: 978-0-9964831-8-6 [e-book]

ISBN: 978-0-9964831-9-3 [print]

Published by JDP Press

Cover design by Lyndsey Lewellen of
Lewellen Designs

Dedication

For John, as always

London, September 1938

CHAPTER ONE

When the butler opened the door and announced "Mrs. Denis and Miss Seville," I entered a drawing room that nearly took my breath away. I was certain it was one of the smaller ground-floor rooms tucked discreetly into the back of the palatial Mayfair house, since we were only from a newspaper and no one important.

However, the use of satin fabrics in a restful green, along with priceless paintings and rugs thick enough to bounce on, left me momentarily speechless. Jane's jaw dropped when she spied the Rubens on the far wall.

The house belonged to one of the oldest titles in England, the Dukes of Marshburn. They'd had hundreds of years to perfect this room, and they'd used the time wisely.

The blonde who rose to greet us was tall and slim like her father, the duke, and had inherited his unfortunate regal nose and weak chin. "Hello, I'm Lady Patricia Saunders-North. Come in, won't you? I thought you might want to ask questions now while you set up the camera. Mimi should have been here by now, bringing my wedding gown and part of my trousseau."

I was startled by her nasally voice. I squeaked out, "Mimi?"

"Yes. Mimi Mareau, my designer and dressmaker."

"*Mimi Mareau* designed your wedding gown?" I hope it sounded more like a professional question and not a screech of excited envy. I was going to meet the famous Mimi.

My idol, Mimi Mareau.

Meet *and* interview, I mentally added with crossed fingers.

"Yes," Lady Patricia replied. "Isn't it too perfect to have a wedding gown designed by a leading couture house from Paris? Of course, she and Daddy are friends. He arranged it for me."

"And she brought the dresses over to London for your fitting?" Just how good friends were the duke and the Frenchwoman? If gossip was to be believed...

"She's over here doing the costuming for a play in the West End, as well as opening a salon here in London. Isn't it too wonderful?" Lady Patricia dropped gracefully onto the sofa.

She didn't offer us a seat. "Mimi'll be traveling back and forth for the next few months, now that her autumn collection has been shown in Paris."

"Will you want your photograph taken today in your wedding dress, or would you rather wear something more seasonal," Jane asked, pausing just a fraction before adding, "my lady?"

"Oh, I thought this frock would do, don't you, Miss—?"

"Seville," Jane answered. "Yes. Your dress will photograph well."

"I doubt Mimi is ready for me to be photographed in my wedding dress. This is just a fitting. There will still be a great deal of work to do on it." Lady Patricia spoke with a note of finality.

"What made you decide to marry in November?" I asked the young woman.

"Everyone will be in town for the Opening of Parliament. Makes it easier to gather all one's friends together for the big day."

While Jane took Lady Patricia's photograph, I asked, "It's only two months away now. Are you getting excited?" I hoped she'd give me a quote that made her sound less like a cold fish. *Daily Premier* readers liked their subject matter in the society columns to sound wholesome and enthusiastic. There was enough bad news on the front pages, with Hitler making threats.

"Of course."

No warmth. No excitement. This was going to be a difficult interview.

"Miss Mareau," the butler intoned like a tolling bell. I hadn't thought there were any butlers left who wore a morning coat, a high, stiff collar, and breeches with silk stockings. My father had once told me all the impressive butlers had disappeared after the Great War. It must be the duke who required the butler to dress like a Regency specter.

"Oh, Mimi," Lady Patricia said, rushing over to give her an air-kiss, "let's see what you brought me."

Mimi Mareau held up a cloth-covered gown in her free hand as she disengaged herself with the other.

"Brigette is bringing in the others. We'll have fun doing a fitting, yes?" she said in a thick French accent.

I almost answered her and had to fight down a squeal of delight. I was excited to see the latest Mimi Mareau designs. The woman was a genius.

Lady Patricia introduced us as being from the *Daily Premier*, and Mimi acknowledged us with a nod and a smile. Her relationship with newspaper reporters was uneven at best, according to gossip.

She was her own best advertisement. She wore a curve-hugging linen dress in pale green with a long blue linen jacket and high heels. She wore a blue felt cloche over her dark, wavy bob. I was surprised to realize she was shorter than me in those ankle-breaking high heels and quite slim. Close up, she looked younger than her forty-plus years.

Mimi managed to appear at once both elegant and energetic. She was everything I imagined her to be from reading the women's magazines. As long as she was in front of me, I would hang on her every word. Her every move.

She made me feel dowdy in my light-wool blue suit with a pale-yellow summer blouse and sensible two-inch heeled pumps.

With summer temperatures lingering into the middle of September and no one declaring war over the Sudetenland yet, we were all dressing in bright colors. Jane hadn't shocked anyone in her Socialist-red blouse. Who knew what threat tomorrow would bring?

A girl at the end of her teens came in carrying a heavy

load of cloth-covered gowns and I helped her put them down, spread out so as not to wrinkle. Mimi didn't introduce her or pay her any attention.

The bride said, "No one will come back here," as she stripped down to her slip and tried on the first outfit in her trousseau.

"Perhaps Madame Mareau could stand next to Lady Patricia while she's wearing this outfit," Jane said as she glanced at the Mareau-designed wool jacket and skirt. She raised her eyebrows, obviously impressed.

As they obliged, I started my interview with Lady Patricia and, without waiting to be asked, took a front-row seat for this fashion show with my notebook on my lap. "Where will you go for your honeymoon?"

"The continent. Switzerland, Germany, France."

"Oh, I would like you and your new husband to visit me in Paris," Mimi said, her eyes on how the skirt hung. The hem was a little wider than had been popular of late. The drape was beautiful, and would work well on someone considerably heavier than this young woman.

"We'll have to see," Lady Patricia said in a stuffy, aristocratic tone.

Mimi's gaze flew to Lady Patricia's face for an instant before she looked down again.

I'd have jumped at that offer.

I sketched the lower part of the skirt as I asked, "Do you have any plans yet for the wedding breakfast?"

"The usual. Eggs Benedict, champagne, bacon, cake—this frill at the cuffs chafes my skin." This last was directed to Mimi.

"Shall we try using a silk cuff and a silk bow at the neck? The white softens the brown and complements the buttons on the front and at the cuffs. Brigette."

"I have it."

I swung my head around. Brigette's accent was English, even though the teenaged girl appeared to be one hundred percent French.

I was still looking at the girl when Lady Patricia said, "I like this belt or whatever this is, sewn in at the waist. Makes me look like I have one."

"Oh, no, my lady. You have a good figure. A noble figure," Mimi said.

"No wonder Daddy likes you," Lady Patricia replied.

There was something about her smile that made me uneasy. I glanced over at Brigette to find her staring at Lady Patricia. I recognized that look. It was hate.

Lady Patricia took off the jacket and skirt, tossing both on a chair in a rumpled heap. Brigette moved silently to the discarded clothes, straightening and hanging the fabric so no wrinkles or soiling could mar the outfit.

The bride-to-be next tried on a light-gray wool winter frock. Large buttons ran in a single line past the belt, all covered in the same light gray wool. My eye was drawn, as it was supposed to be, by a dark brown and gray cape built into the dress.

"These go with it," Mimi said as she produced a pair of dark brown gloves with wide cuffs that spread to cover the bottoms of the sleeves.

"Ooh," Lady Patricia said as she pulled them on. "Now

all it needs is a dark brown hat. I already have the shoes."

"I have a swatch if you'd like to take it to your milliner and have her design something to go with this."

Mimi Mareau was a terrific saleswoman, with a helpful suggestion when needed. Too much of that could be annoying, but not the way Mimi handled it. I kept sketching the frocks as I asked questions. "Where did you meet your fiancé?"

"On the French Riviera."

"Is he British? I'm not familiar with the name 'Frederiksen,'" I said, hearing the click of Jane's camera.

"No, Aren and his family are Danish. They are leaders in brewing, shipping, and cheese making. And related to the Danish royal family."

She made it sound like only a rich, royal family would be good enough for this daughter of an English duke. "So, you'll be moving to Denmark?"

"Aren is going to be the Danish ambassador to the Court of St. James. We'll be living in London for the time being." Lady Patricia walked off to change again, assisted by Brigette.

"You have great talent for drawing," Mimi said, looking over my shoulder.

"Thank you." Praise for my drawings from a famous designer was to be savored. Pride bubbled up inside me.

"What is your name?"

"I'm Olivia Denis," I said, holding out my hand.

She shook it. "I hope you won't print your sketches in the paper. Your drawings are good enough to give away my newest designs."

Her snappish tone squished my pride. Hurt, my own tone was sharp. "Didn't you show similar designs at your couture house last month?"

"Ah, but that was in Paris." She kept on a stiff smile. Behind it, I was sure she was gritting her teeth at my impertinence.

"I'm sure there were many Englishwomen in the audience." It didn't take long to get from one city to the other, either by aeroplane or train and boat.

"I will be showing my designs at my own show here along with the local couturiers on the twenty-second of September," Mimi announced with queenly serenity.

"So you'll have your own salon here?" I knew I sounded eager.

Too eager, apparently. She ignored my question. "I might buy your sketches for an advertisement, but otherwise I don't want to see them in the *Daily Premier*." Beyond her smile, the rest of her face was stern.

"Don't worry," I told her. "Sir Henry would never print any of my sketches. I draw only to assist my writing." They helped me figure out how to describe clothing for the society pages of the paper. Something I wouldn't admit to her.

"That's a shame. They are very good." It sounded like grudging respect. I probably glowed with pride, since the words came from Mimi Mareau.

At that moment, Lady Patricia stepped before us in a stunning wool tweed suit with a sable fur collar on the long jacket. I had never seen tweed hang so gracefully before. It had to be the cut of the fabric. No wonder people paid so much for Mimi's creations.

"What do you think?" the aristocrat said to the designer.

I interrupted with, "I've never seen tweed fall so smartly. You are to be congratulated. Everyone is going to be asking for this suit."

"Thank you," Mimi said, obviously pleased.

"Don't print that in my story," Lady Patricia ordered. Jane took more photographs.

"Oh, no, I wouldn't. By the way, my lady, have you chosen your bridesmaids yet?" I asked to get past what the young woman obviously thought was a faux pas.

She had just reached the third name when she exclaimed, "Mummy!"

I turned to see a horsey-faced woman of about fifty. The Duchess of Marshburn.

"Hello, darling." The woman marched past Mimi without a glance and gave her daughter a hug and an air-kiss. "How is the wedding coming?"

"I was just telling the reporter from the *Daily Premier* who my bridesmaids are." Lady Patricia twirled around for her mother to see the fabulous drape of the skirt. "What do you think of this?"

"Lovely, dear, but wouldn't it be better to go to her shop for a fitting? We can go over to Paris any time." The duchess's mouth turned down as if she'd tasted something bitter. She still hadn't acknowledged Mimi's presence in the room. Oh, the fascinating things I saw that I couldn't put in my articles.

I was frequently reminded by our society editor,

Miss Westcott, and by Jane, that society columns were for people with a title or money to present themselves to the world in their best light. The boys in the newsroom reported any scandals.

"There is no problem coming here," Mimi said to the duchess's back. "I'm opening a salon in London while I work on costuming for a West End play. You must come and see my salon on Old Burlington Street. Number thirty-one."

When she heard the address, the duchess spun around and faced the designer. "A play? Good. You'll fit in among the actors."

Mimi's coloring changed to a reddish shade. She kept a smile on her face, but now it showed her teeth. "Your husband has been very generous in finding a location for my salon."

"That building belongs to the estate. And how is he collecting his rent?"

I held my breath while Lady Patricia gasped, "Mummy."

Mimi turned a brighter shade and the smile slid off her face.

"Pounds or francs?" With that, the duchess strolled out of the room with a smirk.

This sounded like the gossip about the duke and Miss Mareau was true. And the duchess either didn't like the gossip or the situation.

"The French have a lot to teach these aristocrats," Mimi murmured in French behind clenched jaws.

"Madame," Brigette replied in French, "I think it's

time to leave."

"I don't have to make any adjustments to the last two outfits. Do you want me to leave them with you?" Mimi said in English.

"Yes," Lady Patricia said, her expression wooden as she stared at the now-closed door.

"I'll change the inserts on the first to silk. You have a lovely day, my lady." Mimi packed up. "I think for your mother's sake we should continue our fittings at the new salon. The suit will be ready next week, as will more of your trousseau."

"But my wedding gown." Lady Patricia sounded like a four- year-old without her favorite toy.

"Come to the salon next week. Let's not upset your *maman*," Mimi answered.

Lady Patricia hesitated before she nodded.

I had enough for my article. "I'd like to see the space where your salon is going. May I go with you, Miss Mareau?" I couldn't hide my eagerness.

"Of course. A preview before we open our doors. But not the photographer. Not until next week, when I will be glad to welcome you before my show." Mimi smiled at Jane, who nodded. One professional to another.

Jane was all packed. "I'll see you back at the paper, Livvy," she told me, thanked Lady Patricia and Mimi, and left.

I said good-bye and thanked Lady Patricia before I hurried after Miss Mareau and Brigette. The Frenchwoman could move quickly when she wanted to on her high heels, sped on her way by the frosty expression of the butler.

By the time I was out the door, Brigette had already commandeered a taxi. I noticed she wore the same comfortable, wide, two-inch heels I did.

"Come on," Mimi said with a wave as she climbed in, leaving Brigette to wrestle the frocks into the vehicle. I squeezed in last and we took off.

"'Livvy'?" Mimi demanded. "She called you 'Livvy'?"

"My name is Olivia. Livvy is a nickname."

"So very British." She didn't make it sound like a compliment.

We arrived a few minutes later, having traveled only a few streets from the duke's residence to a well-heeled mix of homes and discreet shops. I climbed out first, followed by Brigette with her hands full. Mimi walked away from the taxi as she pulled her keys from her handbag. The cabbie sat there, his hand out and a stern look on his face.

The price of the interview was, at the very least, the taxi fare.

I was last to walk into the four-story and attic brick building. Past the black wrought-iron fence guarding the stairs leading to the basement, past the black-painted door, and into the front room on the ground floor.

Inside, the air smelled of paint fumes despite three twelve-over-twelve pane windows open at both the top and bottom. A ladder had been left lying on the drop cloths in the empty space.

Through the doorway into the back room, I could see a large table with a sewing machine, a few chairs, and a rack holding cloth sacks that contained either stage costumes or priceless designer gowns.

I was getting to see this shop before almost everyone else. I could have cheered from the excitement.

"Don't touch the walls. The paint is still wet. Fleur, are you upstairs?" I followed to see Mimi shouting up a staircase that opened into the back room. "With the play and the salon both opening, we've been rushed. Fleur? Reina? Where can they have gone?"

Mimi returned to the front room and gave me a tour of how she envisioned her sales rooms would look. After she pointed out where everything in the lobby would go, we went up a sweeping staircase to a larger room on the first floor where she planned to hold shows and a back area with fitting rooms. She had a lot to get completed in one week.

From her description, it would be chic. Mimi was a genius, and I could hardly wait to see her showcase.

"Who's Fleur?" I asked when she finally paused for breath.

"My chief cutter," she said, heading down the grand staircase to the ground floor. "Reina is my chief seamstress, and Brigette my chief fitter. I brought them with me so we could keep up with the costumes for the play while we have the building finished to our liking."

Brigette came in from the back room. "Neither Fleur nor Reina are upstairs." Her nose quivered. "This paint smell is horrible. Do you want me to hang Lady Patricia's dresses in the basement?"

"What's in the basement?" I asked.

"Storage. We don't have enough room to store garments as well as cut and sew fashions on the second floor," Mimi said, sounding annoyed by the lack of space. "And I don't want this paint smell to get into the finished designs."

I followed Mimi and Brigette into the back room on the ground floor, where the staircase led both up to the floors above and down to the basement. The paint smell was almost overpowering where we stood by the sewing machines.

"The fumes may be just as bad down there. Is there any ventilation in the basement?" I had no idea if I was trying to curry favor with Mimi to get more access for my story or I was simply nosy about what a couture house looked like behind the scenes. Maybe I was curious about the workshop of someone with this much talent, imagination, and boldness.

I started down the stairs. Mimi flipped a switch and a couple of bare bulbs shone from the ceiling, showing a rough, dry stone floor. At the bottom, I found the paint smell was nearly as strong as on the ground floor. At least it didn't smell musty. To one side was a door to the outside and two windows set high in the wall. I walked over and tried the door. It was neither locked nor bolted. "The odor is nearly as strong down here. Perhaps an open door will clear the air."

I stuck my head out to find the door led to a long flight of steps going up to the pavement on Old Burlington Street beyond the wrought iron fence. When I turned to come back in, I gasped.

In the dim light at the back of the basement, beyond the racks of clothes and in front of a row of trunks, a man lay face down in a heap.

CHAPTER TWO

I walked closer and peered at the man. Blood had oozed from the large wound in the back of his head onto the stone floor. "Don't come down here," I yelled.

"Is the paint odor strong down there?" Mimi called down. "I was assured—"

"No. Get a bobby," I interrupted.

"Why?" I heard footsteps on the stairs. "I have done nothing wrong." Then Mimi was next to me. "Who is he?"

No tears. No shrieking. Just an angry-sounding question. For which I didn't have an answer. "I don't know."

"Is he dead?"

Between the blood and the fixed look of the eye I could see... "Yes, I'm sure he is. We need to get a bobby. Now."

"Brigette. Get a bobby," Mimi called up the stairs.

Brigette must have been listening, because she said, "On my way," and then I heard quick footsteps fade.

Mimi walked closer to the body.

"Don't touch anything," I said.

She bent over and stared at the man's face. "I have seen him before."

"Where?"

"Here."

"Why was he here?" I asked.

She straightened up. "No. I am wrong. I have not seen him before."

"But you just said—"

She interrupted, "He looks a bit like one of the painters. That is all."

Maybe. I'd hold off judgment until I could speak to the painters. Mimi had first sounded very certain about her recognition, and then very firm in her denial.

"Hello?" came from upstairs.

"Fleur? We are in the basement," Mimi replied.

As I heard the footsteps on the steps, I said, "Please don't come down. Brigette has gone for a bobby and we mustn't touch anything."

"Where have you been?" Mimi demanded as Fleur reached the bottom step. They both ignored my request.

"I went for lunch. How did the fitting go?"

"Well, until the duchess arrived."

Fleur laughed. I guessed she knew the truth about the relationship between Mimi and the duke and pictured a catfight. She appeared to be Mimi's age, in her early forties, but stockier and blonder. She wore an ordinary-looking blue suit, an unadorned hat, and stacked heels, making her forgettable next to Mimi.

Then she saw the body. She abruptly grew silent and crossed herself. "Who is he?"

"I don't know. Where is Reina? Did she go to lunch with you?" Mimi demanded.

Fleur didn't seem upset by her tone of voice. "Reina went to shop for the thread you needed. I've not seen her since you left."

A heavy tread upstairs announced Brigette's return with a bobby. They came down the stairs, and after one look at the body, the young man said, "Please, everyone go upstairs and stay there while I call for reinforcements."

We slowly climbed the staircase. I was in the rear. Once the bobby saw us go up, he went out the basement door and shut it behind him.

"Where is he going?" Mimi asked.

"He's phoning this in at the closest police call box," I told her. I had seen one at the end of the alley.

"Fleur." Mimi led her employee around me and back down the staircase to the body. I followed them, wondering what they were doing.

Fleur gave the man a quick glance and then a closer look. The two women exchanged looks and then returned upstairs.

I followed them up. "Who is he?"

Mimi said, "I don't know."

I looked at Fleur. She'd obviously recognized him.

Fleur answered with a shrug.

I heard footsteps in the basement and looked down to see the bobby had returned.

"Brigette, did you know the man downstairs?" I asked.

"I never went downstairs. Who is he?"

"No one we know, *ma chére*," Mimi told her in a determined voice, giving me a stern look.

Whoever the poor man was, Scotland Yard would find out and then I'd find out from the news desk.

Hopefully before I came for the opening of the couture house the next week.

"Hello. Why is everyone back here? What is wrong? Where are the painters and carpenters?" A woman of about thirty, with the slenderness and dark coloring of Mimi and Brigette, spoke in French as she came in the front door and joined us in the back room. Her suit was well cut and her hat was lovely, but her shoes were the same stocky heels of the other two women with Mimi.

"The painters will return any time now," Mimi replied in French. She seemed to take a deep breath before she added, "There's a problem in the basement."

"Oh?" The new arrival moved to start down the stairs.

The rest of them blocked her path. "There's a dead man down there. The police are investigating," Fleur said.

"What?" She looked from one face to the next. "No!"

"Reina, you haven't met Mrs. Denis. She's a reporter for the *Daily Premier*," Mimi said, interrupting her in English with a forceful voice. "Mrs. Denis, this is Reina, our lead seamstress."

I nodded. Reina looked stunned. I doubted she'd heard a word Mimi said.

"What is your first name, Mrs. Denis?" Fleur asked. To an Englishwoman, it was an odd question, but I'd only been told their first names.

"It's Olivia. My friends call me Livvy."

"A very English name," Mimi said with a heartiness that sounded forced.

"What happens now?" Fleur asked, glancing down

the stairs. They all turned to me, as the only local woman present.

"They'll take photographs of the crime scene, dust for fingerprints, ask all of us where we were when they figure out what time the crime was committed, and tell you not to go downstairs until they release the crime scene. Much as it would be done in France."

"Such a thing would not happen in France," Mimi said.

"Will they blame us because we are foreigners?" Brigette asked.

"No. If you didn't kill that man, you have nothing to worry about." I spoke with the certainty of English justice.

"Ha." Mimi gave a Gallic flap of her hands that said what she thought of English justice. I suspected she was thinking of the duchess.

We could hear more men moving about in the basement, and in another minute, the sounds of painters and carpenters coming back to work through the front door after a long lunch break. I hoped the police wouldn't make them stop once they made their statements. I was anxious to see the finished Mimi Mareau couture house in London.

But I also wanted to know who the dead man was and why he was in the basement.

Suddenly, Reina broke away from our group and dashed up the back staircase toward the upper floors. At a nod from Mimi, Fleur followed her at a slower pace.

Mimi, Brigette, and I stood together in silence until a

stern-looking man in civilian clothes came up from the basement. He introduced himself as Detective Inspector Smith and asked for our names. He had his notebook out, and by the speed and constant motion of his pencil, I suspected he wrote down every word we said.

I explained that we'd all been to a fitting where I was taking notes for a newspaper article. When we arrived at the salon, we noticed the high level of paint fumes. Since outfits were stored in the basement, we thought to check how strong the smell was down there.

He demanded details and was particularly interested that I was the one to go down to the bottom level alone.

"Not quite alone," Mimi said. "As soon as she said to call a bobby, I came down to see what was going on. This is my *maison*. My responsibility."

"Right. Did any of you recognize the dead man?"

We all shook our heads.

"So, who lives here?"

"Brigette, Fleur, Reina, and I currently reside upstairs," Mimi told him.

"And where are Fleur and Reina currently?"

"Upstairs."

"Right." He made a move to climb the stairs.

"No. I will call them down." Mimi stood on the landing and shouted up. "Fleur. Reina. The police want to ask you about the dead man and where you were."

"*Oui.*" Footsteps could be heard in the stairwell, along with hushed, rapid French.

The detective might not speak French, but I was fluent. I made out "...nothing you can do now. Don't get yourself..." and "...not right. He..." Someone in this house knew the dead man. Maybe all of them recognized him.

When the two women joined us, Fleur appeared unruffled, but Reina's eyes were red and swollen.

Inspector Smith immediately jumped on this. "You're upset. You knew the dead man?"

"No."

"And you are?"

"Reina."

"Last name?"

"Belleau. Reina Belleau."

"Reina, do you know how a dead man came to be in your basement?"

"No." She glanced at Mimi and then stood straighter. "There has been a death here. The building will now be haunted." Her accent was thicker than I had noticed when she first came in.

"You have more to fear from a killer than a ghost, and we'll need your help to catch him," the detective said.

I wished him luck with that. I could sense these women were closing ranks, but that might have been a reaction to dealing with the police in a foreign country rather than an attempt to hide the identity of a murderer.

"No. You cannot save us from evil spirits. This is the devil's work." Reina's English was now almost incomprehensible.

"What I need right now is the identity of the man so we can find his family." Detective Inspector Smith sounded like he was struggling to remain patient.

"I do not know this man," Fleur said. "I am Fleur.

Reina and Brigette didn't see him, but I do not think they would know him."

"Well, let's find out. Ladies, let's go downstairs and see if he looks familiar to any of you."

Mimi shot Fleur a look that clearly said *Don't say another word.*

"No. His spirit walks down there. I will not go down," Reina exclaimed.

"Inspector Smith, did the man have any identification in his pockets?" I asked. I was afraid Reina would become hysterical if pushed to view the body, and I wanted to get my questions in before she began to wail.

"Nothing," he said. "His pockets were totally empty, as if someone removed everything after they killed him."

I looked at the detective and raised my eyebrows. If Mimi and her assistants had killed him and emptied his pockets, they wouldn't have left the body in their own basement or be so obviously upset about his death. Well, Reina wouldn't be. I wasn't certain what the others felt.

And I had no idea if they were involved.

"We've only been in London a week, *monsieur.* Before that, we didn't have access to this building. We were in France." Suddenly, Brigette had an authentic French accent, where before she'd sounded English.

"That's not exactly the moon. You could have been coming here regularly."

"Perhaps this has something to do with the last tenants?" Mimi suggested.

"We'll be certain to check that out. Now, if I can get all of you to step down to the basement to view the body, we can clear up this matter and I won't have to bother you again." The detective gestured for us to go down the stairs.

I went first, followed by Brigette. Reina came down in a cluster with Fleur and Mimi. Inspector Smith was last.

Bright lights had been set up in the basement, making the stark whitewashed walls glow and showing every little mortar crack in the stone floor. Under this glare, the body, on a white-sheeted gurney, had lost any semblance of humanity. Now his face was completely visible.

I looked down and shook my head as I tried to memorize his features. Brigette glanced down and said, "No."

Mimi, Reina, and Fleur stepped up together with Reina in the middle. They said "No" in unison and turned to leave.

"Wait, ladies. Take a good long look. Are you certain you've never seen him before?" the detective asked.

They shifted to face the detective more than the body. "We are certain," Mimi said.

He glanced at all of us. "All right, then. Thank you. Just don't leave London without letting me know."

"Where are you taking the body?" Reina asked.

"To the morgue."

I winced.

Inspector Smith must have seen my reaction because he said, "It won't be up to you to identify the body. Why did you look sick?"

"The morgue was where I saw my husband after he was murdered. I wouldn't wish that experience on anyone else."

"You were widowed very young, Olivia," Mimi said, sympathy and curiosity written in her eyes.

"I was twenty-five." I didn't want to say anything else. His death was so recent I hadn't quite finished my expected year of mourning. Any reminder of the person I'd lost still kicked me in the stomach.

All four of the women reached out and patted my shoulder or touched my hand. Their simple gestures of sympathy put me squarely on their side. Unlike their suddenly thickened accents and stubborn denials to the police, their touches seemed genuine. For the moment, I'd help them hide their relationship with the murdered man, whatever it might be. And I felt sure at least Reina had prior contacts with the dead man.

But I wouldn't shield a murderer.

We were allowed to go back to the ground floor. Reina kept going up, her heels clicking on the stairs. With manners drilled into me since childhood, I thanked Mimi for showing me her new salon as if nothing untoward had happened.

Upstairs, the sound of hammering and sawing had resumed. The police apparently hadn't started asking the workmen questions.

Mimi stared at the ceiling as she showed me to the front door. "I'd hoped to be happy here. Now I am not so sure."

"Will you tell me who he was someday?" I asked.

"Perhaps. If I learn. I cannot see the future."

Drat. I'd hoped Mimi would have fallen for my trick. She was incredibly talented, more so than I'd realized before today. But I still couldn't tell if she was telling me the truth.

"Who's running your Paris couture house while you're here?" I asked, wondering at the possibility of the whole fashion house leaving the country. "And who will make all the frocks for the show?"

"More staff will come over next week to help with the show." Mimi gave a Gallic shrug. "My manager, Simone, is running my Paris salon. The top assistants are Fleur, Reina, and Brigette are there as well. Who knows, in time I may have two separate couture houses."

Not only was Mimi a brilliant designer, she was also a clever businesswoman. The articles on her in the French press said she had started with nothing and rose to the top of her profession by incredible talent, hard work, and determination.

And she sounded determined to stay, even with a body in the basement.

There was nothing newsworthy in what she'd told me, but it didn't matter. Nothing I learned would earn a byline. I'd been at the *Daily Premier* for almost a year and I'd never seen my name in print.

My pay was earned by my secondary duties. The publisher of the *Daily Premier* thought having my name appear in a byline would endanger my other role, as smuggler and spy.

I doubted this would be one of those occasions when

the publisher would want me involved.

* * *

I wrote up and turned in my articles on Lady Patricia's upcoming wedding and Mimi Mareau's *maison* in London, wondering if I'd hear more from Mimi about the murder victim.

The article on Lady Patricia featured Jane's photograph of her with Mimi. It didn't feature my byline. My article on the new couture house was reduced to a notice.

Two days later, I was called to Mr. Colinswood's office. I went upstairs to the foreign desk where he was editor. He waved me in, his ear to the telephone receiver and a cigarette burning in the overflowing ashtray. I walked in and sat down, waiting for him to finish his call. By the way he was rapidly scrawling notes on a sheet of scrap paper, there had to be a story breaking somewhere.

He hung up and said, "Lord Runciman has been recalled from the negotiations about the Sudetenland to confer with Chamberlain."

I shivered, knowing war with Germany was that much nearer. Captain Adam Redmond, British army officer and my very good friend, was that much closer to danger.

"But that's neither here nor there," Colinswood continued. "What you need to know is the identity of the man found murdered in Mimi Mareau's basement. Elias. That's his *nom de guerre*. A German communist and a Jew. The Nazis have been looking for him for some time. No one knows how he got out of Germany."

"Had he been hiding in that building? I've done a little digging and found out it had been empty since June, until Mimi moved in." I couldn't imagine what a wealthy Paris fashion designer and a German communist had in common.

"Don't know. I only know I was told to put you in the picture and send you up to see Sir Henry." Mr. Colinswood rolled a sheet of paper into his typewriter, obviously anxious for me to leave.

Sir Henry Benton. The publisher of the *Daily Premier* and our boss. After my husband died, he'd saved me from having to move home with my father by offering me a well-paying job, but it came with certain odd requirements. Sir Henry used my facility with foreign languages and knowledge of foreign diplomatic procedures to help his late wife's Jewish family escape Nazi territory.

I went up to Sir Henry's office on the top floor. His secretary sent me right in, where Sir Henry greeted me from behind his massive desk. "Olivia. Good. Colinswood told you?" At my nod, he simply said, "Good."

I took a chair opposite him without being asked, something I would never do as a lowly society reporter, the job he officially hired me for. But in the task I suspected I'd been called up here for, as Sir Henry's personal inquiry agent, we were more equal.

"You need to know I attended a meeting with Elias," Sir Henry told me.

"Does Scotland Yard know?" I didn't want to step on the toes of the police. They had an official murder investigation to carry out.

"Someone in our group is alerting them to his reason for being here."

"'Our' group?" What group was Sir Henry involved with?

"We call ourselves 'the committee.' Mostly a collection of wealthy Jewish businessmen and professionals, with a few like-minded Christians, determined to help save as many European Jews as possible before war traps them inside Nazi Germany and its client states. Because of Esther, James and I are involved."

Esther Benton Powell, Sir Henry's only child by his German Jewish wife and my closest friend from our school days, had been raised as a Christian after her mother's death. Sir Henry had been born a Presbyterian in Newcastle, but that didn't stop him from helping his in-laws.

Sir Henry leaned back in his massive stuffed desk chair. "What I want, Olivia, is for you to learn who sold out Elias. I suspect a leak in our group, a turncoat who led a Nazi assassin to a meeting with him. Here, in the supposed safety of London."

CHAPTER THREE

I shut my eyes and considered the impossibility of what Sir Henry asked. He wanted me to ferret out a specific Nazi sympathizer in a city that had too many of them.

I opened my eyes and stared at Sir Henry. "If you don't believe Scotland Yard can solve this murder, how do you expect me to?"

"Oh, Scotland Yard will solve it, but the killer is not the danger." He leaned forward, watching me closely. "Thugs can be bought for a shilling, especially the ones in Mosley's group. I want to know—no—we need to know who gave away Elias's identity and location. That's the person Scotland Yard won't look for. But that is the person who will lead others to their deaths."

"You don't believe Mosley's British Nazi group is behind Elias's murder?"

"No." Sir Henry shook his head. "They haven't the brains."

I leaned back to make myself more comfortable. "Then I am going to need to know everything you know about Elias and the names of everyone in this group who knew he was in town." The more information I had, the more chance I had of finding the person he sought.

"Elias had found a way to move German Jews out through Poland and then across the Baltic to Scandinavia.

We know it was a sophisticated plan involving forged papers and Swedish and Danish fishermen and had been attempted twice. Both times successfully."

"How do you know this?" The breadth of Sir Henry's knowledge was amazing.

"Elias met with several of us five nights ago. He had left with the second group of refugees using his escape route. He needed more money to keep the route open, to pay both the forgers and the fishermen."

"Had you given him money? There was none found on him." Once more, in my mind I saw his body crumpled on the basement floor and my stomach churned.

"There's a group who had agreed to send money by way of a Swedish bank. We'd given him a couple of pounds for while he was in London, but not enough for someone to kill him over."

"Considering the times we live in, I'd suspect his work rather than robbery would be the motive. There was nothing random about this attack. Are these people friends of yours?" I asked.

He shook his head. "You're going to have to be very tactful with them. I'm tolerated because I'm wealthy and male. By helping my late wife's relatives resettle here, safe from Nazi Germany, I'm considered trustworthy."

"Wouldn't Esther be a better person to approach this group?" Esther was my best friend, starting in boarding school and then at university. She seemed like the logical person to work with this committee.

Sir Henry nearly came out of his chair. "I don't want her traipsing around London with my grandchild."

She was four or five months pregnant with her first child, and with that attitude, I suspected Sir Henry was driving her crazy. "What does Esther think?"

"No, Livvy. You are not to ask her. I forbid it."

"If she finds out you are keeping her from doing something in London that she no doubt agrees is very important, then you are going to be in trouble." Esther had been instrumental in having me travel to Nazi-controlled territory twice to help her mother's family escape.

Esther couldn't go because of her heritage, and that would make her more determined to help out in London.

"How is she going to find out?" he demanded.

"This is Esther we're talking about. Do you really believe we can coordinate on something this involved without her finding out?" And I didn't want her mad at me.

"But she's carrying my grandchild," came out in as close to a wail as I'd ever heard from him.

"How about if I come over to the house tonight? Have Esther come over and we'll discuss this like rational adults. Presumably she knows some of the people in this group and can give me some suggestions, if nothing else."

"She knows some of them better than I do," Sir Henry said in what sounded like a grudging admission.

"Then I need to speak to her." I held his gaze.

"Is Redmond in town?"

Adam Redmond was the only reason I'd try to postpone a special assignment from Sir Henry. "No, he's somewhere for the army." It was that unknown *where* that kept me awake at night.

"Come to dinner. We'll dine at eight. You'll not only have to convince me; you'll have to convince James."

James Powell was Esther's husband. So far he'd been more reasonable than Sir Henry about this pregnancy, allowing Esther a measure of freedom around London. However, at the word *murder*, he was likely to become more difficult.

I nodded and headed downstairs to my desk, thinking about the impossible task given to me. Germany was the most powerful country in Europe. They'd taken over the Rhineland and Austria. It appeared that, at any moment, they'd take over the Sudetenland. And while Hitler might want another war, England didn't. Too many people remembered the losses in the Great War.

Besides all the people who didn't want another war, the Jews were unpopular. Some aristocrats were in debt to Jewish bankers, while working men wanted all foreigners kept away from hard-to-find jobs, which meant it wouldn't be hard to find Nazi sympathizers in London. But how would I find the one who killed, or brought in the assassin to kill, Elias?

* * *

Shortly before eight that evening, I arrived by taxi at Sir Henry's London home. Esther greeted me with a hug when I entered, saying, "I am so glad you agreed to do this, Livvy. Elias didn't deserve to be murdered. He may have been a communist, but he cared about people. About families."

"Had you met him?" Another reason to involve

Esther if they had met.

"Yes. Come and sit down. Dinner's not quite ready."

As she turned sideways, I caught a glimpse of her profile. Esther was beginning to show. "How are you feeling?"

"Fine. This baby is agreeing with me. And how is Adam?"

"Well, the last I heard."

"He's disappeared again?"

I nodded.

"Oh, Livvy." She gave me another hug. "I know how much he means to you."

"I lost Reggie. Not hearing a word from Adam for days and weeks on end is getting on my nerves. Especially with all this war talk. I can't lose him, too." A sob escaped as I spoke.

Esther patted me on the back before I took a deep breath and pulled myself together.

We bypassed the formal drawing room to join the men in Sir Henry's large, book-lined study. The footman offered me a glass of sherry, which I accepted. Everything to eat and drink here was delicious, I knew.

"Glad you could join us, Livvy," Sir Henry said, coming forward to shake my hand. As I was wearing two-inch heels, I could see over the top of Sir Henry's head. I wondered if everyone who grew up in Newcastle in the Victorian age was short.

I blinked away my idle thoughts and said, "I'm eager to hear more about this business."

"Quite. Sit down and we'll tell you," Sir Henry said.

James Powell came forward and said, "Thanks for helping, Livvy. Esther has involved me in this, too." James was as Church of England to the bone as I was. Esther was Anglican, and had attended St. Agnes School with me, but the faint memories of the mother she had lost as a child and fears for her mother's family had pushed her into action. Action made necessary since the moment Hitler began showing his true colors.

I grinned. "Knowing Esther, do we have any choice?"

"All right, you two. Sit down and listen." Esther had put on her bossy voice, but she'd matched it with a smile that reached her eyes.

We sat.

"Elias came into Britain a week ago on the ferry that sails the Esbjerg to Harwich route. His documents proclaimed him to be Jan Kryszka, Polish national." Sir Henry paused. "They were very good forgeries. And that was one of the reasons Elias needed money. Forgeries of this caliber don't come cheap. He also needed to bribe Swedish and Danish fishermen and Polish border guards when they cross out of Germany."

"How much success had he had?"

"The first group, who also used the Esbjerg to Harwich ferry, had three families totaling eleven people. The second, two families and himself, had a total of twelve."

I had more questions. "How exactly does this work?"

"The refugees cross the border from Germany to Poland when his bribed guards are working. Once into Poland, they are taken to a place where they receive new identities and burn their old papers. Then they are taken to the coast where they board fishing trawlers. Once they are in Sweden or Denmark, they are led to Esbjerg and put on the ferry to England," Sir Henry said.

"Presumably, anyone against bringing German refugees into England would want to stop Elias. Is there anyone like that in your group?" I asked.

"No." Both Esther and Sir Henry spoke at once.

"Did anyone else know he was in the country? Did he have any known enemies here? How many knew he was a communist?" I had questions. I really hoped they had some answers.

"He was keeping his visit secret, since he was on a list of assassination targets drawn up by the Nazis. He'd barely escaped attempts on his life twice while in Germany. We all knew he was a communist, but he said political affiliation shouldn't matter in such perilous times. The Nazis are everybody's enemy."

Sir Henry set down his glass and stared at me. "His enemy is a Nazi sympathizer here in London. But how could anyone find him? I don't know. We took precautions. He took precautions."

"He did say he had personal business here," Esther said in a quiet voice.

All three of us turned to look at her.

"When I attended the meeting with Father, I had a chance to say a few words to Elias. I asked how he was enjoying London. He said he'd never been here before, but he was meeting an old friend while he was in town and was looking forward to their visit." Esther looked at each of us in turn.

Now I had even more questions, but at that moment, the footman signaled Sir Henry, who said, "Let's go in to dinner. We can discuss this afterward."

Dinner at Sir Henry's hadn't changed since my university days. Sir Henry was widely read and had fascinating stories to tell, most of them humorous. The food was excellent, the company charming.

But Sir Henry had one rule. No talking business at dinner. No one said a word about Elias.

Still, he was the ghost at the banquet.

After dinner, we went back to the study for our coffee. After we were settled, I said, "Did Elias mention who this friend was? Or where he was staying or meeting this person?"

"Elias was staying at the Hotel Gloucester, where one of the group members had made arrangements for him. He wasn't observant, so there weren't any restrictions on where he could eat," Sir Henry said.

"Not an Orthodox Jew?" I asked.

"No, and he didn't mention who this old friend was," Esther said. "Another thing in his favor was he was wiry, athletic. I don't see how anyone could have won a fight with him, if there was only one person."

"The communists have been involved in all sorts of strikes and dock brawls here in England. Is it the same way in Germany?" James asked.

"It was until the Nazis consolidated their rule. The communists have been outlawed there for years," Sir Henry told him.

"Then maybe he was out of practice in fighting," I suggested. "But do we know how he died? Have you seen the autopsy report?"

"I had one of the local desk reporters get a copy," Sir Henry told me. "Elias died from several massive blows to the back of the head. The first one would have rendered him unconscious. He didn't put up a fight."

"That means he turned his back on his killer." I looked at the others in the room. "He knew that person, and wasn't afraid of him."

"Or her," Esther added.

Her words immediately made me think of Mimi. She hadn't seemed surprised to find his body in her basement, and she'd appeared to have recognized him. "The body wasn't moved?"

"No."

"Then he was killed in the basement of a house in Mayfair. One that was rented a week or so ago to Mimi Mareau for a couture house."

"Mimi's moving to London?" Esther said, suddenly excited. "Then are the rumors true, about her and the Duke of Marshburn?"

"I know the duchess can't stand her," I told her.

The two men looked at each other with puzzled expressions.

"You haven't heard of Mimi Mareau?" I asked them. "She's a French fashion designer. I did an article about her opening a showroom in London just the other day. I had an exclusive, and you turned it into an announcement." I glared at Sir Henry.

"You had an exclusive with the tenant of the building where Elias was found? I didn't realize you had this contact, Livvy," my boss said. "Can you get in there with Jane again?"

"Not until next week, when she's ready to open for business."

"Good. Get in there as soon as you can."

"Will you print the story this time?" I countered.

"Yes, of course. I need you to keep an eye on this Mimi. Marshburn is known to have Nazi sympathies. Does Mimi?"

"I don't know." It seemed odd to think of politics and high fashion at the same time.

"I'm sure she's not alone in that building," Esther said.

"No, she's living there with three other women, her chief assistants, while they get the building ready for their first showing. At the same time, they're designing and producing the costumes for a West End play."

"What play? Who's putting it on?" Sir Henry asked.

"I don't know. She just said a West End play." I should have asked, but then we'd found the body. "During the day, there are painters and carpenters all over the ground and first floor."

"More people to have seen Elias in the basement," James said. "Men who wouldn't want to share job opportunities with immigrants."

"If the director or playwright or anyone from the play has been in that building, they might have seen Elias. They might know him from some encounter in the past.

We need to check up on them, too," Esther said.

"We?" Sir Henry exclaimed.

"This isn't Berlin," Esther said, crossing her arms. "I believe in what Elias started, and I want to see it continue. The best way I can do that is to help Livvy find the traitor in the resettlement committee."

James gave a loud sigh before he said, "Essie, my love. You might not only find a traitor. You might find a killer."

That started an argument that wasn't going to be solved that night. Meanwhile, I had to be up bright and early in the morning for work at the *Daily Premier.* Including any special assignments Sir Henry might find for me.

I wished them all a good night and retreated before I was drawn into a family argument.

* * *

The next morning, I told Miss Westcott that I had permission to follow up on my contact with Mimi Mareau and was going over to her couture house. Miss Westcott raised her eyebrows, but she waved me away from her desk.

I suspected she had already guessed I had a secondary role at the newspaper, a role no one would tell her about. I also suspected she could be trusted, even with a secret of this magnitude.

Knowing where I'd be going, I had dressed to catch Mimi's eye in a cream and light-gray striped suit with a dark blue blouse that tied at the neck with a bow. I paired it with a white lacquered straw trilby with a dark blue band and two-tone blue and white shoes. Leaving nothing to chance, I even put on a new pair of silk stockings.

I took a taxi across town, marking down the cost to get reimbursed, and knocked on the door of the house on Old Burlington Street. Reina opened the door, showing me a room full of drop cloths and painters on ladders. "Come on, we'll go to the back."

We carefully stepped over and around a maze of painting gear. The back room had been altered, too, with a new coat of paint and more racks full of hanging cloth bags and new shelves full of boxes.

"On your own?" I asked.

"Yes. Fleur and Brigette have gone to the theater and Mimi is—out."

"Which theater is it?"

"The Danish Princess."

The Danish Princess theater was a little on the small side and a little east of the West End theaters where musical comedies written by uncelebrated bards were performed by unknown actors. It was great fun and wonderfully cheap. Adam and I had gone there a couple of times.

"Will Mimi be back soon?"

"I doubt it." Said in a French accent, it sounded more dramatic than I guessed she had meant it.

I took a stab at getting some information while Reina was away from the others. "My condolences on Elias's death. He was a friend of yours?"

Her head jerked around as she looked squarely at me. Then she bit her lip and her eyes grew moist. "We grew up in the same town on the German-Czech border."

"In the Jewish quarter."

She took a step or two away from me as she glanced over her shoulder. "Keep quiet."

CHAPTER FOUR

Reina's eyes widened with fear. "If Mimi finds out people know I'm Jewish, she will fire me. And what business is it of yours?"

"I work for one of the men who was paying for Elias's stay in London and is raising the funds to continue his work."

"You know about his work?" she whispered.

"Yes. I helped my boss get some of his relatives out. I know how important Elias's work was. My job is to find out who was involved in his murder."

"Good. I won't sleep well until I know the person who did this is dead."

There was clearly a lot more I could learn from Reina. "You're Mimi's best seamstress. You said if she found out, she'd fire you, but she'd have to be a fool. And Mimi's no fool. You'd be snatched up in a second or be able to open your own shop."

"She does business with Jews if she must. She is quite willing to sell expensive gowns to them. But openly employ a Jew? No."

"Then why do you stay?"

"She's been building her reputation since the Great War. Everyone listens to her. Even you."

I nodded. That was true.

"If I leave, she will say bad things about me and I

won't be able to work again. And I have no desire to starve."

"It can't be that bad." Mimi seemed like a reasonable person.

"Ha. I grew up with starvation. I have no wish to repeat the experience."

Hunger was a powerful motivator. Still, I couldn't believe Mimi Mareau, who designed such beautiful gowns, would be so vindictive toward someone who worked so hard for her. "So you stay."

"So I stay. Please, keep my secret."

I nodded. "Had you made plans to see Elias?"

"No." She looked over her shoulder and trembled.

"Did you know he was staying at the Hotel Gloucester?"

"No."

"Did you know he was coming to London?"

"No. How could I?"

"From someone in your hometown."

She gave me a look that said I was an idiot. "I haven't heard from anyone there in a year or more."

"Do you know of any threats to him in London?"

"Threats?"

"Someone killed him. Was he aware of any enemies here in London?"

"He had a price on his head, thanks to the Nazis. They'd already tried to kill him twice in Germany. He was badly wounded in one attempt. He had enemies everywhere."

"How do you know any of that if you hadn't spoken

to him?"

"My cousin in Paris has some contacts. She—she told me." She still looked scared, but a stubborn glint in her eye told me I wouldn't be able to shake her on that story.

"Why was he in the basement? Did he come to meet you?"

"No. How would he know I was here?" She looked around her as if looking for another answer. "Besides, Mimi sent me off to buy some fabric and thread for the play costumes. When I returned, you had already found his body. That was the first I knew he was in London."

She looked at me and sighed. "He'd had enemies for many years. In the end, he waited too long to escape. His enemies cornered him and killed him."

The evidence told me something else. "No, Reina. He was killed by several blows to the back of the head. He turned his back on his murderer. He trusted his attacker."

With a horrified look on her face, Reina clapped her hand over her mouth and raced up the back staircase.

I was left standing in the back room, wondering why my words had shocked Reina. What had she thought or known that sent her racing away from me?

Moments later, I heard the front door open and Mimi's accented tones floated in, giving the painters specific orders on how she wanted the walls to look. She walked in and looked surprised. "Olivia. Did I forget an appointment?"

"No. I came over to ask when would be a good time for Miss Seville and me to do a feature for your opening. Reina was good enough to let me in to wait for you."

"Excellent." Her expression was still quizzical. "The main salon is finished, and the front room should be ready tomorrow. Could we plan on Monday afternoon?"

"We'll arrive about one in the afternoon on Monday. We're both excited to see your new salon." That was true. My problem was how to question her. "The police haven't been too bothersome, have they?"

"Only the one day. By the next, we were again working without distraction."

"What was that man doing in your basement, did you ever find out?" She had some idea. I was sure of it.

"I don't know. Very strange and very sad, to die alone like that."

"Alone except for his killer," I said, looking straight at her.

"Yes." She stared back at me. "If there's nothing else..."

Curiosity and my love of French fashion design made me add, "Could I have a peek at the costumes for the play?"

She smiled. "Of course. It is a musical comedy about Gypsies. I am using some of the details in my evening gown designs. Bright and cheerful in this anxious time."

Which meant that by the end of the year, every ball gown in every shop in London would display flounces or peasant tops, copying Mimi.

Walking over to one of the racks, she opened a cloth clothing sack to show me a brightly colored, full-skirted frock with layers of petticoats beneath. "This is the basic costume for the women in the play. Clean, colorful, playful. The men will wear high boots and open-collared white shirts. They sing and dance about thieving and no one is hurt. The audience will love it."

"I'm sure they will." I reached out and touched the ruffled skirt, admiring the work that had gone into it.

"So unlike real Gypsies. Nasty, thieving cretins," Mimi grumbled, covering up the dress again.

I was surprised at her sudden rant against Gypsies. "We don't have many in London. And few in the countryside." I'd heard there were many in Germany, and Hitler was shoving them aside to make room for his Aryan backers.

"You're lucky. We have them in France. They're thieves, burglars, highwaymen. Filthy. And always with a clump of children and dogs hanging around." She changed her scowl to a smile. "But on stage they are a colorful presence. They are delightful to design for."

As I lowered my eyebrows to a more neutral expression, she said, "I wonder if you would like to take on a commission for me."

"What is it?" I hoped I didn't sound too eager. I was fascinated by both Mimi and her fashion house. And it would help me in finding out more for my assignment.

"I'd like some sketches of my works for *advertisements*." She pronounced it the French way. "I want the outfits to look like someone is wearing them without the details of a face or head. So all the attention is drawn to the clothes."

"I'd be glad to." It would give me an excuse to spend time here without being as obvious as I'd been.

She named an amount that seemed stingy, but I'd have done it for nothing but the experience.

"It sounds good. When do you want me to start?"

"Now would be good. Let's see what you can do with this." She opened up another clothing bag, took out a simple rust-colored evening gown with a deep vee in the front and wide straps over the shoulders, and hung it over a mannequin.

I pulled over a chair and sat. With my reporter's notebook on my lap, I began to draw. "I'll have to bring over sharper pencils to do this justice."

"This is just to tell me if you can do the job." Mimi walked out of the ground-floor room, leaving me to try to create the folds and drape of the gown.

A half-hour later, I was finished. I stood in the stairway and shouted, "Mimi."

I heard her high heels clicking on the stairs before I saw or heard her. "*Oui*?"

When I showed her my drawing, she nodded. "It is a good start. You need to do something vague with the body, and it needs to be crisper, and it needs to be on a separate sheet of paper, but you will do for my advertisements. You have talent, Olivia."

"Thank you."

"If there's nothing else?"

I couldn't think of another question to slip in to the conversation that would help with the investigation. "Until Monday."

She was ushering me toward the front door when it sprang open. The force seemed to come from the size and personality of the man standing in the doorway.

The Duke of Marshburn.

Training immediately kicked in. "Your Grace," I said with a hint of a curtsy.

"How do you do?" he said and then looked past me. "Mimi."

"Your Grace," she replied with a smile. It was the first genuine smile I'd seen on her face since I met her. Then she remembered my presence and introduced us.

This was the first time I'd seen the duke up close. His deep, resonating voice matched his tall stature. I thought I'd get a kink in my neck looking up at his face. "Are you a client of Miss Mareau's?" he asked.

"No, I'm a society reporter for the *Daily Premier*. We're doing a feature on her new couture house. She does such fascinating work. And to think she can carry on with a murder on the premises." I tried to sound amazed.

I knew of Marshburn's approval of the Nazis and the Nazis' disapproval of Elias. I hoped the duke would say something useful.

The duke shot Mimi a look over my head that was less than friendly. "Such an unfortunate thing to happen. I don't know why a murderer would decide to hide a body in the basement here."

"It has nothing to do with us," Mimi said. I couldn't determine if she meant those words for me or the duke. "Now, Mrs. Denis, I will see you on Monday."

She ushered me toward the door. "Good day."

I had no choice. "Good day."

* * *

I set up the interview time with Jane before going back to my mundane tasks in the society page offices. The grand and powerful were off shooting animals at magnificent house parties and sending back tidbits for society reporters to turn into copy. Having been raised among these young people and their mothers, I was frequently called on to translate reports of visits and tours for my coworkers.

It was close to quitting time when Miss Westcott told me to pick up the phone. It was Esther, and she sounded like she was in a hurry. "Livvy, there's a meeting of the committee tonight to discuss what to do about Mr. Elias's network. Please come. Everyone you need to meet will be there. Unless Adam is back?"

"No. He's not," I grumbled. "Will you be there?"

"Yes, along with my father. We can introduce you to the people you need to meet for this investigation."

I picked up a pencil. "What time and what's the address?"

As it turned out, I had to travel straight from the office to the meeting, wearing the cream and light gray wool suit I'd had on all day. It wasn't terribly hot and humid, but I still felt wilted. The bow on my blue blouse refused to look perky by then, no matter how I tried to tie it in the ladies' room after work.

I felt even worse when I climbed out of the taxi at a sprawling house in Blackheath and walked inside to discover I was the last to arrive. The footman showed me into an elegant ground-floor drawing room where every seat was taken by people in evening attire and the meeting was already in progress.

Sir Henry glared at me, but Esther smiled. The footman brought in a dining room side chair for me and set it near the door.

The speaker, a thin middle-aged man with a thick head of gray hair, stood behind a podium between the windows. Finishing the point he was making, he turned to me. "Yes, young lady?"

I found myself facing a roomful of suspicious faces. I wanted to sink into the thick carpet, but I mustered all the confidence I could dredge up and said, "I'm Olivia Denis, here at the request of Sir Henry Benton and Esther Powell."

Everyone turned to look at them on the other side of the room.

Esther spoke up first. "Livvy has traveled to Berlin and Vienna for me to help my mother's family escape. She's so obviously English that she has no trouble getting in and out, and she speaks fluent German and French. I think she may be able to help with this problem."

"But will she?" the speaker asked, and all eyes bore into me.

I stared back. "Before, I traveled at the behest of Sir Henry, who's my employer. You need to get his support before you ask me."

"And that depends on exactly what you want her to do and whether her tasks involve traveling," Sir Henry said.

The speaker nodded, a grave expression on his face. "That's to be decided. We—"

A man about Sir Henry's age, with jet black hair and a thin face like a hawk, said, "The situation in Czechoslovakia is grave. The British and French are going to capitulate, never mind what their alliances and agreements with Czechoslovakia say. By spring the whole country will be awash in Nazis. Where will the Jews be then? We need to act."

"We all agree the situation is grave, Abram," the speaker said. "But with Elias dead, can his network continue? Is there anything that can be done using his methods?"

A pretty, dark-haired young woman sitting near Esther let loose a sob and looked around as she mouthed her apologies. She set her handbag on the floor with a thud and buried her face in a handkerchief. The young man next to her patted her back as he gave her a comforting smile.

"Leah," the speaker said, "I know you come from Prague and must be worried for your family and friends, but now is the time we must be brave. We will find alternative ways to rescue as many as possible. To send them to Palestine."

"Or here. Or the United States," the man called Abram added in a sharp tone.

"Yes," the speaker agreed with a sigh. I guessed he was a Zionist, and this was probably an ongoing disagreement he and Abram had concerning British-controlled Palestine.

"We're going to need those young men to fight the Nazis when they attack Britain," Abram said. "We must get as many out as possible before it's too late."

A stocky, middle-aged man with thinning hair and a broad face rose and spoke to the gathering. "We need to contact Elias's organization. Find out if anyone can take over the reins. If not, then we might want to turn our attention to resettling as many of our Czechoslovakian brethren as we can while we can."

"Elias gave us no way to contact his network, if there even is a network," the speaker countered, still standing resolutely at the podium.

"Daniel," Abram said, ignoring the speaker, "we might as well contact the head of the Jewish community in Prague and ask if any of them want to emigrate now. They'll be able to leave in a better financial state today than they will be in a few months under Herr Hitler."

"Abram," a man across the room said, "the Germans may take the Sudetenland, but they're not going to take the rest of Czechoslovakia. Why would they?"

"Because Hitler wants to take over the world and kill every one of us," Abram answered in a loud voice.

"Before he does," the stocky man called Daniel said, "let's send word to the community in Prague and see if they want our help."

Murmurs of agreement circled the room.

There was more discussion about Elias and his death, but nothing that would help me pinpoint the leak that led an assassin to him. As soon as the meeting broke up, Esther came over to me. "The least we can do is feed you dinner, since we've ruined your evening."

"You didn't ruin my evening, but I'd love to have

dinner with you. Won't James mind a guest being sprung on him at the last moment?"

"He had to go to York. Father and I have already been invited by Daniel Nauheim and his son and daughter-in-law. You'll round out the table."

"Esther, I can't just show up at their door." I'd never met any of these people. Why would they invite me to dinner?

"My father's been singing your praises to Mr. Nauheim. He said to bring you along because he wants to meet you."

"To size me up for whatever plot is being hatched, you mean."

"Livvy." Esther glared at me. "You did a great deal of traveling before you went to work for my father. And you solved your husband's murder. It's your experience that Mr. Nauheim is interested in. Come on. I'll introduce you."

"All right." I knew Esther wouldn't be satisfied until I met these people. And found the traitor.

Esther tugged me forward to where Sir Henry was speaking to the stocky, broad-faced Daniel Nauheim. She made the introductions as the young woman who had sobbed and the man who'd comforted her joined us. Esther explained they were David and Leah Nauheim, Daniel's son and daughter-in-law. We shook hands and then all of us headed out to the automobiles.

I caught a ride with Sir Henry and Esther. Sir Henry had no more than given his chauffeur directions when he said, "Nicely done, Livvy. They won't be so quick to send you off on a fool's errand if they know they have to convince me first."

"Doesn't anyone know the dead man's colleagues?" I asked.

"He trusted no one. The people he brought out were aware there were others involved in their rescue, but they don't know names or how to reach them."

Wonderful. A whole group of people wanted me to find a man's murderer, but no one knew the identity of the man's friends or colleagues.

There was no way to know if any of his friends were in London. Worse, I was beginning to suspect one of the members of the committee, all of whom were in London, was the killer.

CHAPTER FIVE

"There seems to be some hope that you, with your knowledge of German and impeccable Aryan credentials, could look for Elias's contacts in Germany," Sir Henry said.

"The committee thought I'd run around Germany looking for this secret organization of Jewish communists? The Nazis would follow me and, if I found them, arrest everyone, including me. Do they think I have a death wish?" They were crazy if they thought that, and if they weren't crazy, I was insulted to be held in such low regard.

Sir Henry shook his head. "I don't think that was what they really had in mind, if and when they'd thought it through. What I'm curious to learn is if any of them could be a possible link to a Nazi assassin in London."

"They all appeared to be normal, prosperous Londoners. Of course, I only saw them together tonight as a group."

"That's who they are as individuals, too," Esther said. "Elias must have been followed. Either that, or someone in the couture house set him up."

"The Duke of Marshburn has a reputation as a Nazi sympathizer," I said and caught Sir Henry's eye.

"I've heard there are parts of the government that believe he'll need to be watched closely if we go to war with Germany," Sir Henry replied.

"He's not just the landlord of that building. I met him coming in as I was leaving this morning, and I didn't see a rent book in his hand. He and Mimi Mareau are rumored to be quite close."

Esther's eyes widened and she leaned closer as I shared my bit of gossip.

"So we have another possibility for the leak. Still, it doesn't get us any further forward." Sir Henry looked out the window and said, "Ah, here we are."

"Here" was a lovely house a few miles outside of Richmond. Built before Victorian excess, the building had classical columns on either side of the door. The nine-over-nine pane windows were favored by the Georgians. For its age, it was well maintained, with gardens trimmed to perfection.

"What does Mr. Nauheim do for a living to afford a place like this?" I asked.

"You sound like a Bolshevik, Livvy," Sir Henry said, helping Esther get out of the auto. Without turning around to see the glare on my face at that slur, he added, "He's the head of the Scotland and East Anglia Bank."

I needed to have some idea of what I was walking into. "Does his son work there, too?"

"Yes. He's a manager in the commercial section." As he escorted us up the short walkway, he added, "Daniel, the elder Mr. Nauheim, is rumored to be on the list for knighthood."

Sir Henry, and apparently soon Mr. Nauheim, earned their knighthoods based on vast wealth and service to the nation. My father was a baronet, an inherited title that in his case came with status but didn't come with money or property. My father was a Whitehall diplomat, a post that didn't pay particularly well.

Certainly not well enough for me and my love of exquisite clothes and posh holidays when I'd first come out into society.

The butler showed us into a drawing room done in golds and yellows with some nice artwork on the walls. All three of the Nauheims rose when we walked in and greeted us warmly. The butler poured us glasses of good sherry before Daniel Nauheim asked me, "How long have you worked for Sir Henry?"

"Less than a year, but he's known me since Esther and I were in school together."

"I was already familiar with her fluency in German and French and how much she had traveled with her father," Sir Henry said.

"And a certain amount of acting ability she employed to get us both out of tight situations," Esther added.

"I lost most of my hair thanks to the two of them and their antics when they were girls," Sir Henry said.

By now I could feel my cheeks heating.

"Spirited. You sound like someone who can handle any emergency," Mr. Nauheim said. By now I had picked up his faint accent. German.

A footman signaled him and Mr. Nauheim said, "Shall we go in to dinner?"

I found myself seated between Mr. Nauheim at the head of the table and Sir Henry, and directly across from

Esther at a table lavishly set for six. I counted the forks and realized after the soup there would be a fish course, a meat course, and a salad course. A heavy dinner that would take a while to eat. We'd no doubt learn a lot about each other as we talked, but I'd be tired at work the next day. Thank goodness tomorrow was Friday.

The soup was gently cooked summer vegetables in chicken stock with a good seasoning. Mr. Nauheim had a good cook. There was silence at the table until Esther finished hers and said, "This soup was wonderful."

"It's an old family recipe," Mr. Nauheim said.

"From Germany," I said, rather than asked.

"You heard my accent," he said. "I've worked so hard to get rid of it."

"It's not at all noticeable," I assured him. "I've heard a lot of accents in my travels with my father and later my husband, and I developed a good ear for them."

"Why did you travel with them?" he asked.

"Both worked at Whitehall in the Foreign Office. My father still does."

"And your husband?"

"Died last year. That's why I went to work for Sir Henry."

"I am sorry. I lost my wife five years ago, and I still find it painful."

"You have my condolences." I didn't want to explain that part of my pain was because my husband was murdered, while Scotland Yard assumed at the beginning that he had committed suicide. "Your son and daughter-in-law must be a comfort."

"Leah is a relatively new addition to our family. And a very welcome one, too." He nodded to the woman in the hostess's seat at the far end of the small table, and she smiled in reply. "It was only David and me for far too long."

I wondered when the woman would speak. I'd not heard her utter a word since we sat down at the table.

I gave my host a reply that would let him take the conversation any way he wanted. "My father lost my mother twenty years ago. I imagine trying to raise me was a struggle."

"You are apparently a free spirit, Mrs. Denis." At least he added a smile.

I was saved from replying as the servants took away our soup course and brought in the fish. It was well-seasoned cod, and silence descended in the room again.

This gave me time to consider what I'd heard at the meeting. When Mr. Nauheim set down his fork and adjusted his napkin, I asked him, "If this has become a matter of contacting the Jewish community in Prague and offering to sponsor them, you won't need me for anything. They can take trains and ferries and use their own passports. So why am I here? Do you know more about Elias's network than was shared at the meeting?"

He considered me for some time through dark brown eyes. "No. I don't. You're here for a different reason."

The way he spoke, weighing each word, made me nervous. "What reason is that?"

"Sir Henry isn't the only one who thinks there is a leak in our group. A leak led a Nazi assassin to the man calling himself Elias. A leak stopped his work in rescuing German Jews. We have to plug the leak, Mrs. Denis, as well as rescue our people. We're running out of time."

Mr. Nauheim was clear on what he wanted. I wished I was as clear at finding a way to uncover this leak. "Do you have any idea of who this person might be? I don't know any of the people on your committee who knew or spoke to Elias. For starters, how well did you know him?"

"Hardly at all. Abram Mandel, the one who is so sure Hitler will take all of Czechoslovakia, is the head of our committee. He was contacted by Elias when he brought in the first group a few weeks ago. At Elias's request, Mandel arranged to provide assurances of support for the first group to the British government. Elias went back almost immediately and brought out his second group, at which time he contacted Mandel again."

He stopped talking as the servants removed the fish course and brought in a beef course. We all remained quiet as we ate, but I chafed under the social restriction. I wanted to learn as much as possible before the hour grew too late. I had to get up early.

Perhaps Mr. Nauheim needed to rise early also, because after he had finished a bit more than half his food, he set down his fork and said, "After Mandel provided guarantees for this second group, Elias asked for funds to pay the forger and the fishermen. Mandel insisted he stay and talk to our committee before he'd provide any money."

"How many people did he speak to?"

"There are sixteen all told in our group, but only ten

heard him speak. I found him to be a forceful and appealing speaker. Charismatic. Very clear on his mission. Any points of disagreement to his plan were quickly refuted with a persuasive counterargument."

"What you might call a natural leader. He was also a good-looking man. Leah couldn't take her eyes off of him," David Nauheim added.

His wife rolled her eyes.

"So you were three of the ten who heard him speak," I said.

"No," David said, "the three of us count as one. One family."

"So instead of ten people hearing him speak at this meeting, there were really—?" The hunt just became larger.

"At least thirty," Mr. Nauheim answered.

Something inside of me sank. "Did Elias have any quarrels with anyone?"

"No," Mr. Nauheim told me. "We made arrangements for him to stay at a discreet hotel since he was worried about coming to the attention of the Nazis, even in as safe a city as London. Everyone seemed pleased to contribute to help with his bills and subscribed to a fund to pay for bribes and forgeries to be set up in a Swedish bank."

"Why a Swedish bank?"

"They are as neutral as they can be in the current situation. And a Swedish bank wouldn't draw as much attention, or suspicion, as a British bank would."

"So you considered Elias to be the genuine article?" Sir Henry said. "A real opposition leader."

"Yes. He was well known for speaking out against the Nazis. The Nazis caught him early in their reign, and he was beaten and jailed. Once he was released, or escaped, no one is sure which, he went underground. He encouraged people to resist the government, and when that was no longer possible, to leave. His last act of defiance was to help Jews escape to the west by traveling east, through Poland and on to Sweden."

"But you have no idea how to get in touch with his organization in Germany?"

"None at all. It must be a small organization. He might have been doing all of this on his own. I've heard he was daring."

I studied Mr. Nauheim for a moment. "Daring people don't often get themselves killed in a London basement."

"That's why there must be a leak."

Pressing him, I asked, "Who?"

He shook his head. "I don't know. I don't like pointing fingers at my friends. It seems so out of character for any of them."

"Perhaps one of them let something slip to someone who's behind the attack," I suggested.

"Then that would mean one of them has unsavory friends." He put up a hand. "No. I can't believe it."

Listening to him say none of them could be behind the attack wasn't getting us any further. "Why don't you just tell me about the ten and maybe something will come to light?"

"Sir Henry and Mrs. Powell you know."

I nodded. Sir Henry was involved because Esther had

been so keen to get her mother's family out of German-held territory. I'd known them forever. There was no way they could be the leak.

"The three of us."

Could he have invited us to throw suspicion away from him? "Tell me a little about yourselves."

"I was born in Germany and went to school there. At the turn of the century, I came to England and went to work for the Scotland and East Anglia Bank. At the time, it was run by some cousins of mine. I married and we had David." He shrugged.

I turned to David. "How did you meet your wife?"

"I met up with some old friends in Prague while I was there on bank business and they introduced us." He gave his wife a smile.

"Have you been married long?"

"Not long, only a year," Leah said in a quiet voice with a thick accent. "I was studying economics at the university. We became engaged before I graduated. As soon as I finished, I came here and we married."

She appeared to be close to my age, and Esther and I had finished university five years before. Perhaps she began university late for some reason or took courses for an advanced degree.

"I went to university at Oxford," David said, "and immediately afterward, Father had me join the bank to learn something practical."

From the smiles between father and son, I decided this was a long-standing joke. I looked around the table at the others. "Have any of you mentioned Elias being here, or anything about his work, to anyone?"

Sir Henry and Mr. Nauheim confirmed that they had discussed Elias's work and requests with others in the committee. The younger generation shook their heads.

"And you don't think any of your servants could be behind this?"

They all denied any possibility that their employees could be involved in a murder. Mr. Nauheim said, "They've been with me a long time. We can speak freely in front of them."

At that moment, Mr. Nauheim's staff removed the last course and brought fresh plates with fruit, crackers, and honey.

When they left, I said, "Tell me about the others."

"The chairman tonight was there with his wife. He was chair simply because the meeting was in their home. They own a chain of department stores. Both of them were born and educated in Britain."

"As dry and unimaginative as our Christian neighbors. That's why they are so successful with their stores," David added.

They had to be successful to live in a house as large and magnificent as the one we'd visited in Blackheath.

"Not all of our Christian neighbors are unimaginative," his father said and gave Sir Henry and me a smile.

"I meant no offense," David immediately said, coloring slightly.

"None taken," I told him. "I need you to speak freely if I'm to understand where to look for the leak."

"Tonight's meeting chairman, along with a successful heart doctor, leads the Zionist movement in London. They want all of us to pack up and move to Palestine," Mr. Nauheim said.

"That sounds like he has an imagination," I replied, looking at David. "I can't imagine that you'd want to, but can new arrivals resettle there?"

"The British government is against it, not wanting to upset the Arabs in the area. The only people arriving there must sneak in," Mr. Nauheim said. "And with our efforts focused on getting as many out of Germany as possible, our group doesn't want the extra burden of smuggling people into another land thousands of miles away from here."

"I'm sure you heard Abram Mandel speak at the meeting tonight," David said.

"Oh, yes. He seems to have a very clear picture of what the Nazis plan to do." I shivered, despite the warmth of the clear September evening. "I hope he gives them more credit than they deserve."

"There's no end to Hitler's ambition. I agree with Abram there. His solution is to rescue as many young people as possible, on the theory that they will make good soldiers to fight the Nazis in the coming war," the elder Nauheim said.

"And we'll need all the warriors we can find when the war starts. From the rumors I hear at the paper, Germany has a several-year head start on us in building planes and tanks and munitions factories." I glanced at Sir Henry, who nodded.

"Abram Mandel and his family have a chain of pharmacies. He served in the British army in France during the war and saw the effects of the gas attacks. He's never forgiven Germany," Mr. Nauheim said.

"Not someone likely to aid a Nazi assassin," I said.

The older man shook his head. "None of us are, but Abram is the least likely."

It wasn't until we were leaving that I was able to ask Leah, "Were you able to follow our conversation? I don't know how fluent you are in English."

"I had to study it in university. It is my fourth language. I understand it, but I have trouble forming the words to speak. It wants to come out in German. Or French, or some combination," she added.

"But you're glad to be here?"

"Of course." Indignation poured out in her tone. "I'm not a fool. I am safe here in England. I don't want to go back. Ever."

Esther walked over and gave Leah a hug. "There's no reason for you to go back. We're very glad you're here."

"Thank you, Esther."

I stood there a little awkwardly, ignored by the other two. These were questions I had to ask if I was to find one traitor in a group strongly opposed to the Nazis.

On the other hand, the traitor might not be part of the committee. Reina, Mimi Mareau's head seamstress, seemed to know more than she was willing to say. I'd have to look closer into the ladies at Mimi's couture house.

CHAPTER SIX

The next night, Friday, I was late leaving work, having once again made a mistake in my copy. I was looking forward to reaching my flat and kicking my shoes off, but when I finally walked the last streets from the Underground stop and unlocked my door, I discovered the light was on in my drawing room, and I could hear men arguing.

I walked to the drawing room doorway and leaned on it as I pulled off my shoes. Captain Adam Redmond, my special friend, was facing my father, Sir Ronald Harper. They were standing toe to toe and their expressions said they were trying to kill each other with glares alone.

"I come home and find my two favorite men," I said as I stepped between them. "Hello, Father. Hello, Adam." My father got a peck on the cheek. Adam, who'd been gone for a few weeks, received a longer kiss on the lips that promised more later.

"He has a key to your flat!" my father exclaimed in horror, interrupting my welcome to Adam.

I turned to find him all gray-haired, black-suited, elegant Foreign Office indignation. "Of course. Otherwise, how could he have let you in?"

"Olivia." My father was scandalized.

Adam kept a straight face, but when I glanced at him,

I could see a smile in his eyes.

"I came to ask you to go to dinner with me tonight, but now I suppose it will have to be the three of us," my father said with an aggrieved sigh.

"I'd be very grateful, Sir Ronald. The food on base is beastly."

"You're very welcome, Captain. And then we can both ask Olivia what she is up to."

Adam's eyes narrowed. "What are you up to?"

"Are you two going to dinner dressed like that? Then I won't dress for dinner either. You don't mind this suit? Good. The chophouse?" I suggested. I wasn't sure how much my father had heard in his position in the Foreign Office, and I wasn't going to give anything away.

"That will be fine," my father said.

"What are you up to?" Adam repeated.

"Can it wait until after dinner? I'm starved." I gave him a smile.

The edges of his mouth tugged up. "Yes, it can. I haven't had a bite to eat since breakfast. Too busy trying to make my connections."

That told me wherever he was stationed, it was in the middle of nowhere again. I was less confident that it was in Britain.

Adam and I looked bedraggled, he in his travel-smudged suit and I in my work-wrinkled outfit. Only my father looked pressed and pristine. We walked the few streets to the chophouse and, since it was early, were seated almost immediately.

Father ordered a bottle of red wine to go with our

chops, potatoes, and green vegetables. As soon as the waiter walked away, he said in a low voice, "Olivia found the body of a dead German in the basement of Mimi Mareau's new salon in Mayfair."

Adam looked startled before he said, "Who was the dead man?"

"His *nom de guerre* was Elias."

"Means nothing to me," Adam said.

We all fell silent as the wine arrived until it had been poured and the waiter left again. My father took a roll and passed the basket to Adam. "He was a German communist and a Jew. We had word that he had developed a smuggling ring. Moving Jews from Germany through Poland and Sweden or Denmark and into Britain."

"Any of this true?" Adam asked me, holding the bread basket out of reach.

"I'd like a roll."

"I'd like an answer."

I glared at him until he passed me the rolls. "It's true as far as it goes," I told him. "The Nazis had been after him for quite some time for stirring up the working masses."

"Apparently, this Elias fellow was out in the open in London and so he was killed," my father said.

As usual, my father had the story halfway wrong. "He knew the Nazis wanted him dead. He stayed out of sight."

"Obviously, they found him." My father made the whole problem sound so simple. Too simple.

"He was killed by blows to the back of the head. There was no place to hide in that basement, and he would never have turned his back on anyone he didn't trust. I don't believe he was killed by a German assassin."

"She's right about that," Adam said to my father. "Nobody being hunted is going to turn their back on a stranger."

My father glanced around and lowered his voice a bit more. "There's a rumor about a Nazi assassin in London. We know nothing about this person. Young, old, male, female. Only that this person is very well trained and can blend in and go anywhere. Downing Street is worried about this killer coming here to attack the cabinet."

"Where did this rumor come from?" I was skeptical and didn't try to hide it. A deadly killer who could transform himself or herself into an invisible man and go anywhere and do anything? It sounded like some of the other myths about the "master race."

"The French."

"That explains it," Adam said with a grin.

My father ignored him. "They've been chasing this phantom for the past two years. This person, who's believed to be French, has murdered half a dozen influential refugees and French politicians sympathetic to stopping German rearmament."

"Why have they not at least written up a description?" Adam asked.

"This person uses poisons or explosives and strikes at a distance. The killings have been clever."

Our meals arrived and we turned our attention to our food. It was quite a while before I could ask, "If they have no idea who this person is, why do the French think he, or she, has come here?"

"The Sûreté found the supplier of explosives. A chemist with underworld connections. Once they found the right pressure to apply, the chemist admitted he had sold explosive chemicals to a French person who had bought extra for a trip 'across the Channel for work.' The chemist claimed he'd handed off the chemicals and received payment at a distance and couldn't describe any identifying features." My father's expression was grim.

"I understand why Scotland Yard is worried about this killer coming here," Adam said.

"Or this chemist could have said those things to throw the police off the scent," I suggested.

"We're keeping an open mind," my father said.

I couldn't picture my father having an open mind, but I kept that opinion to myself. "Has this killer ever been suspected of sneaking up behind someone and hitting them over the head like Elias was?"

"No. I agree that this killing has nothing in common with the murders committed by this assassin, but we need to keep the presence of a Nazi assassin in mind. Not you, Olivia," my father added, "you've had quite enough to do with murder and with smuggling people out of Germany."

"I still haven't heard how you got involved with this murder," Adam said to me.

I gave him a shortened version, leaving out the Duke of Marshburn and my fascination with Mimi Mareau's fashions.

Adam stared at my father. "You can't fault her for

that. She had no way of knowing what she was walking into."

"But once involved, I'm sure she and that publisher of hers will not only walk in further, but jump, skip, and run into the middle of this murder investigation." My father finished his glass and poured himself more wine.

"That's not fair." I knew it was true, but becoming involved was my choice.

"Sir Henry has sent you to Germany twice. He'll probably find a reason to send you there again to help out more of his late wife's relatives and Elias's relatives, too." My father was glaring at me now.

"Elias's killer is here in London. I don't need to go anywhere, unless you want me to chase after an unknown German assassin." I glared back at him.

The look of horror on his face was almost laughable. "I would never dream of sending you after a killer. And especially not to Germany."

He'd been furious when I went to Nazi Germany and then occupied Austria for Sir Henry in an effort to get Esther's mother's family, and their valuables, out safely. Sir Henry had me on a hunt again, but this one was in London.

"This was no unknown German assassin," I told him. "The man known as Elias turned his back on his killer. He knew him."

"Any idea what the murder weapon was?" Adam asked me.

"No. There was nothing obvious in that basement that could have been used as a cosh. Whatever Elias was killed with, the killer took it away with him."

"Or her," my father added. "No murder weapon. No fingerprints. And the killer wasn't seen. Sounds like the French assassin working for the Nazis to me."

* * *

Adam and I spent the rest of the weekend lazing about my flat, eating out, going to the cinema, and one night we attended a party where we danced the night away. Once he left at noon on Sunday after a fond farewell, I knew I wouldn't have long to wait before I heard from my father.

It took half an hour. I answered my phone, knowing whose voice would come out at me. "Olivia, get dressed. I'll come around to pick you up for luncheon at the Greenbrier."

That required something smarter than anything in my work wardrobe. I chose a lavender and gray outfit appropriate for tea with the queen. Well, if it was a very large tea party, and if I wouldn't be noticed. I paired the frock with gray heels, a matching bag, and a hat with a turned-down brim designed to be worn tilted to one side.

Father picked me up in a taxi and we rode to the Greenbrier, the elegant restaurant and hotel that hadn't changed since Edward VII frequented its private salons with Queen Alexandra—or with one or another of his many mistresses.

Once we were seated, the first words out of my father's mouth were, "You need to straighten your hat."

"It's designed to be worn this way."

"Why?"

"Because it's fashionable."

"Seems a bit slovenly to me." Then he turned his attention to the wine list and the menu.

We were almost at the end of the meal before he said, "I've set up a meeting for you with General Alford for this afternoon."

"General Alford?" I blinked. The general was or had been Adam Redmond's commanding officer, and Adam worked on clandestine matters. "Because of the body I found?"

"Because of where you found it." My father then tasted his coffee and said, "This is quite good. They've always made good coffee here. Even during the war."

It was obvious I wouldn't get any more out of him. That left me drinking my tea while wondering what Adam would make of me visiting his sometime boss on a Sunday afternoon.

After we finished, we took a cab to the area of Whitehall, Whitehall Place, and Whitehall Court, the streets around the War Office. I hoped General Alford was more imaginative than the men who named the streets.

The general met us in the lobby, led us to a small ground-floor conference room, and offered us seats. The chairs were solid and straight-backed, guaranteeing no one would fall asleep during a meeting. "Now," he began, "tell me about the place you found Elias's body."

"It was toward the back of the basement of the building at number 31, Old Burlington Street. The basement is being used for storage for finished frocks and costumes for a play and who knows what else."

"Can you be more specific?"

I tried to picture details without remembering Elias's body lying there. "There were some trunks against the wall opposite the outside door. They possibly contain fabric and other things Mimi might need for her business. The door to the outside leads to a flight of cement steps going up to the pavement. There also a wooden staircase halfway between the trunks and the outside door leading upstairs inside the building."

Looking over, I found Alford nodding as if I'd made myself clear.

"Was the door to the outside open or closed?" he asked.

"Closed."

"Locked or unlocked?"

That stumped me for a moment. "I don't know. I opened it from the inside without any difficulty, and I didn't see a key, but I suppose I wouldn't have needed one from the inside. The bolt was off."

"Will you be going back to the dressmaker's shop?"

Calling Mimi Mareau a dressmaker was like calling the king a member of the aristocracy, but I let it go. "I'm going there tomorrow afternoon for an article I'm writing for the *Daily Premier.*"

"Good. You're an intelligent girl, Mrs. Denis. We want you to look around. Talk to the staff. See if any of them are acting suspiciously."

"Don't you have people who can do this?" It sounded like I was about to be used, and I found that very distasteful.

"No. You speak French fluently, you understand fashion, and you know a number of their customers from your time at school. You're perfectly placed to do a little snooping."

At that, my father sat forward, his eyes widening in anger or horror. "I don't want my daughter snooping like some American private eye in the cinema. It's dangerous. It's unseemly."

"I wouldn't ask her if it weren't necessary," General Alford assured him.

"Why do you want me to snoop around?" If I was going to be used, I'd like to know why.

The general leaned forward slightly. "This is in the strictest confidence. Elias, not his real name, was helping us. He was providing up-to-the-minute intelligence."

"Elias was a British spy?" And he was murdered in Mimi's basement?

"Well, he was spying for us. Not quite officially. And his name was Josef Meirsohn."

I found that hard to take in. "I thought this Elias, or Meirsohn, was smuggling Jews out of Germany." At least that was what Sir Henry believed.

"He was. It was quid pro quo rather than a cash transaction. We'd let in his groups of refugees and he'd bring us intelligence. On this last trip, he told us a French assassin working for the Nazis was, or would soon be, in London and he had an idea of how to find this person. No one had been able to identify this French assassin before."

CHAPTER SEVEN

I blurted out the first thought to cross my mind. "So he smuggled people into Britain and had identified a French assassin. Where did you meet? Here at the War Office?" That would destroy any cover he might have.

"Of course not. We met at his hotel." The general appeared annoyed that I would think the army would be so foolish.

"How did he plan to find this unidentified French assassin?" I expected to discover I would become the bait to set the trap.

"He said he hadn't had any better luck identifying the assassin than the Sûreté had, but he'd learned this person would arrive in England and get in contact with an English nobleman. The nobleman would provide details of the assassin's next attack."

"This was all he told you?" There wasn't much to help us.

"Yes." General Alford looked a little embarrassed.

"Did he name the English nobleman? Did he name the victim?" Something that would help us?

"No. Nothing." The general's face reddened. "He thought we could follow every peer of the realm until one of them led us to a Frenchman."

"Impossible." My father sounded shocked.

"And then he was found dead in Mimi Mareau's

basement." Not much help, but it did point the finger at the four women living in that building. "That would mean you think the assassin is a woman."

He shook his head. "Not necessarily. There must be a couple of men associated with the salon. Hopefully you'll meet some man working there soon if you haven't already."

"Do you suspect the Duke of Marshburn?"

Both my father and the general looked at me with horrified expressions. The general said, "Good heavens, no. He's a duke, no matter where his political beliefs might take him. Besides, he wasn't in the right country to have carried out assassinations we know were done by this mystery person."

"Tell me about these assassinations." I needed information, and little was being provided.

The general cleared his throat. "You cannot divulge this information to anyone. The so-called French assassin has killed half a dozen French politicians and refugee leaders, all by poison or explosions. No two methods were exactly the same. The French government has been completely frustrated. No suspects. No descriptions."

"It must be difficult when the murders were carried out at a distance. Poisonings, explosions." I could see why the police were unsuccessful.

"But there were elements in these attacks that indicated the assassin wasn't too far away. The weapons, if you will, could only have been sent short distances and over short times," the general said. "Since Elias had been on a Nazi assassination list for a couple of years, we don't know if he was the French assassin's target. Someone else could have executed him."

"So Elias could have been killed by any number of people for any number of reasons." What a mess. How could I find his killer among competing suspects? I probably didn't know most of them yet.

"Will you do this for us? For Britain?" Alford asked.

"What do you want me to do? What am I looking for?" This assignment seemed too vague to succeed. The French police had failed. Why did he think I could do better?

"Talk to people. Keep your eyes open. We want to hear what you find unusual. Questionable." General Alford scrunched up his face. "Oh, use your initiative, girl," he snapped.

I suspected General Alford was totally out of his depth when dealing with women or fashion. Even if I somehow stumbled over information that led right to the assassin, Alford wouldn't see the significance.

I hoped someone else was involved in this investigation. I hoped someone else was in charge of capturing the assassin. "I'll look around. I can't promise anything."

"I'm sure you'll do very well," the general said and gave me an uncertain smile.

After we left the building, I asked my father, "How did you get mixed up in this business?"

"Alford came to see me. You remember he was my commanding officer in the war, and when Scotland Yard told him who had found the body, and where, he recognized the name." He sighed. "While I was telling him not to get you involved, he was asking questions about your background."

"And he heard I speak French—"

"And he'd heard about your involvement in finding Reggie's killer—"

"Of course, he did." I allowed myself to sound annoyed. It had been almost a year since Reggie's death, and still, all anyone seemed to say about me was, "Wasn't she clever, finding the traitor who killed her husband?"

"The trouble is, Olivia, you have a talent for finding out people's secrets. And at this time, with all the difficulties Herr Hitler is causing, having a talent like yours is bound to be noticed." He made it sound like I had been bragging.

All I wanted was for everyone to forget.

* * *

After lunch the next day, Jane and I settled into a taxi and rode to Mimi Mareau's couture house. I still didn't know how I would handle General Alford's request.

There was now a discreet brass plaque next to the black-painted door saying *Maison Mareau*. We rang the bell and Brigette answered the door wearing a deep rose-colored smock.

"We're here for the tour Mimi promised us," I said.

"She hasn't returned from lunch," Brigette said as she opened the door more and let us in. Once again, I was surprised by how British she sounded when she spoke English.

When I complimented her on her lack of an accent,

she said, "A few years in an English boarding school will cure you of any accent."

I could see the front room now appeared to be copied from a country house drawing room, down to the comfortable chairs and worn rugs. I almost expected a retriever or setter to stroll in and curl up on the rug. "It looks a great deal different than the construction zone I saw last week."

"The painters and carpenters just finished the changing rooms upstairs this morning."

"I can't imagine Mimi wants us to see the changing rooms," I assured her. "What does the basement look like now that the police are done making a mess there?"

"They didn't make a mess," Brigette said.

"I'm surprised. May I see? They made a mess of my flat when I reported a burglary." I tried to sound annoyed, but I only managed to sound less eager than I felt.

Brigette shrugged. "Sure."

I hurried to the back room on the ground floor, which was empty of people at that moment, and galloped down the stairs. There was no key in the lock of the outside door, exactly the way I remembered. The windows were still shut. The bolt was still off.

Turning the other way, I found the racks held more covered costumes and gowns than last week. The boxes and trunks were still pushed against the far wall. There was no sign of blood. I couldn't picture Elias lying there anymore.

It was just an ordinary, but clean, basement.

I marched back up the stairs. When I reached the top, I heard Mimi saying, "Where is she?"

I came out of the back room, all grace and polish. "Hello, Miss Mareau. Ready for your interview? I imagine you want to be photographed in your workshop, looking over Reina's or Fleur's work."

"There's no magic in that. I'd like to be photographed in our new showroom looking at one of our designs on a model. As I will look on Wednesday for my fashion show." She snapped her fingers. "Brigette, put on the blue gown. And put up your hair."

Brigette headed up the wide, carpeted front staircase as I said, "There are four British designers who have been readying their salons for weeks for their shows this Wednesday. Don't you feel ill-prepared?"

"Why should I? I'm not some provincial seamstress with no experience. I'm Mimi Mareau. I've been putting on fashion shows in Paris for years."

There was no argument for that. "How many weeks a year do you plan to work in England?"

"I don't know. I expect for a few weeks after the Paris autumn and spring shows so I can bring a uniquely British slant to the newest fashions."

I scribbled furiously as I marveled at how good her answer was.

Mimi settled onto one of the chairs and lit a cigarette. "Many of my clients are British or American, and this new salon will be more convenient for them. Plus, we'll cater to special English and American tastes." She waved Jane over to take her photograph.

"Who will manage your London salon while you're away?"

"I haven't decided yet."

"How many of your employees will be working here while you are in residence in this salon?"

"You've met Fleur, Reina, and Brigette, my three right hands. Several seamstresses, another cutter, and an assistant to Brigette for the fittings arrived from Paris this weekend. My clients will keep all of us busy, but at *Maison Mareau*, we are at our best when facing a challenge. And the models for the show, wonderful girls, arrive tomorrow."

"Did the body of the dead man in your basement interfere with getting the salon ready to open?"

As I hoped, mentioning the dead man rattled Mimi. "No. Why should it?" she snapped.

"It might be considered—inconvenient." Like having to question a woman whose talent left me in awe on behalf of a general who didn't understand artistry or genius.

"So?" She stared at me as if she didn't understand how a dead man could be important.

I tried to explain. "The police would have blocked access to the basement and the frocks stored down there as well as stopping people from working by asking them questions."

She shrugged. "It was a minor inconvenience."

"Did any of you know the dead man?"

"Of course not." The man's temerity to die in her salon, not the waste of her time, seemed to anger her.

"Then why was he in your basement?"

"I have no idea." She stubbed out her cigarette. "Come upstairs and I will show you where we display our fashions and where customers come for fittings. Bring your camera," she added to Jane.

We followed her up the grand, carpeted front staircase to the first floor. The paint was the same color as downstairs, a pinkish beige, but here the furniture was modern. Instead of armchairs, there were black leather upholstered ottomans and curved padded benches to sit on. Neither looked comfortable. The floor was painted a shiny black.

She led us to a silver metallic cloth curtain at the back of the room and pushed it aside to reveal the doorway into the back of this floor. "This is where the magic takes place," she said, walking through.

I followed her to find a well-lit area with a number of closet-sized changing rooms and racks to hang outfits. The walls and floor were the same colors as on the other side of the curtain. The insides of the tiny chambers were mirrored on all sides and each contained a black leather ottoman.

"I'd like to take a photo of you inside one of the changing rooms," Jane said, and Mimi posed in the entrance to one so you could see her reflection in the mirror without getting Jane in the photo. She gestured Jane to set up on her right.

After she took the photo, Jane turned away to put her head near mine and murmured, "She had to practice, and practice hard, to give me an angle to photograph her that was so perfect."

"Brigette," Mimi called out behind us, "are you ready to go into the showroom in the blue gown?"

The girl stepped out of one of the small spaces, her hair piled up. She looked elegant in the sweeping gown, her posture erect and her chin up. "How do I look?"

"Breathtaking," I said.

"Let's go into the showroom," Jane said, walking through the curtained opening and checking her light meter.

"Once the gowns are designed and the customer is measured, how many frocks can you make in a week?" I asked as Mimi and Brigette posed for Jane.

"By sending seamstresses to and from Paris, I can handle any demand we may have in either city," Mimi said, her head up, one fist on her waist with her arm akimbo.

I jotted her response down. "Are Reina and Fleur here so I can get their photographs for the article, too?"

"Fleur's not returned from lunch. You'll find Reina upstairs with the seamstresses. You'll have to use the back staircase to get to the next floor."

I thanked her and took off through the changing room and then up the stairs, hoping to get a word with Reina before Mimi stopped me. I heard Jane say, "That shot wasn't any good. Let's try once more."

When I reached the second floor, Reina was showing three women the stitching on a wool tweed skirt. All four wore deep rose dusters like Brigette's that had to be the uniform for this fashion house. Reina looked over at me and I waved for her to come over as I walked forward.

Setting down the skirt, she met me in the middle of the room.

"Reina, who was he?" I asked her in German in a low voice.

A shocked look crossed her face.

"The dead man. Who was he?" When she didn't answer, I said, "Well?"

After a moment, her shoulders drooped. "Josef Meirsohn. I told you, we came from the same village. He went away to university and I never saw him again."

General Alford was right. And my guess that Reina knew Elias's real name paid off. "Do you know who would want to kill him?"

"*Nein.*"

"Come down here, Reina. We don't have all day to take your photograph," Mimi bellowed up the stairs.

She grabbed my arm. "I'm afraid to have my picture taken. If Josef was killed because of something from the old days, they might come after me next."

I made a quick decision. "Don't worry. No one will see it." But it might prove useful in the investigation. "But why was he here? Had you arranged to meet him here?"

Instead of answering me, she rushed downstairs. I followed and then Jane and I had the three women pose as the sound of the front door banging shut reached us. "Anyone here?" Fleur shouted in French.

"Yes, come up here," Mimi yelled back.

Fleur came up but hesitated when her gaze fell on Jane and her camera. "Oh, no. I look a fright."

"Get in the photo," Mimi said.

"I haven't brushed my hair."

"Come over here. I'll comb it," Reina said.

"No. You're too rough." Fleur pulled out a brush and walked into the back area where there were mirrors.

We waited about two minutes before Mimi called out, "Fleur?"

There was no answer.

Mimi cursed in French and stormed into the back room. "Where are you?"

"Here."

The two women came out, Fleur transformed by a dramatic drape of fabric over her head and shoulders. Only her eyes peeked out from beneath the black velvet.

She was completely unrecognizable.

They lined up then with Jane looking annoyed. It would make a terrible picture. Before Jane could snap the shutter, however, Mimi yanked the fabric away from Fleur's face.

CHAPTER EIGHT

I suspected Fleur looked shocked in the photo as the flash went off.

"Let's try that again," Jane suggested.

Fleur and Reina both said "*Non*" and hurried toward the back room and the staircase.

Mimi shook her head at her assistants' antics. Then she looked at me and said, "Do you have my drawing?"

I pulled it out of my handbag, awaiting her decision with trepidation. I wanted her to like my work. To like me.

Although I was spying on her for a general.

Mimi studied the paper. "It's good, but not quite right." She then pointed out several things she wanted changed. "Corrected," she called it.

My pride tripped and landed, nose first, on the pavement.

After a few more questions, Mimi showed us down the grand staircase and out the front door. She was gracious, she was charming, and she couldn't wait to get rid of us. The door nearly hit me on the backside as I left.

"That was a little strange," Jane commented as we looked in vain for a taxi.

"I want a copy of the picture of all of them. As large as you can blow it up without it getting fuzzy," I told her.

"Why?"

"I don't know. I have this feeling that having a record of what these women look like could be useful."

Jane stopped and stared at me. "You're doing another project for Sir Henry. The last one sent us both to Vienna. If this one sends you to Paris, count me in."

I understood her interest. I would like a newspaper-paid trip to Paris, too. "So far, it doesn't take us any farther than a few steps to the basement entrance."

Jane nodded and off we started. When we reached the cement stairs leading down to the basement where Elias, or as I now knew, Josef Meirsohn, died, I veered off and left Jane on the pavement without saying a word. I walked down three steps and bent to look in the window. Without light inside, I couldn't see a thing through the dirty glass.

I went down the rest of the steps and carefully turned the door handle. The lock must have been set on the latch because the door opened easily. I held up a hand to Jane, who was waiting up on the pavement, and went in, quietly shutting the door behind me.

If the now-dead man had come here for anything, it had to be in the trunks and boxes at the far end of the room. I tiptoed across and began to open them. The first few were empty, but I finally opened a trunk that held vials and little boxes and medicine bottles. I opened one of the tiny boxes and found a fine gray powder inside.

Just as I closed up the trunk, wondering at the reason for such things to be at a couture house, the ceiling lights came on.

The last thing I needed was to be caught snooping at

the site of a murder. Especially by the murderer.

My heart hammered against my ribs when I saw a woman's shoe appear at the top of the open staircase. I crept to the back side of the racks of gowns, hoping whichever one they wanted was in the front. Hoping they'd just take it and leave so I could escape.

I ducked down, hiding as best I could as footsteps sounded coming down the wooden stairs, and then heels clicked across the stone floor. They seemed to pass me. Then I heard what sounded like a box or trunk opening and the clink of glasses.

A moment later, the heel clicks crossed the floor again and started up the stairs. When they sounded as if they were most of the way up, I rose. All I could see was a pair of two-inch sensible heels in blue and the hem of a blue skirt that moved gracefully as the wearer disappeared from sight. Then the light clicked off.

I pictured the four women who had posed for the photographs just a few minutes before. Brigette's gown had been blue, but it was long. Mimi had worn gray, and she was always in stylish high heels. But both Fleur and Reina had worn blue day-length dresses and sensible shoes.

I tiptoed back to the door and slipped out into the sunshine, easing the door shut behind me and leaving it on the latch. I was grateful to find only Jane waiting for me, but my heart didn't stop pounding until we were safely in a cab on our way back to Fleet Street.

It took me until the end of the day to write up what I thought was a coherent article on my interview with

Mimi Mareau. Miss Westcott looked it over and shook her head, waving me away.

I went down to the photography section and asked for Jane. She was still in the darkroom, so I sat and waited as the others cleared their desks and left.

Jane came out about twenty minutes later. "You waited for me? Well, here are the best two shots for your story, and here's the photograph you wanted, blown up as much as I dared. It's awful. Brigette and Mimi both moved."

"It's the other two I want the photo for," I said as I studied it. Fleur's eyes were wide with surprise as Mimi grabbed her scarf, but it was a very good likeness. Reina looked frightened, but then I realized that was her usual expression. "Don't lose the negative to this one."

Jane nodded and leaned against a scarred desk. "What's going on? And what scared you in that basement?"

"What makes you think I was scared?" I said with all the bravado I could manage.

"You fled that basement as fast as you could without being too obvious and raced past me to signal for a taxi."

I felt my cheeks heat. Jane knew me too well. "Sir Henry wants to know who told an assassin that the man who was murdered would be in the basement. Probably a Nazi killer because the dead man had been leading German Jews to Britain." And spying on Nazi Germany. "I thought he might have gone there to look for something in one of the trunks, or put something in one of the trunks."

"Did you find anything?"

"Several were empty. One contained a lot of powders and vials and bottles. And then I was interrupted when one of the women came down and clattered glassware around. I hid so she didn't see me, but I didn't see what she was after or which trunk it was."

"Well," Jane said, her attitude all business and formal, "you'd better report to Sir Henry, and I'm off for the day. I'll keep your negatives safe for you."

I took the two photographs for the article and dropped them off with Miss Westcott, who'd already covered my copy with red ink. Then I went up to the top floor of the *Daily Premier* building.

Sir Henry's secretary had covered her typewriter and was powdering her nose in preparation for leaving. "Is he there?" I asked, and she nodded, gesturing toward his door.

I wished her a good evening as I walked past and knocked.

"Come in," boomed a man's voice.

I opened the door and slipped in, shutting it before Sir Henry noticed his secretary hadn't left yet. I knew he often kept her late when he was working on stories, even ones that might not make it into the newspaper.

"I was at Mimi Mareau's couture house this afternoon. Neither Fleur nor Reina wanted their pictures taken, but Jane managed to get one, with the help of Mimi." I laid the photo of the four women on his desk.

Sir Henry picked it up and studied it. "These are the four women staying at the house when Elias was murdered?"

"Yes."

He looked from the photograph to me, holding my gaze. "Which one did it?"

"I don't know." I knew he didn't want to hear I'd failed.

"Have you been able to eliminate anyone?"

"Brigette is only eighteen or nineteen. I think she's too young. Reina is Jewish and knew Elias from the days of her childhood when he was Josef Meirsohn. She's been frightened ever since he was killed. And I found out they keep the basement door on the latch, so anyone can come and go that way without being seen upstairs."

"You've been busy." He studied the photograph. "Why does this one look so surprised?"

"That's Fleur. She wrapped her head up in that piece of black velvet and Mimi pulled it off just before Jane shot her photograph."

"Why would she do that?"

"She doesn't want anyone seeing the photograph to recognize her?" I suggested.

"Perhaps she's wanted by the Sûreté."

I blinked. "For what?"

"For what, indeed? Does Mimi strike you as the type to hire a wanted criminal if she has the right skills for her business?" Sir Henry said with a faint smile.

"Yes." I took a deep breath. "When I came into the basement from outside, I checked some of the trunks and boxes. Most are empty, as you'd expect since they moved a great deal of goods from Paris for making frocks, but at least one trunk had vials and medicine bottles and boxes with strange powders in them. Another mystery."

"Perhaps one of them is ill."

"Perhaps." I wasn't convinced, but I admitted to myself that it was the most logical explanation.

"What's your next step?"

Well, it wouldn't be to tell him that I was expected to report in to the War Office. I still found their request to be unpalatable. "She's hired me to do a drawing for an advertisement."

He raised his eyebrows. Then he said, "Do it. It gives you a reason to go back there."

I pulled my drawing out of my bag and showed it to him as I pointed out the changes Mimi wanted.

He looked impressed. "She knows her stuff. And your drawing is quite good."

"Thank you." I must have beamed at the praise. "Also, I need to cover the fashion show she's putting on as part of autumn fashion week for aristocrats and the newspapers on Thursday. There will be five shows that day, but Jane and I need to cover Mimi's show. That will give me another chance to look around."

Now came the difficult part. "I need to find someone who could commission an original gown made by Mimi. Or a suit. I would suggest Esther, but her shape isn't permanent."

"Are you suggesting that the paper pay for you to have a dress made by Mimi Mareau?" He sounded both amused and outraged.

"No. Who would believe a reporter would have the

money to buy couture?" I wished I'd have that much money one day, but I wasn't expecting it to happen. "I need someone I can tag along with to fittings as a sisterly advisor." I had plenty of friends who were successful, friends in positions of influence, but no one with enough money to have a Mimi Mareau frock.

"I think we need to get Esther to suggest someone from the committee," Sir Henry said.

"If there's someone there who can act like she has known me for a while and would listen to my suggestions." I'd met them all once. Would any of them be willing to bring a stranger along while they spent a lot of money so I could snoop around the fashion salon?

He picked up the phone and dialed. The rotary wheel had barely come back to rest when he said, "Esther, that was quick. We need your help."

She must have given an eager response because he said, "Nothing like that. We need your advice on someone in the committee who would have a garment made by Mimi Mareau and would be willing to take Olivia along as a close friend to advise her. It's to help with this Elias investigation. No, you can't. The dress would never fit after the baby comes."

He pulled his ear away from the receiver and I heard a frustrated scream. Then he put his ear back and listened for a moment. "Very good. I'll tell her. Good-bye, dear girl."

When he hung up the phone, he said, "Esther will work on this and call you tonight when she has everything ready."

I raised my eyebrows. "That sounds like I will need to take time off from the society page desk on occasion."

"I suspect I'm going to have to bring Miss Westcott into our confidence." His expression said he wasn't looking forward to it.

I stopped at the greengrocer on my way back to the flat and bought a few summer vegetables and then went to the butcher for a bit of ham for dinner. Then I stopped at a bakery for two rolls, one for dinner and one for breakfast the next morning.

I was eating my dinner at the dining room table with a book and a glass of red wine when the phone rang.

Marking my place in the book with my napkin, I hurried into the hall and answered the phone.

Esther's voice came out of the receiver. "Livvy, can you meet me for lunch tomorrow? The Savoy? One o'clock?"

"Yes, your father will fix it for me. Is this about Elias and Mimi Mareau's salon?"

"I think I have the solution. You'll meet her at lunch."

"Ooh, mysterious." I hoped she could tell from my voice that I was joking.

"Not at all. I think you'll remember Leah Nauheim."

"Of course, I remember her. But why is she willing to help me? Why would she bring me along to order a new frock?"

"Her English isn't strong, and you can go along as her interpreter. She won't go to Paris because it's too close to Germany, but her husband has more than enough money for designer frocks. She thinks of this as a perfect situation."

"Does she know I'm going to snoop around and try to discover clues as to who killed Elias?"

"David knows about it and he's convinced Leah she won't be in any danger from the killer. They're both on the committee, and she's willing to help."

"Good. So you've arranged for us to meet tomorrow and see if we can work something out? Esther, thank you." My enthusiasm must have traveled down the telephone line.

"No, thank you. It's good to feel I can help."

"You'll be a very big help if you can convince Leah Nauheim to act like we're good friends."

* * *

I showed up at the Savoy dining room at the appointed time the next afternoon, having told Miss Westcott that I had to cover a meeting for Sir Henry. The look in her eyes made me certain she would check.

When I arrived, Esther and Leah both rose from the couch where they were waiting in the lobby.

My blue patterned dress with tiny pleats running from shoulders to cleavage was the height of fashion in the office, but both Esther and Leah made me look like a Newcastle coal miner's wife.

Esther kept on a bright red jacket with a gray fur collar and a wide hem that hid her waistline, but it was Leah's clothes I wanted to see. She didn't disappoint. She wore an ice-green linen suit with a raspberry blouse that just peeked out at the neckline. Her hat was a raspberry felt turban.

I suspected it was from Selfridge's, but her slim build and delicate bone structure made anything she wore as elegant as any couture design.

Esther and I air-kissed cheeks and Leah and I said it was a pleasure to see each other again as we followed the maître d'. We were formal and polite and even Esther, guaranteed to be lively, was somber.

We ordered clear soup, roast beef with vegetables, fruit ice, and a nice red wine, and then discussed fashion and what Leah could expect at Mimi's salon. It wasn't until our soup had been delivered and we were sure to be left alone for a few minutes that Leah said, "Livvy. May I call you Livvy?"

"Please."

"Esther has told me what you did to help her relatives escape." There was no need to mention where they escaped from. "This doesn't have anything to do with her relatives. Why are you willing to help?"

"I found Elias's body. And then I found out he was doing what I had been doing, but on a bigger scale and with a lot more risk. That took courage. What happened to him was a tragedy."

How could I explain that I admired this man I'd never met? He took risks to help his fellow man. I'd done nothing compared to what he'd accomplished before his killer stopped him, but I suspected he acted for the same reasons. Fair play. Right and wrong.

Leah gave me a hard look. "You're a Christian. You could tell Sir Henry you're done with the Nazis and danger and helping people escape. Why are you willing to help?"

I stared back at her and said in an even tone, "This is what Sir Henry hired me to do. I'm only a fair interviewer and a terrible newspaper writer. If I told him no, he'd sack me, or at least cut my wages to those of a junior society reporter. I need the money."

"Oh, no, Livvy, he wouldn't. And he says you do a very good job," Sir Henry's daughter said, loyal to both her father and me.

"Of course he would, Esther. Your father and I have a business arrangement. One that suits us both." I gave her a smile as I admitted something I wouldn't ordinarily say. "And we both know that I'd be bored if all I did was report on charity teas. Besides, I like these other assignments. I've found I like snooping around, seeing if I can outwit those who try to stop me." I felt as if I could help balance the scales on the side of right.

Even if I didn't, I'd still have to snoop for General Alford. And I couldn't admit to that.

I turned back to Leah. "So will you help me get into Mimi's salon in a capacity where I won't be noticed?"

CHAPTER NINE

Leah studied me, looking doubtful. "You are a reporter. Do you know anything about fashion?"

"I can sketch gowns, and I have a good eye for color and pattern, but I don't have any original ideas. I only know what I see ladies wearing. For example, I suspect your suit was originally from a designer's collection, and then made up for Selfridge's."

"You are right. And it was originally a Schiaparelli."

"It's beautiful."

She nodded.

We finished our soup and it was replaced by the roast course. As I ate, I wondered if she could she pull this off.

When she finished with what little she ate of her lunch, Leah said, "What makes you think going to this fashion house with me will make you invisible?"

I smiled. "Don't worry. That's my problem." Actually, I had no answer. "Can you act as if we've spent a great deal of time together while I've acted as your translator? I'm going to need to know details about your wedding, your house, and where you came from. You'll need to know about my flat, my job, and my late husband."

"He was murdered," Esther said, drawing a surprised look from Leah.

"You'll need to know a great deal more about Reggie

than how he died."

"How did he die?" Leah asked, and for the first time, I heard compassion in her tone.

I told her how the police had thought it was a suicide, and how I knew it couldn't be because Reggie couldn't pull a trigger with his right hand. And how he died trying to stop a Nazi sympathizer in his office in Whitehall from giving away the nation's secrets.

A succession of expressions crossed Leah's face, showing what she thought of each part of the story as I told it to her. I had thought at dinner at her house that she had been aloof. Now that I was getting to know her, I was discovering she wasn't.

"I'm going to have to go through your wardrobe so I know the styles and colors and fabrics you prefer," I told her.

A smile crossed Leah's face. She didn't often smile, but her face was radiant when she did. "It sounds like fun. Are you up for this, too, Esther?"

"A chance to look through your clothes? I wouldn't miss it."

"Can we do it this afternoon? I do not know what David or my father-in-law would think of the three of us rummaging through my dressing room. They are at work, so we will not bother them."

I had to ask. "Is your husband going to be upset about the cost of a designer dress?"

"No. He likes me looking nice and doesn't worry about the price as long as it doesn't scream 'shamefully expensive.'"

"You are so lucky."

"I am," she said with a dreamy smile. Then she blinked. "Will this present a problem at the newspaper?"

"I'll take care of that," Esther said, and the three of us made plans to go to Leah's.

We took a taxi out to Richmond after lunch. In the daylight, I could see their home was a large brick building situated in a good-sized garden. My flat would fit into a corner of the house. "This is out in the countryside. Does your husband find the commute difficult?"

"No. He travels to the bank with his father, or has the chauffeur drive him to the train station. Daniel always has the auto take him straight to the bank."

Then we went through the front door, up to her dressing room, and spent a pleasant couple of hours going through Leah's outfits.

I had to admit to being struck by jealousy.

"Well," Leah asked after we had "oohed" and "aahed" over her wardrobe, "you must have many suggestions to make."

"I think the only thing you could possibly lack is a gown from Mimi Mareau," I told her. "But you have such beautiful gowns."

"I was thinking more of a tweed suit. Something for autumn and winter. Something very English," Leah said.

I couldn't hide my smile. "This is where I have some expert knowledge. Mimi has designed a wool tweed suit with a sable collar that has a fantastic drape to it. It's part of the Duke of Marshburn's daughter's trousseau, and when the girl tried it on, I told Mimi everyone was going to want one."

"I don't want what everyone else is wearing if I'm paying couture prices," Leah said.

I shouldn't have been surprised at her frugality. Even the wealthy Jews in Eastern Europe guarded every penny. They'd been through tough times in every land over the past centuries.

"It's not the color or the fur that makes this suit, it's the cut," I told her. "A woman named Fleur is her chief cutter and I think she's the one who's figured out how to cut tweed so the drape, particularly the drape of the skirt, is so delightful."

"Do I tell her I want a suit cut the way she made a suit for the daughter of the Duke of Marshburn?" Leah asked, looking at me with disbelief.

"No, we will," I told her. "I am going to be your translator." I pulled out my reporter's notebook and showed her the sketches I had made while interviewing Lady Patricia.

"Oh, that skirt is nice," Leah said.

Esther mock whined, "Why do I feel like I'm pregnant at just the wrong time?"

"I'll still have these drawings when you're looking for something new for your wardrobe, and I'm sure Mimi Mareau will be happy to make something for you," I assured her.

"But I'm going to miss out while you snoop around her salon," Esther complained.

"Your father would rather you didn't put yourself in harm's way," I said. "That's why he hired me. And in the meantime, you need to talk to anyone you think is in a position to talk to an assassin."

"That would be no one," Leah said.

"How well do you know the people on the committee? You've only been married a year," I said.

"They are the people I've seen the most of since I came to this country. They are all very English, and they are teaching me to be very English. None of them could possibly talk to an assassin. Or be a murderer," Leah insisted.

Esther glanced at me, and I saw doubt in her eyes. I couldn't hide my investigations for her father from Esther, of all people. And Esther couldn't hide her doubts from me.

After Leah and I made plans to meet as soon as she could get an appointment, Esther and I shared a taxi into town. "While you and Leah will be looking at the latest fashions, I'm going to pay calls on the women of the committee. I'll ask a lot of questions about families, which they'll think is because of the baby, and maybe I'll find the link to Elias or the Nazis."

I didn't know whether I should tell her or not, but I murmured, "You might listen for the name 'Meirsohn,' too."

Her eyes narrowed. "Why?"

"His real name was Josef Meirsohn."

"Why did he change it?"

"He was using a *nom de guerre*. Maybe to hide his identity. Maybe to protect his family. I'm sorry, Esther, but it's part of the mystery."

Esther lowered her voice to a whisper. "There's something else going on. Something bigger than one murder."

"Right now I'm just trying to gather facts. When we know something, then it'll be time to make connections."

"You sound like a detective." Esther sounded amazed, but she managed a smile as she spoke.

"I was hoping I sounded like a reporter." I gave her an answering smile. I still wasn't happy about reporting to General Alford. That felt too much like spying.

"Even if my father won't let you tell me what's going on now, I hope you will when it's over. There's a big difference between murderer and assassin." Esther stared at me.

I couldn't hold her gaze.

* * *

I wished life would return to its normal quiet weekday pattern, but that wouldn't happen for a host of reasons. My mind was churning over what I'd learned from General Alford and what he hoped to learn from me. Reina was afraid of the person who killed Elias. Or Josef Meirsohn, as she had known him. In the center of it all stood Mimi's salon.

And everyone was on pins and needles waiting to see what Hitler would do in Czechoslovakia.

On Thursday, Jane and I could barely find room to stand in the first-floor showroom during Mimi's first London fashion parade. She had managed to make it uniquely British, with tweed suits alternating with French-inspired evening gowns.

The other two shows we'd covered that day had shown the same mixture of British tweed and pearls alongside French elegance and glamour. We snagged glasses of champagne of much better quality at Mimi's than at the shows we'd been to before we reached hers. Everything, from the décor of the showroom to the imagination shown in the fashions, was just a bit more sophisticated, a tad more dazzling, than at the other two salons.

I wondered how the two shows covered by the other team from the *Daily Premier* would stack up.

I was surprised to discover one of the models in Mimi's show was Lady Patricia. She had the looks and self-confidence to walk purposefully around the room for two turns while showing off different outfits, both times wearing Mimi-designed evening gowns. I couldn't imagine why she'd do something so close to actual work.

As the show wound down and customers and reporters swarmed around Mimi, I slipped behind the silver metallic curtain in a search for Lady Patricia. I found her dressed in her own clothes watching the back staircase from one of the dressing cubicles.

Two people, a man and a woman, were on the staircase landing. The woman, a blonde, wore the deep rose duster of a Mareau salon employee, but I couldn't quite see her face. The pair exchanged a few furtive words, and then hurried down the stairs while Lady Patricia walked toward me.

"You showed off Mimi's designs very well," I told her while trying to swing around her.

"Thank you." She kept blocking my way.

"How did you get to model in her show?"

"I asked her. Daddy's paying her enough for my trousseau. She could hardly refuse." She smiled one of those girls' school smug smiles I'd learned to hate years ago.

"Who was the man by the back stairs?" All I could tell from my vantage point was a very tall man had been talking to one of Mimi's employees. From where he stood on the top step, I could clearly see only a dark wing-tip shoe and cuffed suit-trousers. The rest of him had been in shadow or hidden by the doorframe.

"What man?"

"I saw a man talking on the staircase. With Fleur." That was a shot in the dark, but from what I could see of the woman, she had looked a bit like Fleur.

Lady Patricia glared at me. "I didn't see anyone."

"You were looking right at them."

"Was I?" She stepped around me to pick up her jacket and bag from a cubicle and disappeared out into the showroom.

I glanced around. The models were dressing, paying me no attention. I bolted down the back staircase. Somewhere below me, I heard a door slam.

I was too late to catch the mystery man—not that I'd know what to ask if I did catch him. There was no reason to think Lady Patricia had anything to do with Elias's murder. Except for her strange behavior and her father's politics.

Stepping out of the back stairs on the ground floor, I

headed toward the front of the building, only to find Lady Patricia going out the front door.

I followed, worrying about what I'd say if I caught up with her. When I opened the door, I realized I didn't have to worry. Lady Patricia was stepping into a smart two-seat tourer in red, the canvas top down, the automobile looking faster and sleeker than anything else on the road.

A man held the door for her. A very tall man who I saw wore the same color suit as the man I had seen on the staircase.

Then he walked around the auto to get into the driver's seat, and I saw his face clearly. It was her father. The Duke of Marshburn, wearing wing-tip shoes and cuffed trousers. He must have come to congratulate Mimi on her show.

As they drove off, I jotted down the license plate number in my notebook. Just in case.

I walked back inside to a great deal of chatter from women talking above me in the showroom. Seeing my chance, I hurried down the basement stairs.

I had reached the bottom just as Fleur stepped in front of me, holding a large pair of scissors. "What are you doing down here?"

Blast. I came up with the first excuse I could think of. "There was a man on the staircase. I followed him down."

"I don't see him, do you?" she asked, staring at me.

"Did you see a man lingering around the stairs?"

"Not while I've been down here." She held the scissors like a knife.

I wondered if it was Fleur or someone else in the

fashion house I had seen talking to the tall man. "I guess he's left already. Fleur, should I call you *madame* or *mademoiselle*?"

"Why?"

"Because in England it is more respectful to call you 'Miss' or 'Mrs.' and your last name. What is your last name?"

"But I am French and 'Fleur' is just fine. Now I suggest you go upstairs where guests and reporters are supposed to be." Fleur gestured with her scissors.

I nodded and ran up the stairs, glad I didn't hear her footsteps behind me. I didn't ask if she'd been the one I'd seen talking to the man in the stairwell. To the Duke of Marshburn. It was cowardice, but I didn't care. Fleur looked like she knew how to handle a pair of scissors to do more than cut fabric.

From downstairs, I heard Fleur call up to me, "In English, it's 'Miss Bettenard.'"

* * *

I didn't finish my article on the three fashion shows I'd seen until Friday morning, in plenty of time for the Saturday edition of the paper. It didn't matter, since there was no room for our fashion news that day. Friday's paper was full of Chamberlain's trip to Germany to negotiate a settlement to the Sudetenland crisis. I read the stories and wondered, not for the first time, where Adam was.

We were very likely going to war, and he was a soldier. I was terrified for him.

That night, I received a call from Leah, saying she'd

made an appointment for the following Monday at Mimi's salon for a fitting. I told her I'd meet her outside the building for her two o'clock appointment.

On Saturday morning, I knew everyone would read about Hitler's demand that the Sudetenland be handed over by the following Wednesday, September twenty-eighth, or he would take it by force. We were closer to war than we'd ever been, and I wondered if anything I learned at Mimi's salon would make any difference.

I read the *Daily Premier* from cover to cover. The stories on the fashion shows had been cut to the minimum.

I spent the morning not knowing what to do with myself. My father was busy meeting the French government in London with our diplomats to work on a mutually agreeable response to Hitler's demands. Adam had vanished into war preparations. I'd already cleaned the flat until it sparkled.

The weather was too nice to stay indoors. I called Reggie's cousin Abby and invited myself to her Sussex home. She sounded thrilled to see me.

She met me at the train station, regaling me on the way to the manor house with stories of her husband, the war hero Sir John, pacing and fuming over "the government's bloody weak-kneed bowing to that bloody little German."

"Surely Sir John doesn't want to see us go to war," I said.

"He doesn't. However, he doesn't see how we're going to avoid it now. Not without the king goose-stepping and shouting 'Heil Hitler.'"

I nodded. "I can't see King George doing that willingly. Sir John is right." The enormity of it hit me. "Oh, dear."

Abby gave a loud sigh.

By silent agreement, we didn't use the "w" word for the rest of the day while we worked in her flower beds. We dressed for dinner, a glum affair with only the three of us.

Their two sons, Reggie's godsons, had gone back to school that week. I missed their chatter and clatter around the house. I was sure the house echoed with emptiness for Abby.

"Nigel will be sixteen in November," Abby said suddenly.

"Darling, don't," Sir John said.

I was about to say *The war will be over before he'll be conscription age,* but then I realized I didn't know. None of us did. And Abby didn't need foolish sympathy.

Any more than I did for Adam Redmond's fate.

CHAPTER TEN

"I don't want this war," Abby said, clutching her napkin in one fist.

"None of us do," I told her.

"I wish Hitler had never been born." She threw her napkin on the table, took a deep breath, and said, "Shall we have our coffee in the drawing room?"

From then until I left on Sunday afternoon, Abby didn't display any more signs of nerves. We both acted as if things were normal and talked about her stunning chrysanthemums and her eccentric neighbors.

* * *

Monday morning, I got right to work on society page announcements and kept it up through my lunch hour. Then I told Miss Westcott that I had a meeting to cover and met Leah down the street from the couture house. We went inside together, where we were escorted upstairs by a young woman with a French accent who I hadn't met in my earlier visits. She wore the ubiquitous Mareau salon deep rose smock over her clothes.

We were seated in the showroom and Leah asked about what type of outfit she was looking for. As she set down her bag, it landed with a thud. The young assistant and I looked at her handbag at the sound, a noise I remembered from the committee meeting. She had to be stronger than her frail appearance led me to believe.

Leah ignored this as she said she wanted a tweed suit and then had me show my drawing of Lady Patricia's tweed skirt.

The young woman, whose name turned out to be Veronique, was surprised at the drawing. "You draw very well, madame, but I'm not sure it can be translated into woolen fabric."

"Lady Patricia, the Duke of Marshburn's daughter, had a tweed suit made for her trousseau that I drew this from," I told her. "Mrs. Nauheim wants a suit cut like Lady Patricia's, but in a different tweed, and she wants some other changes. Obviously, she doesn't want a copy of Lady Patricia's suit."

"Obviously," Veronique said, her eyes widening more. "I'll get Madame Mimi, shall I?"

We both nodded.

Mimi arrived a few minutes later. "You've been giving away my new designs," she said to me accusingly.

"There was no way I wouldn't tell my good friend about your marvelous tweed suit, since she's been looking for one."

She considered that for an instant before a smile crossed her face. "I'm glad you find it marvelous. There will have to be stylistic changes."

"Of course," Leah said. She looked pleased to be getting an original, or the closest thing to it, from Mimi Mareau. "I'd like a tweed in a light shade. And the fur collar in a light shade, as well."

"Very good. And I'll make some changes to the

pockets and buttons," Mimi said.

Since I hadn't drawn the pockets and buttons, Leah was content with that.

Mimi led us to a dressing room in the back as she asked Leah to disrobe down to her slip and called Veronique back to take measurements. I noticed two of the other dressing rooms were occupied, but their inhabitants were too busy to pay any attention to us.

The cubbyhole where Mimi deposited us was near the back stairs. I kept an eye on the stairs and a minute later I was rewarded with a view of Reina going down them. I could hear Mimi's voice somewhere, but she was out of sight, no doubt working with another client.

I whispered, "I have to question that woman," and gave a small wave to Leah. She looked puzzled but nodded slightly before I slipped down the back stairs. Peeping in, I didn't see Reina in the ground-floor workroom where two seamstresses were busy at their machines. I took a chance and went down to the basement.

There were more trunks against the back wall now than when I was down here before. Reina was reaching into one of the old trunks I hadn't looked in when she must have heard my footsteps. She turned toward me, a guilty look on her face.

I hurried over to her. "What's wrong, Reina?"

"You shouldn't be down here."

"You want to know who killed Josef," I said, using the man's real name.

She nodded, tears springing to her eyes. "He was my

friend when we were children."

"Tell me about him."

"He was a year or two older than me, perhaps thirty-two now, and the smartest boy in our village school. He was daring, stubborn," she said with a smile, "and handsome. His family was among the wealthiest in the village and he had relatives in Berlin, so they sent him there for schooling. Later they said he was going to university there, then law school. That was a few years after the war."

"What is your family name, Reina?"

"Blumfeld. Mimi tells everyone it's Belleau."

So Mimi had to know Reina was Jewish.

"Did Josef come here to meet you the day he died?"

"He asked if there was a safe place to meet. He said he was in danger and wanted to give me something. To keep it safe for him. He said it was important. I told him about the basement and the door kept on the latch for the workmen."

"How did he know you were in London? Both of you had just arrived here." It proved to be an unlucky meeting for Josef.

"I went to Oxford Street to look in the shops at the fashions. To see what was *au courant* here." She looked defensive as she added, "Mimi thinks we can work all the time, but it is not my fame, my money. It is hers. I have no wish to work that hard for someone else. Let her work that hard if she wants."

Reina shook her head. "I saw Josef coming out of a hotel entrance and we ran into each other on the pavement. We only spoke long enough to arrange the meeting here."

She lifted a bolt of light green silk from the trunk. "Now you need to go back upstairs. I have to take this up…" Her voice trailed away as a length of pipe fell from the center of the bolt and fell to the floor with a clank.

One end showed traces of blood and hair stuck to it.

"Do you know how this ended up in your fabric?"

She shook her head, her eyes wide.

"Don't touch it. I'll call the police." And then Mimi would know I was in her basement again asking questions. I didn't want her to be aware of my interest in this murder. I had come here because I was thrilled with her glamour and her style. Her vision for women's clothes.

But we found a body, and everything changed.

"Thank you for…" Reina shuddered and dashed up the stairs, clutching the fabric to her chest.

I went up to the front entrance and used their phone to call the police with my finding. When I hung up, the girl at the desk demanded, "What are you doing?"

"The murder weapon was discovered downstairs. The police have to retrieve it."

"Madame won't like it."

"Why didn't they find it the first time?" I asked the girl at the desk as if this were her fault.

"Because they are incompetent," Mimi said as she strode down the last steps of the front staircase toward me. "Come. Let us talk in the back room, away from the customers," she hissed into my ear.

When we were on the other side of the door, Mimi said, "They left a couple of bobbies, peasants, to finish searching the basement, and I caught them fooling around with some of the costumes for the play. Stupid boys. I told them off and said they should do their jobs. I watched them closely after that, and they were soon done and gone."

Thereby missing the murder weapon. Had Mimi caused this by accident or did she not want the lead pipe found?

The constables were probably bored or annoyed from having to deal with a demanding foreigner. Keeping that thought to myself, I asked, "The day I found the body, I opened the door from the inside without needing a key. Is the door always kept unlocked?"

"It is sometimes kept unlocked during the day because the theater moves costumes out as they need them. And when the carpenters and painters were decorating the showroom, I made them bring their supplies through the basement. We would look like peasants if they brought their wood and ladders through the front door of the salon. Then, the basement door was always kept unlocked."

We heard footsteps on the back staircase and then Fleur came down to join us. "What is going on, madame?" she asked Mimi before she looked at me suspiciously.

I answered for her. "I had to call the police to retrieve the murder weapon. Reina found it hidden in a bolt of cloth."

"In my fabric? Which one?" Mimi exclaimed.

"Green silk."

"Oh, I hope it wasn't damaged." Mimi rushed back up the stairs.

I smiled as I stood motionless, hoping the bobbies would hurry up and arrive. "Mimi seems to trust you completely, Fleur. How long have you worked for her?"

She brushed invisible lint from her deep rose duster's sleeve. "Three years."

"Funny. I thought you'd tell me longer than that."

She gave me a haughty look. "We have a great deal of mutual respect, two artists with fabric. We trust each other."

Her unspoken words were *We don't trust you.*

I understood that. I didn't trust them, either. "Where are you from, Fleur?"

"The north."

That was hardly an answer. "The north of what?"

"That's not the business of a society page reporter. Mimi is the story here. Not me."

Fleur was right. Before I could think of a way to learn more about her, a uniformed constable and a detective arrived and I led them to the basement with Fleur following. They took possession of the piece of lead pipe and asked me a few questions about finding the murder weapon.

By the time they finished, Reina appeared and they began to question her. As I hesitated, Fleur said, "I think your friend is waiting for you on the first floor."

I went. When I reached the first floor, I found Leah was dressed again. "I've been measured," she whispered, "but I'm waiting for Mimi. Did you have any luck?"

"We found the murder weapon."

Leah gasped and trembled before she collapsed onto the ottoman. I'd have to remember to watch what I said in front of someone so nervous.

At that moment, I heard the designer's voice coming toward us, saying in French, "You should have asked, Veronique."

"But I thought you had decided on the design already."

An instant later, Mimi came in with Veronique behind her. Switching to English, Mimi said, "Let me show you what I have in mind." Her sketch showed the slightly flared skirt that was the best part of her design, but a lack of fur on the collar. Leah didn't seem to mind.

"Where does the jacket end?" Leah asked.

"Stand up," Mimi said, and then held out her hand flat to demonstrate. It was a long jacket, hitting below the hip in the style made popular that year in Paris. "The buttons end at the waist. It is a very manly jacket, but the skirt and blouse are womanly. Feminine. The blouse has a simple rounded neckline with tiers of fabric down the front to be worn inside the jacket."

"Won't it be too frilly for tweed?" I asked.

"*Non*," she replied.

Leah and I looked at each other with widened eyes.

"You just wait," Mimi said with a smile. "You will love it."

"And it will be a light color?" Leah asked.

Mimi pulled out a swatch of light shaded tweed in a

soft wool. "And you see this blue here?" She pointed to a thread in the weave. "That will be the blue of the blouse."

"Yes," said Leah, "I think that will do nicely."

Giving me another reason to be jealous of her wardrobe.

* * *

I returned to the *Daily Premier* building and went straight up to see Sir Henry. His secretary sent me in immediately.

"Livvy," he said, looking up from the papers on his desk, "I've heard from Miss Westcott. She wants you to cover the concert at the Royal Albert Hall tonight for a list of attendees and descriptions of their gowns."

I knew that to mean a list of socially important female attendees, beginning with any members of the royal family who might attend, and a mention of their evening frocks. Since the Royal Albert Hall was round, with a number of entrances, this was an almost impossible feat. "I'm in trouble?"

"You're in trouble."

"I went to Mimi's salon, where Reina and I found the murder weapon."

I thought he was going to spring from his chair. "Did you call the police?"

"Of course I called the police." Did he think I was stupid? "I'm worried, though. Reina had known Josef Meirsohn—Elias's real name—since childhood and she found the lead pipe. She's Jewish, too. But she's not the assassin."

"Where was the weapon?"

"In a trunk in the basement, hidden inside a roll of green silk."

Sir Henry was looking astounded by this point. "Why didn't the police find it? It was in the basement."

"It's possible the pipe was hidden there later."

Sir Henry's eyebrows rose more as he said, "Does that sound likely?"

"No." Then I told him what Mimi had told me. "She can be intimidating," I added. Still, it wasn't Mimi's fault if the police didn't do their job.

"That's no reason for them to be less than careful in their search," Sir Henry muttered. "How many people could have accessed that trunk?"

"Anyone coming from upstairs or outside. At the time, the door to the basement had been left on the latch for the workmen. And the trunk was unlocked."

"It could be anyone in London," he muttered.

"Has Esther learned anything?" I asked.

"What?" His voice changed to the roar all of his employees knew to fear.

And I feared firing. Taking a deep breath to stop the trembling in my diaphragm, I said, "She's going to talk to the other ladies of the committee about family. With her expecting her first child and recently bringing her mother's relatives over from Vienna, it will be an obvious topic of discussion."

That appeared to mollify him. "She can't get into any trouble talking to those ladies."

"How many people knew Elias would be in London? Surely not many. And he knew that the Nazis wanted him silenced."

"Had he arranged to meet anyone in that basement when he was killed?" Sir Henry looked at me expectantly.

"Reina told me she met him leaving a hotel on Oxford Street purely by accident. He said he was in danger and wanted to meet her someplace safe to give her something. She told him about the basement. She's the only one there who's mentioned having met Elias."

"Give her something? What?"

I held Sir Henry's gaze. "She doesn't know. Did the police find anything of interest on him?"

"Nothing. His pockets were emptied before they arrived." Sir Henry was scowling now as he thought.

"I think Reina may be the key to finding out who Elias knew in London and what he was doing." But she was frightened. Would she talk to me?

"Reina again. You're going to have to get her away from the others and have a long talk with her. She could know more, and that could put her in danger."

I nodded at Sir Henry's instructions. "The only way I'm going to get the full story out of her is to get her away from Mimi." But would Reina be willing to leave the security of the salon?

CHAPTER ELEVEN

I went downstairs to speak to Miss Westcott, who was still working, and get my assignment at the Royal Albert Hall.

She handed me a ticket. "After the concert, I want you to attend the reception backstage for the guest conductor. That's where you'll find the women we'll want to mention in our article. And try to get some quotes."

"Yes, ma'am." I needed to get this murder out of my head. Attending this concert and reporting on the notable attendees was a good place to start.

Then I had another thought. "Will there be any room in the paper for a description of gowns if we're going to war?"

She gave me a steady look. "We're not at war yet. Get the descriptions."

I dressed in the dark blue gown with the silver shoes and bag that was my favorite evening wear. I looked dashing. It was too bad Adam wasn't here to see me. Sutton, my doorman, left his usual spot to go outside and whistle for a taxi for me. He went so far as to open and close the taxi door for me.

And then when I reached the Royal Albert Hall, I found my seat on the edge of the orchestra level below the stalls. In the aisle seat next to mine was the music critic for the paper.

He greeted me with "Mrs. Denis, what are you doing here?"

I edged past him and sat. "I'm to go to the reception for the guest conductor and describe the ladies' gowns."

"Watch you don't get too close to him. He's a bottom pincher. Slavic and full of himself."

I could imagine getting quotes from some of our aristocrats that would never make it into the paper.

When the concert was over, the music critic rose and said, "Have to dash if I'm going to make my deadline. Good luck with the conductor." Then he hurried off, chuckling to himself.

I headed toward the backstage area where they always held receptions. It was large, brightly lit, and stuffy in this unseasonably warm weather. In the winter, I recalled, it was frigid. I slipped my notebook and pencil out of my bag and circled the room, discreetly writing notes on the ladies I recognized as being the most prominent.

One of them was the Duchess of Marshburn, in what I was willing to bet was a Mimi Mareau creation. The fabric was black, but it was cut and sewn in such a way that the gown seemed to flow down her like a waterfall. On someone young and with a good figure, the dress would be breathtaking. On the duchess, middle-aged, horse-faced, and thick in the waist, it was a nice setting for her jewelry.

If Mimi was as clever a designer as it appeared she was, she would have known such a gown would make her lover's wife look slightly foolish, or vain.

I looked around, but I didn't see Mimi at the reception. I didn't see the duke, either.

I spent about forty-five minutes covering the reception and getting some drawings of the best frocks. As I turned to leave, a shriek nearby made me turn my head in time to see Mrs. Mandel, wife of the pharmacist on the committee, pull a young woman away from the guest conductor. The lady gave the conductor the blackest look I'd seen in a long time.

I headed toward the trio, annoyance with the conductor warring with the chance to get a scoop.

The conductor smiled slyly and murmured, "At least Germany knows how to put you in your proper place."

Mrs. Mandel turned pale. The young woman I guessed was her daughter looked like she had seen the devil. Then they both turned and walked out of the hall.

I followed them at a trot. "Mrs. Mandel. Is your daughter all right?"

She stopped and turned to face me. After a moment, a vague look of recognition flashed across her face. "That terrible man should keep his hands to himself."

"Yes, he should, but I don't suppose he will. I'm Mrs. Denis," I added, holding out my hand.

"I know," she replied, giving me a firm handshake. "I'm on the committee with your friend Esther Powell."

I looked back at the hall. "I didn't know the conductor is a Nazi. Why did they invite him?"

"He's not. He's Polish. The Poles can't stand Germany, but they agree with some of their policies. They don't like us, either."

This wasn't the time or place, but I took a chance on asking questions about the murder. "Did you get a chance to meet Elias?"

"My husband went to the meeting where he spoke. He said Elias was a logical thinker, but he was able to put a great deal of passion into his words. Passion you don't expect from a lawyer. Although it makes sense, considering what he's seen in Germany."

"He said he hadn't seen his wife in several years," her daughter said. "I think that would make him anxious to stop the Nazis so he could rescue her."

"Your father never mentioned that," Mrs. Mandel said.

"I asked him. Elias. After the meeting." The girl, who was probably seventeen or eighteen, looked at her mother as if unsure whether to continue.

"Mrs. Denis, this is my daughter, Valerie," Mrs. Mandel said by way of introduction.

I nodded my greeting and then asked, "What did he say?" I tried to keep the demand out of my voice so as not to frighten the girl.

"He hadn't known where his wife was. When he was jailed, she disappeared, and he never heard from her again. Isn't it sad?"

Reina was from the same village and was the right age. Did they really meet up here in London by accident? How did they both feel about finding Elias's spouse?

Did Reina know the dead man's wife? Or was she the missing Mrs. Elias?

Mrs. Mandel tsked me away from my thoughts as she said to her daughter, "You've only been out of school a few months and already your grammar is deplorable."

"Not at all," her daughter said with a smile. "I'm quoting him. It must be from his translating from German into English to speak to me."

"Your father said his English was very good although heavily accented. But the way you quote him, it almost sounds like he found his wife again. How strange." Mrs. Mandel frowned as she led her daughter toward the waiting taxis.

I followed slowly, more determined than ever to get the entire story from Reina. No wonder she was first shocked and now worried, if Elias was her husband and then she'd found him murdered.

* * *

I went into work the next morning, wrote up my notes on the reception for the Nazi lecher masquerading as a conductor, and left the report on Miss Westcott's desk. Then I repinned my hat, pulled on my gloves, and dashed out of the building.

Bus traffic was with me, and it didn't take long to get to Mimi's *maison* on Old Burlington Street. I walked in the front door, and a woman I hadn't seen before wearing a deep rose smock said, "Name?"

"Olivia Denis. I need to speak to Reina."

She looked up from the schedule of appointments in her hand and said, "Reina?"

"I'd like to speak to Reina, please. It's important."

"It may be, but she's not here." She dismissed me with her smile.

I wasn't leaving without some answers. "When will she be back?"

"I don't know."

I didn't have time to play games, and this Englishwoman with a purposely stuffy attitude was annoying me. "Will she be back today?"

"I doubt it," came out with a smirk.

I found myself developing a strong dislike for her. "Why?"

"Reina's gone back to the salon in Paris."

"And Mimi?"

"*Madame* went with her."

Wonderful. How much did Mimi know about Reina's background? And did that put them both at risk from Elias's killer?

I turned and marched out of Mimi's salon. Once outside, I rushed back to the *Daily Premier* building, snagging a stocking on a rough metal edge on the bus. Ignoring what would no doubt turn into a ladder, I hurried straight up to the top floor of the newspaper's headquarters. A sign on Sir Henry's door said he was in conference.

Could nothing go right? I knew better than to interrupt. Especially since this was private business, not a breaking news story.

I left a note on Sir Henry's secretary's desk and rushed downstairs to Mr. Colinswood's office. For once Colinswood wasn't on the phone. When I knocked, he told me to come in and shut the door. He slipped his new reading spectacles off and blinked as he looked at me. "Sir Henry's tied up with something," he said. "I take it your news is important."

"I need to go to Paris."

He stared at me in silence.

"You know that Sir Henry wants to know who led Elias's killer to him in the basement of Mimi Mareau's new fashion salon?"

He nodded.

"Her top seamstress grew up in the same village as Elias. The seamstress and I found the murder weapon yesterday. And now I've learned he has a wife who may still be alive and could be anywhere. The seamstress could be his wife." Especially since she hadn't mentioned anything about a wife.

"You think she's his wife and she killed him." He was still staring at me.

"I think she's his widow and he was in the basement to talk to her. But I don't think she killed him."

He tapped a pencil on his desk. "Where does Paris come into it?"

"When I went to Mimi's salon this morning to speak to the seamstress, I was told that Mimi and Reina had both left for the salon in Paris. I need to talk to them."

"You're certain this is important to your investigation?"

"Yes."

He grumbled and lit a cigarette. "France and Great Britain will be at war with Germany at any moment, and you want to go to Paris to talk to a suspect in a murder inquiry? Are you mad? What if you can't get back from France?"

CHAPTER TWELVE

"Is it that bad?" I hadn't considered being trapped on the continent at the outbreak of war in what I thought of as my hunt for a killer. And it was foolish of me to ignore what was happening in the world to suit my investigation.

"Sir Horace Wilson is taking a letter from Chamberlain to Hitler saying if Germany attacks Czechoslovakia, France and Great Britain will attack Germany," Mr. Colinswood explained.

My stomach sank. I didn't know where Colinswood got his information, but his sources were usually spot-on. I nodded.

"If this blows over, and I hope to God it does, come back and ask me about a trip to Paris to talk to a murder victim's wife." He gave me a sad smile.

I nodded and left his office.

Back in the society page offices, I went through the motions of doing my job, but my heart wasn't in it. I wondered where Adam was. I wondered whether I'd lose my job, since there wouldn't be much use for a society page in the midst of war.

That night I listened to the radio as closely as my fellow countrymen did while Prime Minister Chamberlain gave a depressing, whiny speech on how this war was so unnecessary. When I awoke in the morning, my pillow was still wet with my tears.

Glumly, my fellow Underground riders rode in silence as we headed for our offices. The only sounds I heard were the rumble of engines and the screech of the brakes of the Underground train cars. Everyone seemed to be in their own little world, carrying their own copy of a morning paper with a gloomy headline. The *Daily Premier* read in huge type: "War looms."

Our phones rang less than usual. Most of our callers apologized for bothering us with trivial news like the birth of a child after asking if war had been declared. We assured them it had not.

Late in the afternoon, word filtered in from the newsroom that Chamberlain was going to Munich to meet with the leaders of France, Germany, and Italy. They still hoped to find a peaceful solution to the Sudeten crisis. I don't think anyone was surprised that Czechoslovakia wasn't invited to the meeting. After all, they were the ones who would have to give up territory.

News on the radio that evening was equal parts vague and resolute.

My father called me near midnight. "I've just arrived home," he told me. "If Hitler buys this deal, it will have won us some time."

"How much time?" I asked him, thinking of Adam.

"That's up to Hitler."

All day Thursday we continued to hold our collective breath. It wasn't until Friday morning as I hurried along the pavement on my way to work that I saw the *Daily Premier* headline: "Peace rescued."

The phones in the office rang at their normal rate with information on births, marriages, engagements, teas, and balls. People appeared ready to consider the recent threat as a bad dream, at least publicly.

Privately, I was still frightened of what would happen next time. I guessed I wasn't the only one.

That was when I decided to propose my trip to Paris to Mr. Colinswood again.

After he listened to me plead, he said, "Can you think of a story you could pursue in Paris? Besides a dead man's possible widow."

"I could contrast Mimi's London salon and her Paris one." I gave him a bright smile. I could tell he was weakening.

"Go over Sunday night. By then we'll be sure that the peace will hold. You have one day in Paris, and come back Monday night. You need to be back in the office on Tuesday."

He lit a cigarette and in a puff of smoke added, "We worry about you when you go on these foreign trips."

I gave a silent cheer. He'd capitulated. "I'd better take a photographer with me. May I take Jane Seville? She took the shots of Mimi's London couture house." Jane would choke me if I didn't put in a word for her going along. Unfortunately, she would also rather have more time in Paris than I'd been given.

"Yes. All right," he snapped. "But only the one day. We're not sending you there for a holiday. I'll have the cash released for your boat train tickets."

I tried to hide my relief. I didn't want to pay for this

trip, particularly since I wasn't sure it would yield any benefits for Sir Henry, the paper, or General Alford. Even if Reina was Meirsohn's long-lost wife, I didn't believe she was his murderer.

* * *

Jane and I talked about it, and in the end decided to travel Saturday night to give us an extra day in Paris. After all, the peace was holding.

We managed to get a little rest on the train to Paris after a rough nighttime Channel crossing. My blue wool suit felt good, warming my skin against the early morning chill seeping into the railcar. After repinning our hats and powdering our noses, we were practically the last out of our carriage. While we had scarcely any luggage, we did have Jane's camera equipment.

I had checked before we left. Mimi and Reina had not returned to London by Saturday afternoon. I just hoped we hadn't passed them in the Channel.

As I suspected, the salon was shuttered on a Sunday. Since neither Jane nor I had any Sunday assignments for the paper, I decided it shouldn't make any difference to Sir Henry or Mr. Colinswood if we went over one day early, as long as we returned by Tuesday morning. And we didn't get trapped in a war zone.

If the mood was jubilant in London, the air was electric in Paris. The headlines in their newspapers were bolder, their streets were livelier, and the cafés were fuller with sharp words and laughter in equal measure. After checking into a small hotel near the train station and having breakfast in a café, Jane went off with her camera equipment and I wandered familiar streets, finally ending up at the Louvre.

I spent hours sketching.

We met up at the hotel and then dressed for an evening in a good restaurant and then a concert. "I can't believe you managed to get us two days in Paris," Jane said as we left the concert hall.

"I didn't. I got us one day, tomorrow, and tickets on the night train coming and going. I'm going to have to sell Mr. Colinswood on us being here on a Sunday."

"Maybe my photographs will convince him. Or your report on the Louvre. You never know."

I was pretty certain I knew. Mr. Colinswood would be angry with my failure to follow directions. "I don't think we should tell him."

* * *

We arrived too early the next morning at the shuttered salon, so we went around the corner and had a leisurely breakfast first. Jane watched the bustle on the pavement and said, "I love Paris. Every street looks like a photograph waiting to be taken."

"If you can take some before the salon opens, go ahead. But I want to get in there the second they unlock the door. I must speak to Reina. And it would be better if I talked to her alone."

"You want me to distract Mimi."

Jane wolfed down her breakfast and coffee and hurried out the door with her camera. I finished at a slower pace and brought the rest of her equipment with me.

I spotted her down the avenue, taking aim at a building across the street. While the Champs-Elysées would be busy at this hour, the side streets off the Rue Saint-Honoré were still relatively quiet. Jane saw me, waved, and rejoined me.

As she picked up one of her camera cases, I said, "It's time. Wish us luck."

"I'll let you do all the talking, shall I? And when you get done, may I take some more photographs until we have to get back to catch the night train?"

"Sounds good to me." If I couldn't get the full story out of Reina, it would be nice if one of us could have a successful trip.

I heard a key turn in the lock as I reached the door. I immediately opened it and stepped inside to greet the startled clerk in French. "I hope to see both Madame Mareau and Reina," I told her. "I'm from the *Daily Premier* in London."

If anything, the young, willowy clerk in the familiar deep rose coat looked more surprised when I spoke. Then Jane walked in with her camera gear and the young woman fled to the back.

I was surprised to see Brigette come out to greet us. In unaccented English, she said, "You want to see Madame and Reina?"

"I didn't realize you returned, too. Did Fleur as well?"

"No, she's running the London salon." Her tone turned suspicious as she said, "What do you want?"

"I want to do a companion piece on Mimi's Paris salon, and I want to talk with Reina."

At that moment, Reina walked in the front door. "Sorry I'm late," she said in French.

"Good. You're here," I told her in French. "You didn't say Elias was married."

She gave a deep sigh, glanced at Brigette, and said, "Come with me."

I left Jane waiting in the front room with a startled Brigette while I followed Reina to an office on the third floor filled with filing cabinets. "Patterns from Mimi's designs," she said, gesturing to the wooden drawers as she pulled her deep rose duster over her clothes.

I didn't have time to be distracted. I suspected Mimi would bring our talk to a halt as soon as she heard from Brigette that I was here. "Tell me the exact conversation you had on Oxford Street with Josef Meirsohn."

"We greeted each other in surprise, and expressed more surprise that we'd met in London. He'd last heard I was in Paris, and I'd last heard that he was in Berlin. Then he said the Gestapo was hunting him everywhere, even in London, and nowhere was safe. I told him about the basement and that the door to the street was unlocked because of the workmen. He said he would meet me the day after the next in the morning. He would have something to bring me that was important. Someone wanted it, and I must hide it for him. Keep it safe."

"Someone wanted it," I repeated.

"Yes."

"A particular person. Not a country or the Nazis. Someone."

"Yes. I'm very sure of that. It surprised me, too."

"Did he say what he wanted you to hide?" I hoped he'd said something clear.

"No. He gave me no hint."

"Then what did he say?"

"He was in danger standing out on the street and had to leave. He said he would see me, and then he hurried away."

"Did he say anything else? Anything at all." I hoped my trip had not been in vain.

"I do not think so."

"Once he went away to school and left your village, did you ever see him again?"

"A few times, when he came back to see his family. Once he brought his wife."

"He was married?" Confirmation of what Miss Mandel had told me.

"Yes."

"But not to you?"

"No." She smiled ruefully. "My family wasn't sufficiently grand for his parents. He married while he was in school. An arranged marriage. His wife seemed quite young. And rich."

"You met her?" This was good luck.

"He only brought her to the village once, shortly before I moved to Paris. She was a city girl, uncomfortable in our village with everyone staring."

"Staring?"

"She was an outsider. She was pretty. And she was too young and quiet for Josef."

"Do you know what happened to her? She needs to

be told—" I was eager to begin a trace.

Reina shook her head. "She died, I think. And then the Nazis came to power and people like Josef, communists and Jewish, began to disappear. Anyway, she never came back to the village and we heard no more about her."

"Do you remember her name?"

Reina shook her head.

"What did she look like?"

"I remember people commenting that she was pretty. Other than that, nothing."

"Did Josef seem to be in love with her?"

"No." She sounded quite certain about that. "It was an arranged marriage. I'm sure they would have learned to care about each other in time, but this was early in the marriage. She seemed frightened and he seemed annoyed that his father was so thrilled."

Interesting. "Why was his father happy?"

"She was from a big banking family. I'm sure she was only from a minor part of this family to have married someone so far beneath her, but his father knew his son had married well. Far above his station, but then everyone thought Josef would do well. His parents felt he should become an employee of the bank, but Josef wanted to become a lawyer."

"What did his parents and his wife think when he became a communist?" I suspected I knew. I wondered if I were wrong.

"I didn't hear about that until after he got out of jail, and don't ask me how he managed to escape or get released. His wife was out of the picture by then. Dead, perhaps, or in jail herself."

"A communist in a banking family. That couldn't have been popular." Perhaps he'd wanted to break with all of them."

CHAPTER THIRTEEN

Reina grinned at me, suddenly looking cheery. "The letter I received from home told me his father was beside himself. He'd had high hopes for his son, and then all his hopes were dashed when Josef became a communist. I imagine Josef would have been pleased."

"He and his father didn't get along?"

"No. And from what I heard, Josef didn't like being ordered into the family banking business by his wife's father."

"Do you remember the wife's family name, or the name of the bank?" Anything to start a search. If she was still alive, she should learn what happened to her husband.

"No. They weren't the same, and I don't remember either one." Reina seemed disinterested in Josef's wife. I suspected Reina had dreamed of marrying him herself.

With a shrug, she added, "Her family was a small part of one of the big banking groups, though, with branches in Berlin, Prague, Stockholm. Everywhere."

"How long ago did you move to Paris?"

"Ten years ago, and I've been with Mimi for eight."

"So Jacob's marriage would have been—?"

There was no expression in her dark eyes. "In 1926 or '27."

"In your hometown?"

She looked at me with raised eyebrows. "In a synagogue in Berlin."

"That will make getting records more difficult." The Nazis had been cracking down on Jewish activities even more since they took over Austria. Who knew what would happen after this mess in the Sudetenland settled down?

This was my one chance, and there was more I needed to know. "Did you see Josef again after your meeting on Oxford Street?"

"I checked the basement as many times as I dared that morning, but he never showed up. When it got close to lunchtime, Mimi told me to leave right then to buy some thread in a particular color that we had run out of. We needed it to sew the costumes for the play and this color is very hard to find in London. By the time I had matched a sample and returned, you were with Mimi and you had already found Josef dead in the basement."

"So the last time you saw Josef alive was on Oxford Street?"

"Yes."

Drat. "And you have no idea what he wanted to give you?"

"None. He didn't want to stand talking on the street where he felt vulnerable. He would have told me if I had been there when he came in the basement."

"Who knew he would be in the basement that morning?"

"I told no one."

But Josef Meirsohn, in his guise as Elias, might have

told anyone on the committee or someone at his hotel or anyone else he had met in London. "Did any of your coworkers see you coming or going to the basement? What about the painters?"

"The painters ignored us. And I found lots of reasons to go into the basement that morning, so it wouldn't have seemed suspicious."

I wondered if that was true. "Did any of the others go down there?"

"Brigette and Fleur both went down there, but they didn't say they found a man lurking in the basement. And I was the last one down there before I went out to look for the thread."

I had to ask Reina the next question. "Could Mimi have sent you to buy this difficult-to-find thread to get you out of the salon for some reason?"

"There is no reason she would have known Josef or wanted anything to do with him. He was Jewish. She and her duke hate Jews. They want the Nazis to control England, so they can force us all to work slaving in their factories or scrubbing floors."

I knew Marshburn was conservative enough to believe in the divine right of kings, and he'd claimed the Nazis were right about the "master race," but I didn't realize he was into hating groups of people other than all of us peasants. "Was Mimi like this before she began to see the duke?"

Reina gave me a smirk. "You mean before she started sleeping with that fabulously rich aristocrat?"

I didn't change my expression as I said, "Yes."

"No." She sighed. "She wasn't that bad. I was better in her eyes than the other seamstresses because I have more talent and work harder. Equal to Fleur. Now she favors Fleur over me, because Fleur is a Christian. And the duke likes her."

"The duke's met her?"

"Of course. He's met all of us. But he talks to Fleur. He says little more than hello to Brigette and he ignores me."

"Do you still keep in touch with anyone from your village who might remember Josef's wife's name or the name of the bank?"

"I have a cousin living here in Paris who fled our village just a couple of years ago. She's working as a domestic. She's younger than me, but she might remember. I'll see her tonight."

"Thank you for asking her. Send me word here of anything she says. Anything at all." I handed her my card.

Mimi bustled in then and Reina slipped my card into her pocket. "There you are. Has Reina been showing you around my salon?" Suspicion dripped from every syllable.

"She's been entertaining me until you arrived," I said, rising. "I'm doing a piece comparing your two salons. It will appear in the *Daily Premier*, so you may want to favor your London salon in what you point out to me."

"Ah, a woman who understands commerce." Mimi turned and left the tiny office. I followed her, knowing I had as much information as I could get from Reina.

I found Mimi had brought Jane as far as the hallway where we started our tour. The original *Maison Mareau* was much larger than the salon in London, with five or six times the workers she would have room to employ in England.

"You don't believe there is as big a market for your clothes in England as in France?" I asked her.

She lifted her hands and threw back her head. "Paris is the center of the fashion industry. There is a market in England, yes, but only a market. The entire world comes to my doorstep in Paris."

I couldn't hide a smile. "I don't suppose you want me to put that in a London newspaper."

She lowered her hands and returned my smile. "No. I do not think that would be good advertising. Speaking of advertising, how is your sketch coming along?"

I thought she'd ask that, so I'd brought the new version along. She studied it for a minute and said, "This is closer." She pointed out a half-dozen tiny flaws and then said, "You have talent."

She spoke as if she were discussing the weather, and I found this time I was sunk by her attitude and not lifted by her words.

We continued our tour, ending in the showroom. It was much like the one on Old Burlington Street, but larger and even more elegant. A sparkling chandelier hung from the ceiling. The floor shone. Champagne was on offer for the customers, even at that time of the morning.

I glanced over to see Brigette helping a customer nearby. "I see you brought Brigette back with you as well as Reina."

"Of course. I never travel without Brigette. She is my assistant. My right hand. I could not do without her."

I was surprised to hear Mimi say that. The girl wasn't out of her teens yet. How could she have become so valuable to Mimi's salon so quickly? "How long has she been with you?"

"Come upstairs." Mimi gestured me away from the showroom toward the back staircase. I followed her, and found myself squeezed into the tiny office again, this time with Brigette and Mimi.

Mimi started speaking in English so it was unlikely her other employees could understand if they listened in. "You're going to keep asking questions until you learn the truth, aren't you?"

I thought of the dead man in her basement. "Yes."

"It's none of your business."

I knew that. I was about to ask if Brigette was in some way connected to Elias, when Brigette said, "Oh, tell her, Mother. It doesn't bother me. I've always felt it makes no difference."

After a moment, Mimi said in a shrill voice, "This is not to be repeated."

I nodded.

"After the war, I was young and full of ideas for my own salon, but I needed more capital than I could raise. The French banks turned me down." Mimi's body and voice seemed to shrink. "I met a Swedish banker, a Jew, associated with a bank here, who agreed to lend me the needed capital at a decent rate, and I took him as my lover."

I looked from daughter to mother and lowered my voice to match Mimi's murmur. "I've followed your career because I like your designs so much, because I'm in awe of your talent, but I'd never read of a marriage, Mimi."

"There wasn't one." Brigette stood with her arms crossed, staring hard at me.

"Brigette was the result of this union." I made it a statement.

"Yes. I'm the half-Jewish bastard," Brigette said defiantly.

Mimi ignored her daughter. "Union? Hah! Not long after I found myself with child, he told me he was going back to Stockholm. When I mentioned marriage, he told me he had a wife and children at home. This had only been a bit of fun. My loan had been forgiven, and I could use my future success to raise my child unencumbered by debt."

I cringed. That must have been a cold good-bye for a young, expectant woman.

"What a cad," slipped out before I could stop it. "Who was this man?"

"His name was David Grenbaum. At least that's what he told me."

"Is this why you don't like Jews?"

She glared at me. "Who told you that? Reina? That girl just wants everyone's sympathy since she doesn't get letters from her mother anymore. I told her to go, to see her mother, but she tells me she is afraid. She doesn't think she could get out of Germany again. Jews. All this drama."

I glared at her. How could a mind that created such beauty harbor such a lack of sympathy? Especially in light of her daughter's parentage. "So I take it the answer is yes."

She shrugged. "Perhaps. Perhaps not. But what I don't like is that they keep themselves separate. They don't try to be true Frenchmen. Different foods. Different dress. Their own areas. Their own rules." Then she straightened and said, "Not a word of this to anyone. And certainly not in your newspaper. You British are too sympathetic."

"We are? To whom?" I'd never heard that before.

Jane appeared in the doorway and said, "Can I get a photograph of you sitting at your desk, madame?"

Suddenly, Mimi was all smiles. "Of course. Brigette, Olivia, out," she said as she sat behind her desk and beamed at Jane.

* * *

When I reached work the next morning, sleepy from being up most of the night on the boat train from Paris, I found a message on my desk to see Mr. Colinswood immediately. I showed it to Miss Westcott, who frowned and waved me away.

I reached Mr. Colinswood's office to find him on the telephone. He glanced up, saw me, and put his hand over the receiver. "Go up and see the boss."

Nodding, I continued up to the top floor. As I approached the secretary's desk, she said, "Go straight in."

Apparently, she had her orders. Sir Henry was in a hurry to see me, and that meant I was in trouble. I tapped twice on his door before I turned the handle and walked in.

"What was that about?" he said in an angry tone before I had the door shut.

I walked over to his desk and standing before it, looking down on Sir Henry, said, "I followed a line of inquiry. An inquiry suggested by the resettlement committee."

"And you took Jane Seville with you?" His tone told me he hadn't calmed down.

"I needed an excuse to get into Mimi's Paris salon, since she has gone back there with Reina and Brigette. I needed to speak to Reina, alone if possible. When Jane points her camera at Mimi, Mimi forgets all about me."

He tilted his head to the side as if considering. "Jane is good at that," he finally conceded. "But a day early?"

I shrugged. "It was our day off. We arrived at the site of our assignment early."

He shook his head. "What is this line of inquiry?"

I knew I had to convince him the trip was valuable. "Did you know Elias, under his real name Josef Meirsohn, was married?"

"No." Sir Henry leaned back in his large, leather-upholstered chair and waited for me to continue. He was interested, and that meant Jane and I were out of trouble.

"He told Abram Mandel's daughter at the resettlement committee meeting he attended. Then he ran into Reina on Oxford Street, quite by accident, and told her he had to see her and give her something. Could that something have anything to do with his wife? Or perhaps his smuggling operation?" Or his spying for the British government?

Or the identity of the French assassin that he hadn't shared with the British?

I wished we had whatever was stolen from his body, or at least knew what it was. It held the answer to this mystery.

CHAPTER FOURTEEN

Sir Henry waved me into a chair. I sat, grateful since I was ready to drop from fatigue. "Reina was from the same village as Elias, and she met Elias's wife the one time he brought her to meet his family. His wife was a city girl from a banking family and very young. She apparently wasn't impressed with her husband's hometown."

"Does this point to anyone on the committee?"

"It points to everyone on the committee. They are members of wealthy families with roots in the same area as Elias, when he was still known as Meirsohn. His wife died or went to prison when he was arrested. Did her family blame him for her death or imprisonment? Was it somehow his fault?"

When I saw I had his full attention, I continued. "And did this thing he wanted Reina to keep safe for him have anything to do with his wife or her fate? The police didn't find it when they searched the body. Reina didn't receive it. The killer must have taken it. Something a political assassin wouldn't bother with."

Then I looked at Sir Henry. "Unless I'm wrong." Unless it had to do with the assassin's identity or appearance. Something General Alford would want.

Sir Henry was frowning now. "What was his wife's name before she was married?"

"Reina couldn't remember, and Elias never mentioned it to Abram Mandel's daughter." I told him what little Reina had told me. "Reina is going to ask her cousin, who also lives in Paris now, in the hopes she can remember."

"Elias would have only been twenty or twenty-one then. The bride must have been about eighteen, so she'd be between twenty-seven and thirty now if she is still alive." Sir Henry looked at me. "You've given us quite a puzzle, Livvy."

"And it means Nazi assassins might not have been involved in his death or even known he was here. He might have died at the hands of an irate in-law."

The thought crossed my mind a moment before Sir Henry said, "Esther is questioning her friends, one of whom might be a killer."

The look on his face told me that if anything happened to Esther or the baby, I would be out of a job. My nice, cushy, well-appreciated position, gone.

I'd be forced to live with my father.

And Esther was my closest friend.

"Do you want me to go with Esther when she talks to the committee members?" He might want it, but where would I find the time? Miss Westcott was already furious with me for missing so much time at work.

The phone rang. Holding up a hand, Sir Henry answered with, "Is Chamberlain headed off to some other crisis?"

Then he fell silent. His expression went from astonishment to amazement to anger.

Oh, my Lord, we're going to war.

Sir Henry finally said, "Was he hurt?"

After a moment, he said, "Well, thank God for that. Keep me informed. What do you mean, we can't print?"

When he hung up, I said, "What happened?"

"Someone tried to kill Winston Churchill with an exploding cigar."

What? How could they...? My heart fluttered before it restarted. And then I wanted to giggle at the foolishness. "Aren't they some sort of joke?"

"Not this one. Some sort of incendiary chemical was planted inside the cigars in a box that went out to Chartwell with the deliveries yesterday. He had lit one but was called out of the room almost immediately. A moment later the room was engulfed in flames. His study."

No doubt where he did his writing and spent a lot of time. I was wide awake and on the edge of my chair. "Was he hurt? Did he lose his papers?"

"No. He's fine," Sir Henry told me. "They had a number of sand buckets nearby, because of Churchill's habit of leaving burning cigars near combustibles. The papers on the desk were destroyed, and the fire put scorch marks on the rug and some books on a nearby table, but they kept it from spreading to the bookshelves and the draperies."

He shook his head. "It could have been a great deal worse. Investigators from the military said the initial flare and the speed that the flames spread told them they were looking at a powerful incendiary agent."

Churchill might just be an ordinary member of Parliament, but he was the most persistent voice for rearmament as the best way to stand up to Germany. And there was no one who wanted him dead more than the Nazis. "If Churchill had been sitting there with that cigar when it exploded, he could have been killed." I couldn't hide the shock in my voice.

"Exactly." He clenched his fists as he looked at me. "I believe the Nazis sent someone over with their newest technology to kill Churchill."

"And we can't print the story? Have the public looking for anyone concocting weird chemicals?" I heard what he'd repeated on the phone, and I didn't think it was a good policy.

"The government is afraid we'll start a panic. And Whitehall doesn't want the Nazis to know how close they came to eliminating their greatest threat in England."

"But who could do this? And how will they catch him?" Then I thought of General Alford and the French assassin who was reported to have come to England. Alford would begin pressing me for results.

"Fortunately, that's not our problem. We only need to find Elias's killer, or the person who led his killer to meet him in that basement. Livvy, I want you to start attending all the resettlement committee meetings until we catch this killer. There is a meeting every week or two. You can tell the members I'm sending you to protect Esther."

"Doesn't that tip our hand that we think one of them is the killer?"

He grumbled through clenched jaws. "Tell them I've made it known I'm searching for Elias's killer, and I'm afraid the killer will know the best way to stop me is to injure Esther. I've sent you to shadow her."

Esther was my closest school friend, and this would be an enjoyable assignment. "How are we going to justify this to Miss Westcott?"

"You don't have to. Remember, she works for me." The growl in his tone told me no one should argue with him about this. This was about protecting Esther.

This would not make me popular in the society page section. "When do you want me to start?"

"There's a meeting tonight. I'll tell Esther you'll meet her at her house."

I hoped the meeting wouldn't last long. I needed some sleep.

"Don't tell anyone about the attack on Churchill," he continued. "I'll let you decide how much to tell them about Elias's real name and his marriage."

I nodded. I had my orders. But first I needed to write up an article on Mimi's French salon to go along with Jane's photographs. And drink more coffee.

* * *

I went straight to Esther's house after work to find her ready and waiting for me with her jacket on. "We're going to be late," she told me. "And why are you coming with me? My father made your attendance mandatory."

"Let's catch a taxi and I'll tell you."

As soon as we were settled in the back seat, I said, "Elias was married to a girl from a Berlin banking family.

An arranged marriage. When he went to prison, she died or went to prison and then died. We have reason to believe his killer might have struck out in revenge."

"Mr. Nauheim came from Germany, but at the turn of the century. Most of the people on the committee were born here. This makes no sense. Do you suspect Mr. Nauheim because he was German born?"

"No. Not really." He seemed like a nice, sensible person.

"Then why are you acting as my guardian?"

"Because your father said I have to guard you with my life or lose my job."

"That's ridiculous."

I gave her a wry smile. "He didn't say that, but I don't want to take any chances. And with your father so worried about his grandchild…"

"He's not worried about me. It's all about his grandchild. He wants a boy. You'd think James and I have nothing to do with it." Esther sounded near tears of frustration.

"He is worried about you. When he lost your mother, you became the center of his universe. Now you're expecting, and he sees that as terribly dangerous."

She made a scoffing noise.

"He's trying to look beyond that to having you and the baby here safely." I squeezed her hand. "And we're looking for a killer. The last thing he wants you to face."

Esther studied my face for a full minute. Finally, she said, "You think one of those nice, ordinary people in the committee is a cold-blooded killer."

"It's a definite possibility." Among others. "I hope it's one of the other lines of inquiry that we're following. Please, don't let anyone know what we're thinking."

"What you're thinking," Esther corrected me as the cab pulled up to the curb. She nearly bolted up the pavement to the door, leaving me to pay and then catch up to her.

Mrs. Mandel and her daughter Valerie were the hostesses of this meeting, and Esther and I paid them well-deserved compliments on their lovely home. The downstairs appeared to be totally decorated in blues and grays, tranquil and refreshing. Then we walked into their large drawing room and found the talk was all about war.

"Hitler will walk into Czechoslovakia tomorrow and we will have to declare war," a man's voice proclaimed.

"Surely not. It is too far away for Britain to get involved," another said.

Clusters of people stood, talking about the threat that had just been averted and the possibility of more trouble for the rest of Czechoslovakia. No one sat.

Abram Mandel moved to the center of the room and shouted, "Ladies and gentlemen, while war has been postponed, we must do what we can to help our brethren in Czechoslovakia. Please, sit down and let's not waste time discussing rumors."

People took their seats amid a sea of murmurs.

"Abram, I've been in touch with Rabbi Vltiva in Prague. He passed along our offer of one hundred sponsorships for young adults and young families and received over five hundred requests for those slots,"

Daniel Nauheim said.

"Can we raise the amount of money for sponsorships to bring in more Czech Jews?" another man asked.

There were more murmurs around the room, and then after hushed consultations with their wives, further offers came forth from the men.

"Come, come. We need to get more of these young people to safety," Mr. Mandel said. "We'll need their help here in Britain to fight the Nazis when war comes."

"Or to build up a Jewish homeland in Palestine," another man I suspected was a Zionist said.

"We can't do everything at once," Mr. Mandel replied. "Let's get as many as we can away from Hitler and his dangerous plans first."

Esther and I sat in silence while around us the men talked, argued, and pushed their own theories about the coming war. The room grew warm despite the cool night outside. Someone opened a window, and none too soon. The talk and the stuffy air were making me sick.

Suddenly, Esther rose. "I'll need a nursery maid in the coming months and I could use a housemaid. Those are positions we're allowed to hire refugees for, aren't they?"

"Domestic workers are one of the few positions open to refugees," Mr. Nauheim confirmed.

"Then you can put me down for two sponsorships. And I'm sure my father would offer a sponsorship, too." Esther gracefully sat down again.

As the meeting continued, she looked at me.

"Your father doesn't pay me well enough to have a

maid, Esther."

"What about your father?"

"My father?"

"Surely Sir Ronald doesn't do his own housework."

"I'll have to ask him first. But you know my father. If I ask him, it will be the worst idea ever."

"Coward," Esther said with a teasing gleam in her eye.

"I am." I admitted it freely and had since we were in school. I knew I had no talent for getting around my father.

"Then I'll ask him, shall I?" She gave me a smug smile.

I felt my eyes widen. At least my father would be polite to her while rejecting her suggestion. "Please. Be my guest."

"Mrs. Denis."

I swung my head around to face Mr. Mandel, who'd spoken to me.

"You work for Sir Henry's newspaper. Do you have any insight on what might happen in the coming days?"

"None at all. I cover society news. I know Sir Henry has been very busy today, so he might have some idea of what the various governments plan to do tomorrow." *Start a terrible war* immediately came to my mind.

"A shame, really," Mr. Nauheim said. "We could all do with some insight into the future."

I didn't want any. The present was frightening enough.

The meeting broke up shortly afterward with an additional seventy-five sponsorships to offer to the

Jewish community in Prague. We spread out over the drawing room and dining room for coffee.

Esther and I found ourselves talking to Mr. Nauheim and his son, David. "Where's Leah? I haven't seen her," I said.

"She didn't come tonight. She's very upset about the situation in Prague," David told me.

"She has family there?"

"Yes. That's where we met. She was living with her aunt and uncle. Her parents are trapped in Berlin and can't get out. And she rarely gets any word from them."

"That must be frightening," Esther said. "My grandfather is in Berlin and very ill, and I can't go to help my grandmother and aunt. They're the only family I have left over there now, thanks to my father and Livvy."

"It's so terrible. The not knowing. Or knowing and being unable to do anything," Mr. Nauheim said, sympathetically patting Esther's shoulder.

"What exactly did you do, Mrs. Denis?" David asked. "Or may I call you Livvy?"

"Please, call me Livvy. I carried out some goods for Esther's relatives, in some cases acting as if they were my own and in others by smuggling them under my clothes. Goods they could sell when they reached here to support themselves until they permanently settle elsewhere. That's the official position of our government—be able to support yourself until you leave. The government fears adding any new names to the dole. In the meantime, the goods help the refugees while they set up a new life here on a permanent footing."

Whichever version was true, it meant most of Esther's relatives were safe. Unless Hitler overran England.

"Livvy was very brave, smuggling these goods past the German border guards," Esther said.

"I was lucky." I didn't realize how lucky until later.

Mr. Nauheim smiled. There was something in that smile that scared me, but his words frightened me even more. "Perhaps Mrs. Denis will be willing to undertake another journey. One that would benefit the entire Jewish community in Prague."

CHAPTER FIFTEEN

"What do you have in mind?" I asked Mr. Nauheim. The way he posed his question made the hair on the back of my neck stand up.

"Nothing for you to look so concerned about. We'll have to see what happens before we need to consider the possibilities." He gave me another smile and said, "I think I'll get another cup of coffee."

As he walked off, I looked from David Nauheim to Esther.

They met my puzzled frown with head shakes.

I convinced Esther to go home then so I could get back to my flat and get some sleep. The night train from Paris meant frequently being jerked out of sleep, and I needed a clear head for the meeting with General Alford that I knew was coming.

But first I needed to answer the question that nibbled on my nerves. What had Esther learned from talking to the families of the committee? "May I come in?" I asked as the taxi pulled up outside her house.

Esther nodded. "I'll make some tea."

Their cook, a sturdy middle-aged woman, refused to let Esther make tea or carry the tray with the teapot and little sandwiches into the drawing room. After the cook left, I said, "She's new, isn't she?"

"Mrs. Rosenbaum. Yes. She escaped from Austria.

She knows my aunt. Her husband was a lawyer before the Nazis took over."

I nodded. While her husband wouldn't be allowed to practice, or hold a job, his wife could work as a cook. "It doesn't seem quite fair for Mrs. Rosenbaum to suddenly be thrown into the workforce."

"It isn't, but she's glad to be in England and glad of the work. And the timing couldn't have been better. My former cook left to help her daughter with newborn twins." When I nodded to the sandwiches, Esther said, "Help yourself."

I polished one off immediately, roast beef and horseradish on a whole wheat roll that had been sliced into quarters. "This is delicious. Mrs. Rosenbaum is a treasure. Now, before I stuff another one in my mouth, what did you learn?"

"Nothing."

"Really?"

She looked at me through wide eyes. "Yes. Really. No one had met him before or heard his name. Valerie Mandel said when he first came in, he appeared to recognize someone, but she had no idea who. There was a whole crowd to greet him, and he didn't appear to speak to anyone longer than to say hello. No one said 'Remember me?' or anything helpful like that."

The Mandel girl had been the first to tell me she'd learned Elias was married. She was either observant or fanciful. I had no idea which. "Does Valerie always study people that carefully?"

"No. Elias caught her fancy. He was youngish,

attractive, daring, and involved in bold adventures. Do you remember when we were that age?" Esther gave me a knowing smile.

Indeed I did. One more reason to pay careful attention to what Valerie Mandel observed.

* * *

By the time I reached the *Daily Premier* offices the next morning, everyone was reading the newspapers, either hunting for a clue to Hitler's next move or for something that proclaimed life had returned to normal now that the Sudetenland was under German control. I hoped General Alford would be too busy to ask for me.

It was gratifying to see the society pages carrying on as if nothing untoward was happening elsewhere in the world. Besotted grandmothers were sending in photos and details of their treasured new grandchildren. Teas were being held. House parties with shooting during the day held masked balls at night. People were still getting engaged, and married, and phoning the paper to tell us about it.

And I doubted I would ever turn in an article that didn't leave Miss Westcott clicking her tongue. I'd improved, or so I thought, but there was always that little something wrong that annoyed Miss Westcott.

As I handed in my first notice of the day, she asked, "Will you be here the entire day today?"

"You'll have to ask Sir Henry," I replied, giving her a smile.

She clicked her tongue and waved me away from her desk.

One of the girls called out, "Livvy. Telephone."

I walked over and picked it up. "Mrs. Denis."

"Mrs. Denis," the gruff voice came out of the line to me. "This is General Alford. I need to speak to you."

"Would after work do?" I asked, my back to Miss Westcott. She didn't approve of personal calls in the office. Come to think of it, she didn't approve of most of what I did. "I can reach your building by six."

"Very good. I'll see you then." I heard a click and the line went dead.

I glanced back to find Miss Westcott studying some copy, her red pencil poised in midair. I dialed Leah Nauheim's number and asked for her when a woman's voice came on the line.

A moment later, another woman could be heard. "This is Mrs. Nauheim."

"Leah? This is Livvy Denis."

"Livvy? How are you?" Her voice took on some warmth.

"Have you checked on your suit lately at Mimi Mareau's salon?"

"No. Thank you for reminding me."

"Do you mind if I check on it for you? I need to go over there and snoop around." I might as well be honest with her. She was doing me a favor. Especially since my calling with my sketch for the ad was getting old. I suspected Mimi would never approve my work.

So why did she ask me to do the sketch?

"Go right ahead. Just let me know when I need to go in for a fitting."

"I'll be glad to. Thank you, Leah. This makes my job easier."

I finished my last assignment of the morning a few minutes early and slipped out while Miss Westcott's attention was elsewhere. I took a bus toward Mayfair and climbed out on Piccadilly around the corner from Mimi's salon.

Strolling up to the black lacquered door, I turned the handle and walked in as if I were one of their wealthy clients.

"May I help you?" said an English-accented speaker at the desk. She was in her twenties and her deep rose coat kept me from judging the quality of her clothes. The same smock I'd seen on Mimi's employees in Paris and here. While I recognized the smock, I hadn't seen the woman before.

"I'm checking on the progress on Mrs. Nauheim's tweed suit. With Mimi back in Paris with Reina and Brigette, I can't imagine much has been accomplished lately." I used the upper-class diction I'd learned at St. Agnes.

"Oh, you're wrong," she told me. "Madame returned last night with Reina and Brigette, and we kept everything moving along in her absence. She was pleased with our progress."

"And the progress on the suit?"

The woman studied the large book on the desk in front of her. "Would next Monday do? At ten o'clock?"

"Yes." I certainly hoped it would. I'd leave straightening out any problems to Leah Nauheim. "Is

Reina here?"

"She's in the building somewhere."

The phone rang at that moment and when the woman's attention was away from me, I slipped through the door into the back room on the ground floor. No one was about, so I dashed on tiptoes down the basement stairs, making sure my heels wouldn't clatter on the wooden steps.

It was a wasted trip. There was nothing down there to indicate why a spy for the British who also smuggled refugees had been killed in this place. I checked the outside door and found Mimi, or someone, had decided to start locking the knob and the latch. It felt like a step taken too late.

The racks were emptier than they had been. Had the costumes for the play been taken to the theater? The trunks still sat along the far wall. I walked over and began to open them one by one.

A few of them contained fabric and thread, fur and leather and buckles. A few were still empty. And the one I wondered about before contained small bottles, tins, and envelopes of powders.

"Livvy?" a quiet voice said from behind me.

I jumped and turned, a guilty look no doubt plastered on my face. My heart stopped pounding once I saw who was there and I caught my breath. "Reina. Thank goodness it was you. Did you reach your cousin?"

"Yes, but she couldn't remember his wife's name. She remembered the name of the bank, though. Mr. Meirsohn was so proud of the family his son was marrying into, he told everyone that soon his son would be related to the Grand Wolf Bank. As a child, my cousin couldn't understand why anyone would want to be related to a bank, or any company. Even more, why would anyone name a bank after an animal? She thought it was run by real wolves."

"Was that the name of the bank? The Wolf bank?" I asked. I'd never heard of it.

"It doesn't sound right, and it doesn't jog my memory. I can't remember the name of the bank or his wife's name. It was a small wonder, since that occurred among bigger concerns. About the time of the wedding, which was hundreds of miles away, we had an outbreak of influenza that claimed several of our neighbors. And then on her one visit to our village, this scrawny young woman, Josef's wife, wanted nothing to do with us. We'd found her as unimportant as she found us."

"One person lost among thousands," I said sadly.

She gave me a sharp look. "When some of those lost are my family and friends, yes. And now Josef is dead. I don't have the time or energy to mourn her."

"What is all this?" I asked her, pointing into the trunk with the bottles and tins.

Reina looked into the trunk and shrugged. "Fleur's. She does the dyeing and sometimes softens the cloth. Those are skills I don't have."

I wanted to keep her talking. "She must be invaluable to Mimi."

"I'm sure she is. She keeps her knowledge secret from the rest of us. It makes her irreplaceable." Reina closed the lid. "And Mimi says we are all to give each other as much privacy as we can. We live too close together in this house to do anything but give each other room."

I nodded. "Is that why you and Mimi went back to Paris for a few days?"

"Partly. We also needed more fabric and supplies. We've been very successful here. We've had far more orders than we expected."

I stared at the now-closed trunk. "Is softening the secret of the sweep of Mimi's skirts? I thought it was the way the fabric was cut, but is it Fleur's secret process?"

"I don't know. I know it's not the stitching. The magic is already in the fabric before I get my hands on it, but I can't feel any difference in the cloth before and after she says she's treated it." Reina took a bolt of red cloth from one of the trunks and then turned toward the stairs. "Are you coming?" It was clearly a command.

I followed her up the stairs. "When did Mimi finally decide to lock up the basement?"

"She didn't. I understand Fleur locked up the downstairs door as soon as we left, saying she didn't fancy being murdered in her bed."

"Are you all still sleeping on the third floor?"

"Yes, and the extra seamstresses from Paris are sleeping in the attic," she told me. We reached the ground floor. "Good-bye," she said and continued upstairs.

"Wait," I said and gazed up the stairs at her. "Will you hear from your cousin again?"

"It depends on when I next go back to Paris," Reina

said without looking back at me, her tread slow and steady on the steps.

I went back to the receptionist and asked to speak to Mimi about the sketch she asked for. She left and a minute later Brigette returned with her.

"Madame is very busy today. We just returned from Paris."

"So I heard."

Brigette gave me a weak smile. "Perhaps you could return in a few days."

I nodded and headed out the front door, ignored by the receptionist, who was helping another client.

On the way back to the office, I heard people on the bus talking about the weather, sports, and how grown-up Princess Elizabeth had become. No one mentioned how close we'd come to being at war.

* * *

Big Ben had chimed six o'clock a few minutes before I reached the War Office. General Alford had made arrangements for me to be escorted by a sergeant to the same conference room where we had met before.

After we greeted each other, I said, "I hope the news will be good now that Chamberlain's trip was successful."

"I doubt it," Alford said in an abrupt tone. "Now, what have you learned about Elias's—shall we call him that— death?"

Since he didn't invite me to sit down, I stood waiting until I had the general's attention. "Elias met with the refugee resettlement committee, made up of Jewish leaders in London, asking for their help in bringing in more German Jews. While there, he mentioned to someone that he was married. A fact I've verified another way."

"I hardly see the point…"

"It is also believed he recognized someone at that meeting," I interrupted. "Since his wife is believed to be dead or in a German jail cell, I think he may have recognized a member of her family, and that person sought revenge for Elias's wife's death."

"It would make more sense if this person had aimed his revenge against Hitler." Alford glared at me. He was not making things easy.

I glared back. "Revenge against Elias would be easier to carry out than revenge against Hitler. Especially since Elias was conveniently in London."

The general sat, signaled me to do the same, and grumbled, "Go on."

I sat and faced him. "Elias was a communist and a leader in the opposition to Hitler. If he hadn't been, he wouldn't have come to the attention of the Nazis quite so quickly, and his wife wouldn't have been jailed along with him. One version of the story I've been hearing is she died in prison. Another is that she died very young before the Nazis came to power. I think either would be enough for Elias to earn the hatred of her family."

"So you haven't looked into this French assassin?"

His words earned him an angry glare. Did he also want me to pull a rabbit out of my navy slant-brimmed hat? "I don't know how I would. That's more in line with Scotland Yard's work. Or yours."

"The assassin has attacked Churchill." Alford's face had reddened and his expression said he'd like to lock me up for being unhelpful.

"I know."

"You know?" His voice rose alarmingly before he grabbed hold of his temper. "How do you know?" sounded deeper, icier, and much more ominous.

"From Sir Henry."

"How the devil did...?"

"I have no idea. I work on the society pages. The women's section. I don't know where he gets political information." I said it in the most innocent tone I could manage, with my eyes wide open.

"Since you know about it, you can help us. We not only need to find Elias's killer, we need to find the person who attacked Churchill, too." The general boomed his orders at me, though I was sitting only a few feet away. "They may be one and the same person. And there's no time to lose."

CHAPTER SIXTEEN

"What do you know about this assassin?" I asked the general.

"Only what the French government and Elias told us. This person is French and experienced in explosives and poisons. He keeps at arm's length, so no one has seen him."

"So it's a man?"

"N-n-not necessarily." Suddenly, he seemed extremely uncomfortable.

"So it could be a woman."

"Possibly. They say poison is a woman's weapon."

"*They* say a great number of silly things," I replied. "What exactly did Elias say?"

"He learned of a confidential German government memo saying the French assassin was going to England and would be there for an indeterminate period of time. The targets were previously selected and would be passed on by a member of the aristocracy."

"Targets. More than one." I shuddered.

"But—kill Churchill? With an exploding cigar?" He didn't sound as if he could believe it.

"Have you ruled out Lady Astor?" I smiled at the thought.

"Oh, she would never—"

"She threatened often enough," I reminded him.

"Although I think she planned to use something more direct than an exploding cigar."

"But that was all in jest," he insisted.

From what my father said, I wouldn't be too sure. Nancy Astor and Winston Churchill began their feud before I was born. It sounded like the feud would only end in death. Or murder.

"Besides, the Astor woman is American, not French. This assassin has had several successes in France against anti-Nazi targets. Under circumstances where the killer must be French." Alford glared at me.

It was all I could do not to squirm in my hard wooden chair.

"You are spending a great deal of time with the French at that dressmaker's," he added. "You have their confidence. If one of them is the assassin, you'll spot it."

"There are a great number of French citizens in London."

"Don't think you're the only one with this assignment. So, are you going to take this on?"

"I'm going to try to find Elias's killer. If it's the same person, then we'll have a real success. I have no idea what someone who builds exploding cigars looks like." It still sounded ludicrous.

"Don't you?" he asked. "The exploding cigars went out to Chartwell in the same shipment as a dress for Mrs. Churchill from Mimi Mareau."

If their information was correct, this was news. "How much do you know about Mimi Mareau?" I asked.

"How much do you know?" he challenged.

"Obviously, not as much as you. I believe she's having an affair with the Duke of Marshburn, who has pro-German sympathies. I know she has a daughter who was born just after the war and she's never been married."

"Know about that, do you?" The general sounded mildly impressed.

"But not much more. What have your people been able to find out?"

He leaned forward, lowering his voice. "She's a conservative, in the way those who have money are against any changes, but back during the war and immediately afterward, she was a socialist. Back then she had a Jewish lover. Now she scorns them."

"Have you been able to determine if she shares Marshburn's Nazi sympathies?" The women who worked for her certainly thought she did.

"She says she does," Alford replied.

I suspected Mimi's politics were formed more by what would do her the most good at that moment. "Marshburn is a good friend of Churchill's, isn't he?"

"They were very close, shooting together and that sort of thing. In the last couple of years, however, since Churchill has started his rearmament speeches in Parliament and in his writings, there's been a coolness between them."

"Yet Mrs. Churchill just got an outfit from the salon headed by Marshburn's mistress." If the two men were truly feuding, I doubted Mrs. Churchill would buy anything from the House of Mareau.

"What difference does that make?" the general

grumbled.

"Possibly none." At least to a man. "Who made the delivery?" I saw a way to investigate the exploding cigars.

"Royal Mail out of Westerham."

I turned to leave. "I suggest you get Sir Henry's permission for me to take a few days off to investigate my idea. If it leads to nothing, we're no worse off than we were."

His grumbling grew louder. "We can't discuss this with a newspaper publisher."

"He already knows about Churchill's brush with death," I reminded him. "If you want my help, you need to get his approval." I reined in my temper in an attempt to reason with the fossil. "To help you, I need to look into some things."

"Such as?"

His tone didn't sound like he wanted my help. I tried to explain without sounding like I was beginning to think he was an idiot. "How did his wife's gown, and those cigars, end up at their door? I know someone who lives nearby, and I can have her introduce me to the people I need to speak to."

And I wouldn't mind a bit of a break from London, and war talk, with my late husband's cousin, and my friend, Lady Abby Summersby.

The next morning when I arrived at my desk at the *Daily Premier*, Miss Westcott looked at me with raised brows and said in a low voice, "Sir Henry wants to see you." In a whisper, she added, "Good luck."

How much had Sir Henry told her? And what had he

learned?

I rode to the top floor in the elevator and climbed out to walk toward Sir Henry's office. His secretary waved me in with a jerk of her head as she continued talking on the telephone. I knocked and entered.

"You certainly have been mixed up with some unusual investigations." Sir Henry studied me for a moment after I sat down. "I told General Alford that I would get an exclusive on anything you learn once this business is finished."

I tried to fight a smile. "Now why doesn't that surprise me."

He sounded eager as he said, "Will you be able to continue your search for Elias's killer at the same time?"

"Not unless Elias's killer blew up Churchill's cigars." My conscience nudged me. "I'm sorry about not telling you that General Alford was using me for this other investigation. I wasn't allowed to."

"I understand." Amazingly, he sounded as if he did understand. What had General Alford said?

"What I plan to do will only take a couple of days. Then I'll be back and we can continue the search for Elias's killer." I hoped that was what would happen. Take care of this before Monday, report into the general, and then head back to work at the newspaper.

"Unless events overtake us. So far Germany has given us some breathing room, but..." He left the thought hang in the air.

My mind raced to finish his words. If Hitler changed his mind, then we would be at war and life would change completely. And it would be too late to find the French assassin or Elias's killer.

Then I thought of Adam, and knew that discovering the identity of either the assassin or the killer was of no importance if we were at war.

"When should we expect you back?"

"I hope Monday, unless I'm on the trail of the assassin," I told him.

"Then you better get going."

I jumped up, surprised at how calmly he was taking General Alford's orders, and headed for the door before he changed his mind.

As I reached for the door handle, he said, "Good luck. We may need a lot of it in the coming days."

I sent a telegram to Abby telling her to expect me on the eleven o'clock train. Then I left a note in my flat for Adam telling him where I'd gone. That was the height of wishful thinking, but I would like to see him again, particularly if we went to war.

Even though the Sudeten crisis was over, everyone felt the weight of "the next time" looming over our heads.

I packed a bag and took a train into the rolling countryside, past farmers harvesting crops, trees turning amber and golden, and the occasional cyclist at a crossing. Abby was there with the car to meet me at the local station with a stack of questions.

"It's not like you to take off in the middle of the week. Is something wrong with your job?" she started.

"No."

"Adam?"

"Good grief, no."

"Then what is going on? And you'd better get your story straight, because John is going to want to know why you're here midweek, too."

Colonel Sir John Summersby, farmer and survivor of the Great War as well as Abby's husband, was a true gentleman and would probably believe any strange story I told him. Abby was the one who saw right through my prevarications.

"I have to tell you, Abby, because I'll need your help, but we need to keep this quiet from everyone else. Even Sir John."

"Is that fair?" She took her eyes off the road to glance over at me. "John is my husband and your host."

"I'm doing this for General Alford."

I was glad there wasn't any traffic on the curving country road because Abby nearly put us into a ditch. When she recovered herself and her driving, only grinding the gears once, she said, "John will understand that. What are we doing?"

"After we take my suitcase to your house, we need to find a plausible excuse to talk to the Westerham Post Office."

"Old Mr. Nicholson or young Mr. Nicholson?"

I stared at Abby in confusion.

She glanced at me again, a smile on her lips. "Old Mr. Nicholson owned the shop and ran the post office for many years. Young Mr. Nicholson, who is older than me, runs the business and the post office now. Then there's young Dickie, young Mr. Nicholson's son. All three are involved with deliveries and manning the counter."

"Surely the founder is retired if his son is older than you." I realized a moment too late how tactless that sounded.

Abby ignored the last of my words. "Old Mr. Nicholson must be eighty, but he still puts in a full day's work. He's a wonder from the old school."

"What I want to do is trace a gown made at Mimi Mareau's salon for Mrs. Churchill and sent from London to Chartwell by Royal Mail." Well, sort of. It was the other parcel I was really interested in.

Abby scowled at the road. "You can't just ask them. They're very closed-mouthed about their deliveries. They're very proud of what they call the trust the public has put in them."

"How far do you live from Chartwell?"

"Ten miles? Twelve? And what is this about Clementine having a frock made by Mimi Mareau?" She said the name with the sort of reverence I had used until I began spending time with the French designer. Until I began to see her narrowmindedness and egotism.

"She did, and Royal Mail delivered it." Then I had another thought. "Any idea where she would wear it?"

"Anything that special would probably be worn for something in London around the Opening of Parliament."

That didn't sound like a promising lead. "Do you see them often?"

"Her? Yes. In Sevenoaks on occasion or in Westerham, usually at Gwynne Waters's home. Her mother is a distant cousin of Clementine's. Him? Rarely.

He's busy with running the country, or trying to, and he comes to Chartwell to relax. Well," she added, "that's what I hear. County gossip. Sir John tells me not to pay any attention."

The reporter in me, or maybe the investigator in me, asked, "Will you be seeing Clementine Churchill again soon?"

"Possibly. Gwynne's having an 'at-home' on Friday afternoon. Lots of talk about gardens. Gwynne's perennial borders are the best in the county."

"Could you ask Mrs. Waters if you can bring me along?"

We pulled up in front of the house. "Of course, Livvy. Now, I've put you in your usual room."

A comfortable room with fabulous views of the garden. "I'll just take my suitcase up and then we can plot about what to say to the Nicholsons."

"Nonsense," Abby said as a maid came out to the car and took my suitcase. "I'd already asked Mary to see to it for you."

I was always slightly amazed by any situation made easier for me by servants. I'd grown up with only a daily cleaner who found me a nuisance. My father told me I should have experienced life in the houses with plenty of servants before the war.

Which reminded me of how much life had changed because of the war. And of all the deaths in those four long years. No one wanted another one. Hitler promised to be much worse than the kaiser.

We settled into Abby's morning room with cups of

tea and began to plot, only to have Sir John knock and walk in. "There you are, old girl. Oh, hello, Livvy. I saw the car out front. Do you want me to put it away?"

"No, thank you. We're going out directly after lunch, so just leave it where it is." Sir John and Abby didn't touch, but the looks of affection on their faces said far more than words.

He turned to me then. "How are you, Livvy?"

"Fine, Sir John. And you?"

"Oh, you know. Doing as well as the harvest." His smile told me that the harvest was going smoothly. "When is luncheon?" he asked his wife.

"In twenty minutes." Neither of us invited him to sit down.

"I'll leave you to it until then." With a hint of a bow, he left the room and shut the door after him.

"Now, what are we going to tell the Nicholsons?" Abby asked, eagerly leaning forward again.

"I want to know every step of the way from Mimi's salon to Clementine's hallway or wherever packages are delivered."

"That would be the kitchen entrance." When I looked surprised, she added, "I think every delivery has cigars and foodstuffs you can't easily obtain in Westerham. At least that's the impression I got from the gardening enthusiasts at Gwynne's."

"And before it reaches the kitchen entrance?"

"Royal Mail would carry the dress, but there would be a daily delivery by Lagrange's van, they supply the spirits and cigars and such to the big houses around here, as well as the greengrocer and the butcher and the baker," Abby said, nodding as if she understood where my questions were leading.

I'd seen the gowns hanging in their protective sacks or wrapped carefully in large boxes at Mimi's fashion house. "I'm going to claim a frock I ordered from Mimi to be delivered here has failed to show up. Then we'll see what we can learn about the route it would have taken."

Abby shook her head as she rose. "Won't work. If it were coming here, it would come from the Royal Mail office in Royal Tunbridge Wells. And now, I should call Gwynne and ask about bringing a guest on Friday."

Abby walked out to the hall where the telephone was. In a few moments, she had Gwynne Waters on the phone and the invitation was apparently cheerfully extended.

Now to hope Mrs. Churchill showed up at the Waterses' home that day. She might have some idea of how that exploding cigar ended up on her husband's desk.

CHAPTER SEVENTEEN

Sir John was already at the table when we walked into the dining room, but he immediately stood and waited for us to sit. As soon as we were in place, a maid brought out the soup. Before I picked up my spoon, Sir John said, "Is your father in good health?"

"Yes, thank you. How are the boys doing?" Reggie had been godfather to Abby and Sir John's sons. Since his death, I tried to take over his role with the boys.

"Very well."

Abby said, "There's no point in asking why she's here. She can't tell you. It's for General Alford."

In his surprise, Sir John half rose from his chair, bumping into the maid. Fortunately, she'd already set down his soup or we would have been covered in the cream-based broth. Once he recovered, Sir John said, "General Alford? Livvy, what are you mixed up in?"

"She can't tell you, John. That's the whole point." Abby took a spoonful of her soup to signal the subject was closed.

I took pity on him. "I'd tell you, Sir John, if I could use your help. But this is out of your usual realm of experience. Please know I appreciate you taking me in while I do a little digging around."

"Ah, women's things. Gossip and gardening and all that." He appeared more relaxed now that he could pigeonhole my activities.

I glanced at Abby. "Exactly."

"I'm sure Alford is out of his depth, too." Sir John smiled. Then he blinked and said, "Be careful. Some of the things Alford has been involved in have been dangerous."

"Not this time." Then I added, "I don't think he'd allow me within a hundred miles of anything treacherous."

After lunch, Abby and I rode over to Westerham. "If claiming to have a frock from Mimi going missing isn't going to work, what story can we tell them?"

"I don't think telling them any story will work. They'll see right through it."

Abby was too practical. I thought for a moment and then said, "You drove me over to Westerham so I could check on the speed of delivery for Mimi and whether the package arrived in good shape. I don't think they'll check with Mimi to find out if I'm working for her or not."

"I don't think it will work either. It's too bold. No one ever checks. They just assume everything is delivered in order unless they get a complaint."

Abby was right. I needed luck more than anything. "Then I suppose it doesn't matter what I say, as long as I can get them talking."

We arrived in Westerham and parked along the edge of the green. The post office was in a store marked "Nicholson's," full of canned goods, sweets, and stationery. When we walked in, Abby ran into an acquaintance and they chatted for a minute or two. Only then did we approach the post office counter in one corner of the shop.

A man, I guessed the younger Mr. Nicholson, came around from the shop counter to the other side of the store where the post office counter was located. He left a middle-aged woman to serve the customers in the shop. Fortunately, there was only one person waiting.

"Good day, Mr. Nicholson," Abby began. "I'm Lady Summersby, a friend of Mrs. Waters, and this is my cousin, Mrs. Denis."

We nodded to each other before he turned his attention back to Abby. "I remember you. How can I help, Lady Summersby?"

"Mrs. Denis is taking on a little commission for Mimi Mareau, the French designer. Being French, she doesn't trust our English institutions, including the Royal Mail."

The man glared at me.

"Oh, not me," I said, holding up my hands. "I know there is nothing as efficient and trustworthy as the Royal Mail, but Madame Mareau has that French distrust of any authority." I rolled my eyes. "I'm trying to assure her that her frocks and gowns arrive by Royal Mail Parcel in a timely manner and quite safely."

"Has she had any complaints?"

"No. Of course not."

"Well, then."

"Perhaps if you told me a little about how her frocks go from her shop in London down here to Westerham, I could explain it to her and relieve her mind."

"Is this about the delivery to Chartwell?"

"She mailed a gown to Mrs. Churchill, yes."

His mulish expression told me this attempt was going to go down in ruin. "Oh, you'll not get any gossip about that from me."

"I'm not asking for gossip, Mr. Nicholson," I said, trying to sound affronted. "I'm trying to learn how Mrs. Churchill's frock got from Mimi's salon to Chartwell so I can get that Frenchwoman off my back."

"Well, if that's all you want."

"That's exactly what I want."

"I don't know the London end of the process, but when the mail reaches Sevenoaks on the train, the postmaster in Sevenoaks takes it to his office and sorts it."

At that moment, a young man of about twenty walked in behind the counter from an outside door and nodded to us.

"Good day, Dickie," Abby said in a hearty voice.

"It's Lady Summersby, isn't it?" he replied as he set down an empty bag made of heavy canvas. "I recognize you from that lost delivery to Mrs. Waters. You remember, Dad."

His father glowered at him before he continued. "When we go over to Sevenoaks to pick up the mail, we pick up the packages, too. Then Dickie delivers it to the house on his bicycle."

"How did you manage a big package like that on your bicycle?" I asked Dickie, letting my amazement show. He was a tall, thin lad, quite fit, but I couldn't see how he could balance a package the size of a dress box for an evening gown on a bicycle. "With all your other mail and parcels, a dress box seems like it would be too much."

"He does, is all. Now, if there's nothing else?" his father snapped.

I caught Dickie's eye and lifted my eyebrows as I gave him a conspiratorial smile. "Thank you."

Abby thanked him and we walked out of the shop.

When she started briskly off to the auto, I said, "Wait. Slow down."

I guessed right. A minute later we'd only walked past two shops when Dickie hurried up to us.

"Were you interested in something specific, asking how I balanced that dress box all the way to Chartwell?"

I smiled. "You couldn't have done it. Not without breaking your neck. How did you get that package over there?"

"Why are you so interested in deliveries to Chartwell?"

"Is there anything interesting about Chartwell deliveries?"

He hung his head. "Yes. And now everyone's asking questions."

Everyone? "How could deliveries to Churchill raise questions?" I tried to sound like a wise older sister and not a snoop.

"The help who live here in the village told everyone about the fire. Then the army and Scotland Yard came down before the end of the day, asking questions and telling us not to talk to outsiders."

I smiled, trying to act like I wasn't an outsider. "I still can't picture carrying a dress box on a bicycle and not taking a spill. How did you do it?"

He turned beet red. "I didn't. I—well, Rex from the vintner's was driving out there, so he offered me a lift. Please, don't tell my father."

"I won't tell. But what did you do with the bicycle?"

"Put it in the back with the goods." He grinned.

"And Rex would need the truck, since he'd have a heavy order to deliver, with Scotch and wine and cigars. You wouldn't take up much room with your mail and your bicycle. Very clever." I smiled back at him like we were sharing a joke.

"No cigars that day, but plenty of fancy canned goods. It was a heavy load. I had to help Rex carry it all in after I took in the mail."

"No cigars? I thought Mr. Churchill went through a box of those a day along with a bottle of Scotch." I guess his reputation was a bit of an exaggeration.

"I had the two packages and a bunch of letters. Rex had his load including the Scotch." He paused a moment, then shook his head. "But there wasn't a box of cigars."

"Two packages, one a dress box, and mail, on a bicycle. How does your father think you could do it?" I still couldn't believe anyone would think it was possible.

He shrugged. Despite his lean build, his shoulders were muscular, probably from hauling and carrying all his life. "I don't think I could have managed it without a ride from Rex, with the mail and the two parcels."

"It was lucky he was going your way." Then I pushed, trying to sound like I was still thinking about balancing on a bicycle. "How big were these two boxes?"

He gestured with his hands the size of a dress box, and then a box about the size of a cigar box. "It must have been gloves or some ladies' thing like that."

It hit me why he thought the box, probably containing the cigars, contained "ladies' things." "Did Madame Mareau send two packages?"

"Yeah. Well, I thought so. They were postmarked at the same time at the same post office in London. While we were driving along, I was re-sorting the mail to deliver on my way back from Chartwell and I noticed the postmarks on the letters and the packages. Hoping we were delivering fast enough to suit the Royal Mail officials."

Then he stopped and said, "Please don't tell my dad. He doesn't want me to have anything to do with Rex. Thinks he's a wild one. And Dad's determined that we deliver all the mail on our own."

"I bet that's what he told Scotland Yard," I said.

"Yeah. I wouldn't dare tell him I'm catching rides with Rex in the van whenever I can. Don't tell on me, please."

"I won't." Especially since my focus was turned back onto Mimi's salon.

When we returned to the automobile, I said, "I wonder if I should return to London immediately and start asking questions again at Mimi's salon."

"You just arrived and already you want to go rushing back to London?" Abby said in a stiff voice. "You'll miss out on anything else you might learn down here about the Churchills and Chartwell and whatever it is you're really investigating."

I quickly smiled to reassure her. "You're right, Abby, as you always are." I looked out the window as we drove out of the village, hearing the hurt in her tone, and fighting down the sensation that I'd forgotten a detail that would prove fatal. "The trouble is I fear I've overlooked something in London. Something rather vital."

"Do you know what it is? Contact the police and ask them to check on it." I heard the challenge behind her words. I suspected she was worried for me, and with good reason. Working for General Alford could be dangerous.

I shook my head. "I don't know what it is. Just a gnawing suspicion that something is very wrong. But I will send General Alford a telegram if you don't mind stopping at the post office in Sevenoaks."

"Instead of Westerham? You don't want to raise the suspicions of the Nicholsons."

"No, I don't. I can think of two explanations, and one of them might be in Westerham listening in."

CHAPTER EIGHTEEN

Abby willingly drove me to Sevenoaks on the return trip and I sent a telegram asking, "Are you certain cigar box delivered that day? At Summersby House, Kent. Olivia."

"There," I said when we were heading away from Sevenoaks. "Let's see if I get a return message."

I spent the rest of the afternoon in Abby's garden laboring in her flower beds. We had cleaned up and dressed for dinner when there was a knock at the door. A moment later, a maid came into the parlor with a telegram envelope for me.

I opened the envelope and read, "Certain." I looked at the hovering maid. "No reply."

"You found out what you needed to know?" Abby asked.

I took a sip of my sherry before I nodded. "Do you think tomorrow morning we could try to find Rex and his delivery van?"

"There's only one vintner in Westerham. Lagrange's. They call themselves a vintner but they also sell fine cigars and imported foodstuffs. Delicacies. Theirs is a black truck. And I believe I can convince Mrs. Lagrange to tell me the order of the stops Rex will be making tomorrow." Abby looked very satisfied with herself.

"Telegrams? Delivery vans? What is going on,

Abigail?" Sir John asked.

"The telegram is from General Alford, Sir John," I told him. "Abby's involved because I need her help. General Alford needs her help." Whether he knows it or not, I silently added.

"Well, Alford wouldn't get you two ladies into too much trouble," Sir John said. I suspected he was trying to reassure himself.

"Shall we go into dinner?" Abby asked, and Sir John escorted us both into the dining room.

We spent the meal making Sir John the focal point of any discussion so he wouldn't feel so left out. All was well until near the end of the main course when Sir John said, "Oh, I invited your father to come stay for the weekend. Get in some golf at the club. He'll be on the early train Saturday morning."

Oh, goody. My stuffy, Foreign Office diplomat father, Sir Ronald Harper, would be down here Saturday morning sticking his long nose into my investigation. And every other facet of my life.

I needed to have my investigation over by the time he arrived, or he'd find something to complain about. I had enough to do without having him involved.

"And we've all been invited to a dinner party at Little Hedges Saturday night," he added with a smile.

"Oh, good. Livvy, you'll like them," Abby told me. "He's something big in shipping, and she's a painter. They're new to the area."

My invitation, and Abby's enthusiasm, meant I had to stay down in the country until Sunday. That had been my original plan, but if we were successful in talking to Rex in the morning, I'd hoped to leave by lunchtime so I'd be gone before my father arrived.

Not being in the same place as my father was always the best plan, as I'd discovered as a young girl.

I slept like a rock that night with the cool autumn air coming in the window. If I'd awakened, I would never have gone back to sleep with nothing but crickets and owls making noise outdoors. Engines and voices and slamming doors were a lullaby to a city girl like me.

After washing and dressing for our morning in a smart blue suit with two-tone pumps and planning on matching accessories, I went down to breakfast. Abby had a country breakfast on the sideboard, with eggs, smoked ham, mushrooms, tomatoes, and toast that wasn't burnt like mine usually was. I dug in.

"Right after you eat, we'll go speak to Mrs. Lagrange," Abby said. "Hurry and finish up. The morning is half over."

I noticed Abby had already cleaned her plate and was finishing her coffee. I obediently raced through a very good breakfast, managed two gulps of coffee, and rose from the table.

We headed out to the car. "Where's Sir John?" I asked as I climbed in.

"He's gone over to home farm to supervise the harvest. I don't expect he'll be home until dinnertime. We can use the morning to track down Rex and visit this afternoon with Gwynne."

I had forgotten about our afternoon get-together

with Gwynne Waters and, hopefully, Clementine Churchill. "Will I have time to change?"

Abby glanced at me. "You look fine." She wore a tweed suit and sensible shoes, what I would call her country uniform.

"Not too 'employed in the city'?"

Abby smiled. "They like glamorous strangers here."

"I'm hardly a stranger."

Mrs. Lagrange, when we entered her shop, looked at me over her long, thin nose as if I were a visitor from another planet. Abby breezed through introductions and added, "I'm looking for a good red to take to a dinner party tomorrow night."

They discussed various options for a minute or two before Abby said, "It's at the Palmers'. Little Hedges. You wouldn't happen to have them on your books, would you? It might give me an idea of what they like."

"Well, Lady Summersby, for you, we might sneak a peek." Mrs. Lagrange picked up a ledger from under the counter in her long, thin hands and opened it to flip through pages covered in a spidery scrawl. "They seem to favor reds from these two vineyards." She set two bottles of red on the counter. They were both French and from expensive vineyards.

Abby studied one of them. "Is Rex taking a shipment out to them today?"

"Yes, Little Hedges, Bruno House, and Chartwell." She leaned slightly over the counter. "You heard about Mr. Churchill's cigar blowing up and nearly burning the house down?"

"No," Abby said with such shock I thought she'd destroyed any chance of learning more.

Fortunately, Mrs. Lagrange took Abby at her word. "If Churchill hadn't set it down and walked out of the room, he'd have been killed."

"How awful."

"Rex had just been out there that morning, but I know we didn't take that cigar out to him. Every three days. That's his standard order when he's home, and we'd taken a box out to him the day before the explosion. I showed the police our records, and in the end they had to accept that box of cigars hadn't come from us." She stood upright as she spoke those last words with her arms crossed and her chin lifted.

"How distressing for you." Abby made sympathetic noises as she paid for the wine.

Meanwhile, I stood there thinking we didn't need to chase down Rex and his delivery van. Mrs. Lagrange and Dickie Nicholson had answered all our questions.

Unless there were questions I hadn't thought of yet.

We went back to Summersby House and spent a few quiet hours readying the flower beds and the vegetable garden for the end of the growing season. Abby was always sure to find a few chores for me that required shoveling, bending, and chopping. I was glad when she called a halt to our work so we could go inside and get cleaned up for the tea at Mrs. Waters'.

"Wear that lovely suit you had on this morning," Abby called from her room.

"Won't I look like too much of an outsider?"

"You are an outsider. You might as well be an event. Make them jealous."

I doubted I would make them jealous, but Abby was right. I should play up my differences, since that's what they would notice.

And notice they did. When I walked into Gwynne Waters's parlor behind Abby, all conversation stopped. For a moment, I was afraid they knew why I'd been so keen to get invited to this afternoon tea.

Then Abby stepped forward to an unremarkable, middle-aged woman and said, "Gwynne, I'd like you to meet my cousin, Mrs. Denis. Livvy, this is Mrs. Waters."

Gwynne Waters walked up to me with a warm smile that reached her eyes. "I'm so glad you could make it, Mrs. Denis."

"So am I. Thank you for inviting me." We shook hands and then she walked me around the room to introduce me to the others. The only one I really noticed was the placid-looking, middle-aged Clementine Churchill, who was dressed in a matronly frock that draped a little too loosely to be at the height of fashion. Her skin and hair glowed softly in a way I could only hope mine would when I was her age.

"Are you a gardener?" one of the women asked. By now I had realized I had to be at least ten years younger than everyone else there, and in most cases, at least twenty.

"I live in a flat in London, so my only chance to garden is when I come to visit Abby."

"What does your husband do in London?" another

woman asked.

The question was a minefield, no matter how I answered. "I'm a widow, so I work as a society page reporter for the *Daily Premier.*" True as far as it went.

I heard various sympathetic noises from around the room.

"Are you here to report on Mrs. Waters's tea?" someone asked.

I gave Gwynne Waters a big smile. "Would you like me to, Mrs. Waters?"

She laughed and shook her head.

"Then I relinquish my pen, and I have a very short memory. If you mention something you want announced in the paper, you'll have to write to us." I gave them all a smile as if that would eliminate their mistrust of me.

It did, but only to a certain degree. At least, they all appeared at ease and willing to speak in front of me, but most of it was about chrysanthemums and vegetables. Nothing interesting was said. And nothing at all about the Churchills. I wasn't sure if that was because of my presence or Mrs. Churchill's.

"Do you know the Palmers?" one of the ladies asked me.

"No. I understand I'll meet them tomorrow night with Sir John, Abby, and my father."

"Who is your father?" another woman asked, and I noticed everyone was listening while trying not to appear to be eavesdropping.

"Sir Ronald Harper. He works for the Foreign Office."

"He and your mother must travel a great deal."

"My mother died shortly after the war when I was quite young. Growing up, I've had the opportunity to travel with him on occasion."

"Where did you travel to?" was asked at the same time as "What did your husband do?"

"I've traveled all over Europe and to North Africa, both with my father and with my late husband, who was also with the Foreign Office." I was expecting more questions, and I wasn't disappointed. I was surprised at the source of the next question.

"What's been your favorite society event to cover so far?" Abby asked.

She gave me the perfect opening. "The London autumn fashion shows held only a couple of weeks ago. I was sent to both Norman Hartnell's and Mimi Mareau's shows. Imagine. The two biggest names in this autumn's fashion shows. The gowns were stunning."

"You went to that, didn't you, Jane?" someone asked.

"Yes. So did Clementine," the woman I guessed was Jane answered.

"I was there." Clementine Churchill spoke quietly.

"Unlike me, I imagine you were able to order at the shows," I said, hoping someone would bring up the delivery at Chartwell.

"I ordered a gown for the Opening of Parliament. Unfortunately, the gown looked much better on the model than it does on me," Mrs. Churchill said to general head shaking and quiet disagreement.

The opening I needed. "Do you have it already? That was quick. Was it from Hartnell or Mareau, and are you pleased with the quality?"

"Mimi Mareau, and the quality is very good. The only good thing to come out of that morning," she answered.

"Oh?"

"There was an incident at her home that morning. Fortunately, it turned out to be nothing, but it could have been quite dangerous," Gwynne Waters said. I thought her summing up was clever. Fortunately, I'd heard the story already.

"Then you've had a lucky escape," I said. "Can you describe the gown for me? I saw the fashion show, and I'm curious as to which dress you chose."

"It was jewel green in the show, but I had it made up in a dark blue. It was cut on the bias with a lot of folds in the bodice."

I could imagine it, although I didn't remember the gown at all. "Quite lovely. Congratulations on your choice," I said. "What have you chosen for your accessories?"

"I found a lovely beaded bag at my usual milliner's on my last trip to town. I'm afraid Gwynne and I came back on the train with a large number of packages."

She smiled at Gwynne who said, "We nearly bought out the glover in our size. We have the same size hands and arms."

"How remarkable," someone said.

This told me the smaller box from Mimi's salon wasn't for Mrs. Churchill. I wondered how it had been addressed.

I rode back with Abby considering the various

possibilities for where the exploding cigar could have come from, and I ruled out every one. Except one. Mimi's salon or someone in London who was keeping an eye on Mimi's salon.

I'd been quiet for so long that Abby finally said, "Is something wrong?"

"I'd like to get confirmation that someone in Chartwell ripped off the brown paper wrapping and found a box of cigars on that morning. And I'd like to know who the package was addressed to."

Abby drove in silence for a minute before she said, "Hmmm."

I looked at her. "Hmmm, what?"

"We need to speak to Mrs. Goodfellow."

"Who is she?"

"Our cook."

"But if she's *your* cook...?" I didn't see how she could help.

"Mrs. Goodfellow comes from a long line of good cooks. Which is why we're very lucky to have her. And why Chartwell is lucky to have her sister, Mrs. Summers, as their cook."

"Who would have been in the kitchen when the packages were delivered." Then I stopped. "Wouldn't she have been busy with the delivery that came from Lagrange's and the packages sent elsewhere in the house to be opened?"

"Whatever happened, she would have seen the packages come in and she would have heard about the fire shortly thereafter." Abby shifted and sped up as she turned her gaze back to me.

I shrank into the seat, hoping we wouldn't end up in a ditch as trees and fences flew by.

"Yes," she said when she finally looked back at the road, "we'll talk to Mrs. Goodfellow when we get home."

Mrs. Goodfellow had just put a chicken in to roast and sat down with a cup of tea. She rose when we walked into the kitchen, but Abby told her to sit down, asked Mary, the housemaid, to also fix us some tea, and sat down across from the cook at the well-scrubbed, well-used table.

"Now, Mrs. Goodfellow, I wouldn't ask this if there weren't a good reason, but my cousin Livvy works for a secret part of the government. She's found out there were two packages sent by mail to Chartwell the day of the fire. Would your sister, Mrs. Summers, have any idea what was in the packages?" Abby looked at her cook with an eager expression.

Directness had always been Abby's strong point, but no one had better trust her with the country's secrets. I could picture General Alford's expression if he heard this conversation.

The woman shrugged her large shoulders. "What difference does it make?"

I sat next to Abby. "We know Lagrange's didn't send out any cigars that day in their deliveries. We know there were two packages delivered by Royal Mail that morning, and one of them may have been the right size for a cigar box. So the question is, was it a cigar box?"

"And you think Royal Mail delivered the cigar that

nearly burned the house down?" She took a sip of her tea. "Well, you'd be right."

"Your sister actually saw the box." That would be very helpful.

"Of course not. She was too busy with the foodstuffs. But the housekeeper, Mrs. Johnson, remarked on the box not two minutes before the house was on fire."

"Did she notice anything about the box or the wrapping paper?"

"It wasn't his usual brand. It was sent from central London, so she assumed it was from someone in the Foreign Office or Parliament currying favor." Mrs. Goodfellow took a sip of her tea and closed her eyes in bliss.

I hated interrupting her rest. "How was it addressed? To Mr. or Mrs. Churchill?"

"She said she could make out the 'M,' but nothing else. Of course, as soon as they saw it was cigars, they knew right where to take them."

"No sign of who sent it or a company name?"

"Now, who would be daft enough to try to kill Mr. Churchill and sign their name to it?" She looked at me as if I were stupid.

"You're right about that, Mrs. Goodfellow. I was hoping the person who did this put someone else's name on the box or the wrapping paper. It would be another clue." One we didn't have.

"Did your sister mention anything else out of the ordinary that day?" Abby asked.

Mrs. Goodfellow shook her head. "The only thing out

of the ordinary was the house catching fire. And what with the Scotch and the cigars that man consumes, I'm surprised it doesn't happen more often."

"The housekeeper hadn't kept the wrapping paper, had she?" I asked.

"Scotland Yard was right down and they collected the paper, the remains of the box, the other cigars, everything. So why are you here, Mrs. Denis?" Mrs. Goodfellow gave me a suspicious stare.

"Because nothing led them to the person who sent the box. That's because they didn't ask the right people the right questions." I gave her a brief smile.

"You found out who sent it?"

"I have it narrowed down to a few people. With luck, we'll soon have her."

"Her?" Abby and Mrs. Goodfellow both said.

"I think so." Despite what people might have assumed, Mimi and her staff were all suspects. Female suspects.

CHAPTER NINETEEN

No matter how often Abby asked, I wouldn't tell her where I expected to find the would-be assassin. It seemed so unlikely I didn't believe it myself, despite the evidence.

Perhaps I didn't have all the evidence.

Abby and I were in the middle of breakfast the next morning when Sir John entered, followed by my father in his weekend wear. Dark gray three-piece suit, old school tie, standing collar, derby hat, shoes polished to a shine. Unless he was on the golf course, that was as relaxed as I ever saw him.

Sir John said good morning and headed to the server to dish up his breakfast. My father came over, gave Abby a small bow and thanked her for inviting him for the weekend. Then he put a hand on my shoulder and said, "How is the sleuthing coming along, Olivia?"

I raised my eyebrows at Abby before I turned to greet my father. "Quite well, thank you."

"Do you have anything for General Alford?"

"Yes."

"Don't expect to get anything out of her," Abby said with a smile. "She won't tell us a thing."

"That's as it should be, Abigail," my father said in his stuffiest tone. "You never know where these things may lead."

"Why don't you get yourself some breakfast? Abby

and I were just discussing our morning."

"We have an eleven o'clock tee time, so we'll eat lunch at the club," Sir John said.

"Don't forget dinner at the Palmers' tonight," Abby said. "Of course you're invited, Ronald."

My father looked slightly confused. "Do I know the Palmers?"

"Doubtful," Sir John said, sitting down with his full plate. The footman came over and poured him a cup of coffee. "He's in shipping and she's an artist."

"She's an event," Abby added.

"I look forward to meeting her," I replied.

"Don't get any ideas. You come too close to being a scandal far too often," my father grumbled as he loaded up his plate.

That was too insulting not to challenge. "When have I ever been a scandal?"

"Your cousins won't speak to you after your behavior at the wedding last spring, and then your aunt's death…"

"My aunt, whom I admired very much, was involved in murder. And Cousin Celia was always a pain. I had nothing to do with it. And I wasn't the one erroneously arrested for murder."

Not having any ammunition to refute my comments, my father changed course. "Before that, you took it upon yourself to find your husband's killer…"

"You thought he committed suicide until I proved otherwise."

"And you're working for that rag."

That was his main complaint. "The *Daily Premier* is

not a rag."

"Sending you off to Austria..."

"I was covering a story." Well, sort of.

"When you should be marrying your soldier friend."

"His name is Adam Redmond, Father, and the more you push, the less likely we are to marry."

"Stop!" Sir John said. "You two will not bicker in my house. I don't want to listen to it."

"Yes, sir," I immediately said.

"You're right, John," my father said as he sat and the footman poured him a cup of coffee. "So what are you ladies up to this morning?"

"There's a harvest festival in Canterbury. I thought we'd go," Abby said.

"Excellent," I said with forced enthusiasm. "Is it near the cathedral?"

"Quite near."

"So you can pray for your sins on the way," my father said.

Sir John, Abby, and I all glowered at him, but my father studied his eggs and ham and ignored our dark looks.

* * *

As the sun set, we pulled up in front of Little Hedges, an eighteenth-century farmhouse improved by twentieth-century conveniences. I suspected the roof had always been slate and the walls stone, but everything else looked recently refurbished. New mullioned lancet windows with beveled glass and a new, taller door where skillful installation couldn't quite hide the change in stone showed that the new owners had spent lavishly.

We walked in and were greeted by our hosts in the narrow hall. They directed us into a cozy drawing room that had originally been two rooms on either side of a fireplace, now joined with a beamed ceiling and a slate floor beneath colorful rugs. The space was all warm and friendly, but the servants who took our wraps and served us drinks were as well outfitted and trained as the best in London.

Apparently, none of the other guests had been inside the house since the renovations either, as we all looked around and remarked on the changes. I was quite taken by the paintings that decorated the room. A man walked up next to me and said, "They're Alicia's."

When I looked blank, he said, "Alicia Crawford."

"Didn't she have a show in London a few months ago?" I'd gone as part of my duties for the newspaper.

"Yes. You've heard of her. I'm glad to know not everyone here is a Philistine."

The paintings were colorful and lively, but they weren't so good that not knowing the artist's name made anyone a dunce. "The Palmers collect them?"

He laughed. The sound made my skin crawl. "Alicia is Mrs. Palmer."

"Oh. I'd heard she was a painter, but I hadn't heard her professional name." Beyond him, I saw Lady Patricia Saunders-North, the Duke of Marshburn's daughter. I stared at her for more than a few seconds. What was she doing out here in the countryside?

"What do you do? Something artistic, I hope." I hadn't

paid any attention to the man talking to me. To my horror, at this point he was so close I was talking to his heavy jowls. He was perhaps in his mid-forties and very well-dressed in an evening coat and white double-breasted vest. He looked the part of a debauched gentleman, and every instinct told me to run.

"No. Nothing artistic at all."

"Oh." He sounded disappointed. "Perhaps you haven't had the right inspiration." He oozed the last words. Now was the time to run.

"Excuse me. I think my father is looking for me." I hastily retreated, glad for once my father was nearby.

"This is my daughter, Olivia Denis," he said as I approached. He was standing with a blonde of about forty who wore a dangling necklace of rubies and diamonds over her thin chest. "Olivia, this is Mrs. Palmer. She's an artist."

"As Alicia Crawford," I said as we nodded to each other.

"Yes. Oh, you were talking to my agent."

"Your agent?" our host asked as he walked up to us. "I'd keep him far away from your daughter if I were you, Sir Ronald."

"My husband exaggerates," the artist said.

"I was at your London showing," I told her. "I covered it for my newspaper."

"The *Daily Premier*," Mr. Palmer said.

He was very well informed. "People have been talking about me."

"You're a local celebrity," Mr. Palmer said an instant

before my father said, "I wish she hadn't taken that job."

I ignored my father and replied, "I'd hardly call myself a local or a celebrity."

"You've come to the attention of a great number of people," Mr. Palmer said. I heard something threatening in his tone. Something ominous. I suspected he'd received his information from Lady Patricia, and I wasn't her favorite person.

I wasn't quite sure why.

I changed the subject. "Right now I'm working on a series of articles on Mimi Mareau and her salons."

"I'm a big fan of hers," Alicia said, smiling. "This is a Mimi Mareau gown."

Her use of color and the sweep of the skirt told me as much. "It's lovely. I think Mimi is brilliant as a designer. Are you a fan of hers, too, Mr. Palmer?"

"She came from nothing. Now she's rich and conservative and holds to the values of others like us." His admiration showed he apparently held the opinions common among aristocrats and businessmen, that the ruling class should make all the decisions and have all the money. Most of them, if it came to war with Germany, would pull together with their countrymen and the residents of the empire. I hoped Mr. Palmer would do the same.

"So your admiration is for her business acumen and not her designs." I meant my words as a general conversation starter, but my father's horrified expression said I'd missed the mark.

"Ah, it's time for dinner," his wife said.

I lined up with my father to go into the dining room and nearly gasped when I saw where we would eat. A series of French doors led outside, but were closed against the night chill. The view in the daylight over the fields must be spectacular.

After we sat, the lights were turned off, letting the silver and china shimmer in the candlelight.

I was seated between a tall, slender, blond man and Sir John, with my father staring at me warningly across the table. For the soup course, I was to talk to Sir John. I knew better than to try to talk to him until he'd nearly finished his dish. Then I said, "How well do you know everyone here?"

He glanced up and down the long table before he said, "I know a few of the neighbors, and you and your father. Abby I know quite well," he added with a smile. "The Palmers, that man on the other side of you, a few other guests, not at all. Not local."

He made it sound like they were from another planet. There was no worse failing in Sir John's eyes than not being local at a country dinner party. In London, he wouldn't have thought twice about going out to dinner with people he didn't know.

Now it was time to switch sides and I found myself nodding to the blond man.

"This is a nice dinner party, yes?" he asked. "The view before it grew dark was superb."

He had a thick accent. Not German. Not Russian. I couldn't place it. "If I may ask, where are you from, Mr....?"

"Frederiksen. I am from Denmark."

It only took me a moment to remember the name. "Oh, you're engaged to be married to Lady Patricia."

"Yes, and then I will take up my position as ambassador to your nation from mine."

"Congratulations on both counts." I decided to see how he would respond to my probing. "You are in quite an important position, seeing as your country shares a border with Germany. That hasn't been a lucky position for other countries, like Austria and Czechoslovakia."

He smiled, and I was reminded of a poisonous snake. "This fish is very good." He took another bite and savored it.

I tried it as well. It was good, but nothing to show such enjoyment over. Why didn't he want to say how he felt about politics or the Nazis? We weren't at war with them. Yet. I made another attempt. "Do you think we'll end up in a war with Germany?"

"It would make no sense. We have too much in common with them. It is not good to fight with neighbors. Still, you fought against them in the Great War, all for the sake of your alliances."

"We have alliances again that may require us to fight Germany." And that was frightening.

He shook his head. "Alliances aren't doing the Czechs any good. Perhaps every country should admit they don't want to fight the Nazis and let them go about their business."

CHAPTER TWENTY

"Let's hope there will be nothing to fight about, that the Germans will let others go about their business, too." No one, even those who believed war with Hitler was inevitable, wanted a war. And my dinner partner's country didn't have the luxury of the Channel between them and Germany.

"No one wants to see England crushed." He held my gaze. "I know it is a subject that vexes the Duke of Marshburn. He is very worried about the destruction of England if they choose to fight Germany."

I stared back. "What about the chances of seeing Denmark crushed?"

"That's why we try to stay neutral. We are a small country surrounded by larger ones." He smiled and added, "This is too gloomy for a dinner party. What do you think of the painting on the far wall?"

It was of a face in orange and purple and I thought it was awful. I was saved from answering by the arrival of the fowl dish, so I could turn back to Sir John. We ate in silence for a few minutes before he said, "Baked chicken with pieces of potato in gravy. Good, solid fare. I like their cook."

"I'm sorry I came tonight."

He raised his eyebrows, but his eyes showed concern.

"The man on my other side says the Duke of Marshburn expects we'd be destroyed by Germany if we fight."

Sir John gave me a smile. A genuine smile. "Thank the Lord we have the navy and the Channel."

"You think we'll be crushed, too?"

"No, Livvy." Then he scowled. "How does this man know what Marshburn thinks?"

"He's marrying Marshburn's daughter."

"That's unfortunate. Marshburn is a defeatist. Pay no attention to those types." He shook his head. "What I fear is a stalemated war like we had last time. Facing each other for months, shooting and bombing, without moving an inch. That's when we lose so many good men on both sides."

Gloomy over his words, we ate our chicken in silence.

Then came the fruit and ices and having to face the new ambassador again. He kept silent as he enjoyed the apple pieces and cherries and delighted in the ices. I was beginning to relax and enjoy my food when he suddenly turned to me and said, "You have a close friend in the British military, don't you?"

I thought of Adam and a British collapse if we fought Germany, and my dinner nearly made a reappearance. I stared at him, angry about how he was tormenting me.

He smiled, which somehow made it worse. "I'm not a mind reader. Someone here tonight mentioned you have a friend in the British army, so you must be worried about him with our current international situation. I wish him well. I wouldn't want to be in his position, to be on the losing side if your government pushes you into a war, but I wish him, and you, well."

"We've been counted out before and ended up victorious." My tone made him lean back slightly and look at me. Then I took another spoonful of my ice, but I found it suddenly tasteless.

"But you are far behind in building tanks and planes. At least this war, if there is one, will be short. The Germans will do no more than is necessary to take control of your island. They've given their assurances to Denmark, and I'm sure they will to Britain, too."

I suspected my anger was sending danger signals from my eyes. "What if we don't want to be controlled by the Nazis?"

The next Danish ambassador nodded to me and turned back to his ice.

All of the locals left the dinner party as soon after coffee was served as was polite, leaving just a few guests behind. I caught sight of Lady Patricia, holding hands with my dinner partner the ambassador while she gave me a cold glare.

I changed direction and walked over to her. "Nice to see you again. Best wishes for your wedding. Is your trousseau completed?"

She looked like she wanted me to go away. "Yes. Mimi did a wonderful job."

I hoped I could goad her into saying something about Mimi that I could use to find the French assassin. "That's fortunate. I suspect her London fashion house won't be around for long."

"Then it's a good thing you don't know what you're talking about." She turned then and walked away. The new ambassador nodded and followed her.

I went outside and joined Abby, all the time suspecting I'd given away more than I'd gained.

Once we were in the auto heading back to Summersby House, Abby went on and on about the clever modernization of Little Hedges.

When I could stand it no longer, I said, "Was anyone else told how Britain will quickly lose the war against Germany and so we should just give up now?"

"No!" My father came close to shouting.

Abby and Sir John both said "No" in puzzled voices.

"Who was saying this?" Abby asked.

"The new Danish ambassador, who is marrying Marshburn's daughter. I was sitting next to him at dinner."

"I wonder if Palmer agrees with him," my father said as if to himself.

"Why?" I asked, able to hear him since we were both in the back seat.

"Just a rumor I heard."

I knew better than to question him further when he said something was a rumor.

"I don't think we need to accept any more invitations to Little Hedges," Sir John said.

"I'm glad we went the once," Abby said. "That house is magnificent. Remember what it looked like when old Mrs. Miller lived there?"

"I was always afraid it would fall down on her," Sir

John said.

"Are you going up to town in the morning or staying for another round of golf?" I asked my father.

"Are you going to church with us?" Abby asked.

"After tonight's dinner, I feel in need of some prayers," I agreed.

As it turned out, I didn't leave for town until after my father had finished his round of golf with Sir John. Abby and I rode bicycles down country lanes, enjoying the fresh autumn air. When I asked my father if I'd be able to reach General Alford on a Sunday, he told me to wait for the morning and then call the War Office. I was eager to tell him what I'd learned, but I was also tired and ready for a quiet evening at home with a book.

But after the tranquility of the countryside and a few hours with a book, I was ready Monday morning for the tramp of a million feet traveling along the pavement and the rumble of taxis and buses as I made my way toward Fleet Street. The weather was still warm and dry, so I carried my furled umbrella and wore a gray, light wool suit with a lavender blouse. I entered the *Daily Premier* building with a spring in my step.

It wasn't quite time to start work, so I picked up a telephone receiver and dialed the number for General Alford's office. He wasn't in, so I left a message.

When I put down the receiver, I heard, "Livvy."

I looked up to see one of the new girls come over with a message slip in her hand. "This came for you on Friday."

The message read, "It's important I talk to you immediately. Something has come up about Josef that you don't know. I must see you as soon as possible, day or night. Reina."

I went over to Miss Westcott. "This message came in for me on Friday. I need to go out for a little while."

"Sir Henry has a lot to answer for," she grumbled. "Go on. Just hurry back."

I took off immediately for the Underground, the fastest way across town at this time of day. Had Reina learned the name of Elias's wife? Had she found another clue in the basement?

And all the time I hurried down the pavement toward Mimi's salon, I was afraid of what I'd overlooked. I hoped Reina wasn't in danger.

But it had been three days.

I pushed open the front door of the salon and tried to catch my breath. The young woman behind the desk looked at me curiously as I rushed toward her.

Finally, I said in a gasp, "I need to speak to Reina."

A man's voice said, "You're too late."

I spun around to find Detective Inspector Smith standing behind me. "What happened?"

"Reina was found bludgeoned to death in the basement this morning."

CHAPTER TWENTY-ONE

"What? No. That's awful." I felt sick, shattered. I couldn't believe it. I was too late to find out what Reina wanted to tell me. Had been desperate to tell me from the tone of her message.

Too late to save her life.

"Why did you want to speak to her so urgently that you're out of breath?" the detective asked.

I opened my purse and handed him the note.

"This could have been written by anyone at any time. The date and time mean nothing," he said, handing back the note.

"Reina called my office," I told him. "No one would forge this. The only thing Reina would have wanted to tell me that was important was the name of Elias's wife. Reina met her about ten years ago. Reina and Elias came from the same village."

"Do you find the fact that Elias was married to be important?" The detective was studying me now.

"Yes. Scotland Yard was informed he had met with a group of financial backers here in London. According to a witness, he recognized someone. At no time did he or any other person there indicate they knew each other, so they were trying to keep it a secret from the other people present. It was after this meeting that Elias told Reina he wanted her to keep something safe for him. Whatever this thing was, the killer took it with him or her."

"You think his wife is here?"

I shook my head. "Various stories say his wife is dead or in a German prison. But a member of the wife's family, blaming Elias for his wife's imprisonment or death, might have killed Elias and then Reina if she discovered their connection."

The detective was scribbling notes in his book. "You know his name wasn't Elias?"

"Josef Meirsohn. Reina also knew his real name."

He stopped writing and glared at me. "Would have been nice if you'd told us."

I glared back. "It was days before I found out, and by then I assumed the army had already told you."

"Anything else we need to know?"

"Reina has a cousin, a young girl, in Paris, who'll need to be notified." I took a couple of deep breaths, upset at the waste of a gentle, talented life. "You're sure it's murder?"

He nodded.

I suspected I wore the same grim expression he did. "When did it happen?"

"Sometime yesterday. They called in a plumber on Friday who came and went by the basement, Madame Mareau's orders, and no one locked up after him. It wasn't until this morning that they noticed Reina was missing and started a search."

"The poor girl. Lying dead while above her, they went about their business, coming and going, and no one noticed she wasn't there." I stared at the ceiling as a shudder passed through me. How awful.

"They were all enjoying a day off here in London, it being Sunday. Someone saw her go out about mid-morning. No one saw her return. And her colleagues said she was often by herself when she wasn't working."

I nodded. That was true of what I'd seen of Reina. "Who saw her go out?"

He flipped through a couple of pages in his notebook. "A woman named Fleur. She was also the one to find the body."

It had been Fleur who looked after an upset Reina when Josef Meirsohn's body was first discovered. Thinking about it now, I couldn't decide if Fleur had acted out of friendship or because Mimi wanted everything about her salon to appear calm. Professional. Innocent of any crime.

In which case, Fleur was Mimi's enforcer, making Reina follow the designer's wishes. I had seen that day how much Reina wanted to cry over the loss of her childhood friend, and Fleur had been her support when Mimi didn't want her to break down.

She had appeared like a sensible older sister. Was Fleur's support out of compassion or brutality?

I wanted to see her one more time. "Have you moved her body?"

"The police surgeon's not arrived yet."

"May I see her? See the crime scene."

He frowned. "Why?"

That was hard to answer. I didn't really know her. I couldn't claim a familial or social relationship. "She'd urgently called for me on Friday. I suppose I just want to apologize for not responding before now."

"Where were you?"

"Out of town at a relative's." Not an informative answer.

"You can tell her, but I can assure you, she won't hear you," Inspector Smith said. He accepted my answer at face value, and I was grateful.

"But Inspector, I owe her that much."

"All right. Just for a moment, and don't touch anything."

I followed the detective downstairs to where a few constables were taking photos and measurements. Reina was between the outside door and the steps, her bloodied head toward the steps as she lay face down on the cold stone floor. "Did any of the neighbors see anyone coming or going from the outside staircase yesterday?"

"Not that we've found so far. We're not holding out much hope." Smith stood at the bottom of the interior steps, making sure I couldn't get past him.

I stood on the bottom step, trying not to gag at the rotten smell that would be absorbed into the frocks kept down there. "Have you found the murder weapon?" I asked.

"No."

"Check all the trunks against the far wall," I told him. "That's where the first weapon was found, after Elias's murder. Reina found it inside a bolt of cloth she was taking upstairs."

The inspector gave a nod to the other man dressed in

a suit who spoke quietly to a uniformed constable. "Have you seen enough?"

I nodded, and then bowed my head, hoping she knew how very sorry I was. "She'd turned her back on her attacker, just like Elias did. Why didn't they fear him? Or her?"

"We'll try to find out," he said in a hard tone.

I went upstairs, letting the inspector get back to work, and found Mimi waiting at the ground-floor landing. "Satisfied?" she asked me. "Reina wouldn't be dead if you hadn't kept asking her about the body in our basement. Now we have two murders here, and I must find a new head seamstress."

My jaw dropped and I was speechless for a moment. "Is that all you're interested in? Two people are killed under your roof, and you're worried about finding a new seamstress?"

The anger in her eyes fizzled and went out, leaving her shoulders slumped. "Of course not. Reina was part of my top management. I knew her. I trusted her. I did not want her to die so cruelly."

"Fleur saw her go out yesterday. Fleur found her today." I stared at Mimi.

"What are you trying to say?" Mimi hissed.

"Do you trust Fleur?"

"Of course, I trust Fleur. And Reina trusted Fleur. She and Reina were friends."

"Are you sure?"

I thought for a second that Mimi was going to physically attack me. "Yes. She was our friend. Now, please leave and let us mourn her in peace."

"She was a Jew, and you good French Catholics are going to mourn her?" There was scorn in my tone.

Mimi looked down and answered me in French. "She was our friend. Our coworker. She was kind and honest. Her Jewishness doesn't seem to matter now that she's been murdered."

"And the Duke of Marshburn? Does it matter to him?"

She looked up then, her dark eyes snapping. "It doesn't matter what he thinks. She was our friend, not his."

"May I speak to Fleur for a moment?"

"I don't know where she is and I'm not going to go looking for her. Call back another day." She pointed toward the front door.

I had no choice but to leave, questions still nagging me.

* * *

My first stop once I reached the *Daily Premier* building was to the top floor at Sir Henry's office. His secretary nodded at my whispered, "May I go in?"

When I opened the door, Sir Henry looked up and said, "Do we have a story yet?"

"Not the one you were planning. Reina, the childhood friend of Josef Meirsohn, also known as Elias, was murdered in the basement of Mimi Mareau's salon. Just like Elias. Exactly like Elias. She left a frantic message for me here at the office on Friday. She was killed sometime yesterday and found this morning." I rattled off the information as if I were reciting dry facts.

"Good grief. She was the source of your information on Elias, wasn't she?"

"Yes."

"And the other story? About Churchill's cigars?"

I sighed. "I have to report in to General Alford. I have information that appears to point to a certain fashion house, but not a particular person. And I have no way of proving it."

Sir Henry leaned forward in his massive desk chair. "You have information linking an attack on Churchill to a building where two murders have recently occurred. I'd say that's newsworthy."

"It's hearsay. It's an indicator for further investigation. By the army or Scotland Yard," I added. With Reina's death, so cruel and unfair, I wanted to quit this investigation. I'd pushed her into revealing the details of a dead man's life, and it may well have led to her murder.

"Most hearsay has evidence to back it up, if you look hard enough." Sir Henry was staring at me.

"I don't know if I want to. I had Reina looking into things she didn't want to see. Then when she called me, I wasn't there. She might still be alive if I hadn't gone to Kent."

"Chartwell," Sir Henry said, nodding to himself. "So you're going to allow this killer to get away with murdering someone who was helping you."

I made a grinding shriek through my clenched teeth. "The whole thing's not fair, but I guess I have to keep going." Sir Henry was right. I had to keep going on this investigation. "Let me report in to General Alford with what I learned in Kent and then I'll see what I can think of to find this killer."

"Good girl," Sir Henry said. "The committee will be interested in this development. There's a meeting Wednesday night on a different matter, but this needs to be brought up."

"If our guess was right, and someone on the committee is related to Elias's late wife, why would they kill Reina?"

"She knew them," Sir Henry said.

"But she knew nothing about this woman. She knew Elias's family." I looked up at Sir Henry as something occurred to me. "Perhaps someone in his family, not hers, is in London, and that is the person Elias recognized at the meeting according to Valerie Mandel. Reina came from his hometown. She would recognize them, too."

"But where would Reina have met someone on the committee?" Sir Henry asked.

I started thinking aloud. "In the synagogue. Walking along a street. It could have happened by accident in any one of a dozen ways. And Reina wouldn't have thought there was any danger. We were looking for a relative of his late wife's. She'd known his family all her life."

"And this member of Elias's family is someone both victims would never have feared turning their back on," Sir Henry said, finishing my thought.

I went to the War Office and gave my report to General Alford, telling him who told me what, and where I believed that led to the next step in the investigation.

As I returned to the *Daily Premier*, a thought struck me with such force I stopped on the pavement and was bumped into by three different people.

Murmuring apologies, I hurried on.

Why? Why would anyone in Meirsohn's family want to kill him or Reina? What difference would it make if someone recognized him or her?

With that thought racing around in my mind, I went back to writing up reports on which notable people spent the weekend at the country estate of which noble title. The newspaper wouldn't include the interesting details on how well romances were proceeding toward engagements or how discreetly affairs were being conducted. Still, there were people who would read our stories and guess where these domestic dramas were headed.

I didn't care who was doing what. I was fed up with the stories we printed, the people we wrote about, the craziness in Mimi's salon. I couldn't wait for the end of the day.

As soon as I was off the clock, I telephoned Leah Nauheim. "How did the fitting go?" I asked after we'd spent moments on pleasantries.

"The suit is going to look terrific. They were behind today because the head seamstress died over the weekend."

"Actually, she was murdered in the basement."

A German exclamation came loudly across the telephone wire.

"Did you by any chance see anyone named Fleur?

She's about forty and blond."

"That wasn't who was murdered?" Her shock sounded in her tone.

"No," I assured her. "A friend of hers."

"No. I don't think I saw her. Is it important?"

"Probably not."

"I think my father-in-law and Mr. Mandel are working on Sir Henry in the hopes that he'll send you to Prague on a mission to help the Jewish community there," Leah said.

"Thanks for the warning," I told her.

"Would you mind?" she asked, doubt in her voice. "Now that the Sudeten has been occupied, it won't be long before they march into the rest of Czechoslovakia like they did Austria."

"I don't mind helping. I would like to get in and get out again before they march." We all knew who "they" were. But Sir Henry had made it clear he wanted me to stay in London and investigate. "That is, if I go. I don't think Sir Henry wants to send me anywhere right now, with two people killed practically under my nose."

"It almost sounds as if you'd be safer in Prague," Leah said, and I could hear her amazement down the telephone line.

"Will you be at the meeting on Wednesday night?" I asked.

"Yes. Will I see you there?"

"In light of this second murder, yes." Not that I thought my presence would do any good. I was an outsider. Esther stood a much better chance at learning any secrets the members of the committee held.

After I returned home and ate a sandwich with my tea for dinner, I called Esther and came right to the point. "I want to pick your brain."

"Anything I can do to help." She sounded eager.

"I'm lost. Your father and I have been playing with the idea that the murderer could be a member of Elias's family. Well, the Meirsohn family, really. Neither Elias nor Reina would have any reason to fear someone they've known all their lives."

"Reina is the seamstress who was found dead this morning?"

"And who grew up a friend of Elias. He was her childhood playmate," I told her.

"You don't expect people you've known all your life to be murderers," Esther said.

"What would make a member of Elias's family kill him? So far, we haven't met anyone named Meirsohn in this business. Could they fear exposure for living here under an assumed name?"

"Reputation might matter in a small village, but this is London," Esther said. "I'm sure his family got over Elias being a communist and a rabble-rouser long ago. Unless they're acting at the behest of the Nazis, for either money or protection, I can't imagine why anyone would hide their identity."

"For people living in a small German Jewish enclave, what kind of a sin would make someone leave their home, change their name, and then years later, kill to hide their secret?"

"Only two I can think of," Esther told me. "Murder and conversion."

CHAPTER TWENTY-TWO

"None of the people in the resettlement committee have converted, have they?"

"No."

"Then you're telling me, if the killer is a Meirsohn, they've killed before. In Germany." If that were true, we were up against someone very frightening.

"Do you know the name of this village?"

"No. No one's ever said." A mistake on our part. Then I realized I might have the key to this riddle. "Reina had a cousin in Paris. I need to find out if Reina received any letters from her while she was here. If I had the cousin's address, I could talk to her."

"And find out the name of the village and whether there were any murders where the Meirsohns were suspected," Esther finished for me.

"Perhaps we can rule out some of the committee on Wednesday night," I suggested.

"I'll be there," she said cheerfully before she rang off.

I thought that was my last call for the evening until my telephone rang about a half hour later. An unidentified male voice said, "General Alford wants you to meet him at the War Office tomorrow at six in the evening."

Before I could object, the line went dead.

* * *

I arrived at work the next morning dressed to visit the fashion salon in a belted, forest-green suit with a belt-banded, brown fedora-like hat with an over-wide brim and brown low-heeled pumps. Miss Westcott took one look at my outfit, raised her eyebrows, shook her head, and looked back at the copy she was correcting.

Walking over to her desk, I could see the copy was bleeding profusely from her red pencil, and for once it wasn't my copy. Cheered by that thought, I said, "I need to go back to Mimi's salon."

"Be sure you get results for Sir Henry," she replied in a dry tone without looking up.

I decided that was permission enough and left.

As soon as I arrived at Mimi's salon, the English girl on the front desk picked up the phone and whispered into the receiver. I suspected I would be booted out immediately.

Instead, Mimi came out and took me into the back room. As soon as she shut the door, she said, "I wish you'd leave us alone. Your interference killed Reina and I'd rather not lose any other staff members."

"I'd like to see her belongings. I'm hoping they'll give me a clue as to why she needed to see me so urgently."

"So you can have the police traipsing through my salon again? We lost another day of work yesterday. Will this happen again today? Or tomorrow?"

I stood there and stared at her.

"Fine. Come along." We started climbing the back stairs. "The police went through them yesterday, but they left everything here. I don't know what I'm supposed to do with them. If this were Paris..."

If this were Paris, I thought bitterly, Reina would still

be alive and so, probably, would Elias.

"I brought another attempt at the drawing for the advertisement," I told her.

Mimi waved a hand in dismissal at the drawing I pulled out of my bag. "I've decided against running anything in the newspapers."

I wasn't surprised, but being so easily dismissed hurt.

She led me past the dressing rooms and the sewing rooms above them to a room on the next floor facing the back. Light-colored curtains matched the spread on the iron-framed single bed. The only other pieces of furniture were a wooden table and chair and a wardrobe. It had the look of a room once kept immaculate but now disturbed by many hands trying not to leave everything in a shambles.

"Madame," a woman's voice shouted from below.

"Coming," she called out the door. "Try not to make a mess," she said and left.

The police had apparently shifted the thin mattress and put on top the items they'd found hidden beneath—an envelope with some pound notes tucked inside and two other envelopes containing letters.

On the table were two framed photographs. One was of a family group in old-fashioned dress. I studied the photo, but didn't recognize anyone. I turned it over and opened the frame. On the back of the photo was written, in a spidery hand, "Blumfeld family, September, 1920" in German. None of those pictured were named individually.

With a shock I recognized the young man in the next photograph. It was the dead man, Josef Meirsohn, in his early twenties. To have kept his photograph this long, and carried it to London with her all these years later, Reina must have cared for him very much.

And that had to be why Mimi and Fleur recognized him when he lay on the basement floor. Reina must have left his photograph displayed in her room.

Then I unfolded the first letter and sank down on the bed to read it. It was written in old-fashioned German, taxing my literary and idiomatic knowledge of the language, and dated a week ago.

Dear Reina, it read, *Whatever made you think of her and her rich relatives? I still can't remember the name of the bank. I think her name was Lise, Elisa, something like that. Her family name was Grenbaum, I remember that.*

Now that the Sudeten has been taken over by the Nazis, I doubt any more of our family can get out. I've heard the Czechs won't let Jews cross the border ahead of the Germans the way they are allowing the Christian Czechs.

Once more, our village is cut off and surrounded by evil men. I dream of Mama at night, but in daylight I know I will never see her or any of our family again.

Please be careful, Reina. Nothing good can come of trying to find a selfish, vain woman like the little beauty Josef married or in helping the authorities. I'm sorry he is dead, but I'm sure someone like her will survive the end of the world.

Your loving cousin,

Deborah

And there on the envelope was Deborah's address. I wanted to talk to her and learn what else she might know about the Grenbaums.

Grenbaum. Where had I heard that name before?

The other letter was sent only to set up a meeting between Reina and her cousin while she was in Paris. I put the letter about Elias's wife and its envelope into my purse before I checked over the rest of the room. All of Reina's clothes were in good repair. A few of them were stylish. I wondered if they were frocks rejected from Mimi Mareau's line.

I didn't find any other photos, notes, or trinkets that held a personal connection to the dead woman. I hoped she'd led a fuller life in Paris and kept her keepsakes there.

At that moment, two laborers brought a trunk into the room and walked away without a word. Curious, I walked over and opened it. Empty.

Mimi came in then and directed a seamstress to pack all of Reina's belongings. I made a point of thanking Mimi for letting me see Reina's room.

"And you didn't find anything, did you? The police certainly didn't."

"I saw where you had seen Elias before he turned up dead in your basement." I pointed to the photograph.

Mimi hugged her arms to her chest. "When I first saw him, I couldn't think where I'd seen him before. Then I realized, and I knew the photograph gave Reina a link to the dead man. This proved she knew him. I couldn't trust the police not to arrest her. And I couldn't trust you not to tell them."

I was reminded once again that I was the outsider here. Then I glanced at the trunk. "Her cousin isn't coming over for her things?"

"No. I received a return telegram telling me to pack up her belongings and ship them to her in Paris." Mimi looked around the room sadly. "She had little enough here. Little enough in Paris as well, I imagine."

Then her tone turned stern. "Out. You're in the way now."

Once I returned to the *Daily Premier* building, I went straight to Sir Henry's office. When I walked in, I told him, "I want to go back to Paris. I want to see if her cousin remembers anything else."

"Do you have an address for the cousin?"

I pulled out the envelope containing the letter. "And I have a family name for Elias's wife. Grenbaum."

"You think that was what she was in such a hurry to tell you?"

"There's no sign of anything else," I told him, "but the police looked over her things first. They might have taken away any clues."

"All right. You can go to Paris," he grumbled. "But wait for the weekend. Miss Westcott was up here this morning, telling me to move you to the international desk. Telling me! Try not to ruffle her feathers for a while, will you?"

I nodded. Miss Westcott was being used by Sir Henry just as I was. I felt sympathy for the dried-up spinster as well as a little fear.

Except for my being a widow, that could also be my fate. Alone, chained to a demanding position, without love.

I went downstairs to my desk and set to work on my official job with renewed zeal.

That evening, I left with enough time to reach the war office at six o'clock promptly. I was escorted to the same conference room as before, but this time there was a surprise waiting for me along with General Alford.

Adam!

He kept a professionally somber expression, but I'm not sure I managed to keep from smiling at the sight of him.

"I take it you two know each other." As I felt my cheeks heat, General Alford continued, "Good. You two need to work together to find the French assassin."

"Yes, sir," Adam said, standing at parade rest.

"Relax, Redmond. We're working with civilians now in a purely unofficial capacity." The general turned to me. "I had the captain question Dickie Nicholson about the delivery and he sticks by the story he told you. A further word with Rex confirmed the details."

"And since we know where the larger package came from, the smaller package sent at the same time and containing exploding cigars must have also come from there." But how were we going to prove it?

"Possibly containing exploding cigars," Adam reminded me. "And possibly sent from Mimi's salon. We only have circumstantial evidence."

"Do you have any better ideas?" I asked.

"No. That's why we're looking into it," Adam responded, sounding a tad annoyed.

I turned away from the general to focus on Adam. "You're obviously not going to be ordering a dress, and Mimi knows I can't afford it, so how are you getting in there?"

"I've been attached to Scotland Yard to investigate the two murders in the basement." Adam grinned at me. "A follow-up investigation."

"Do we know each other?" I found it hard to hide my feelings for him.

"I could be Reggie's cousin again. That worked well the last time."

"Last time?" General Alford asked.

"When I was hunting for my husband's killer." I saw the general raise his eyebrows before I looked at Adam. "I could know you from a previous story for the *Daily Premier.* I've been bold enough for Mimi to believe I'd do anything to get the information for the newspaper."

Adam nodded. "That sounds plausible."

"Good. Now, where do we start?"

"Oh, no. There's no 'we,' Mrs. Denis. Captain Redmond is in charge of this investigation. You have no part in it. You are a reporter for the women's pages. Anything you learn at that dress shop, anything at all, you pass on to Captain Redmond. Is that clear?"

"I found you a good lead on where the exploding cigars came from, and all you can say is I'm not part of the investigation?" My voice began to rise. I was furious. I worked hard to find out as much as I had. Information they hadn't learned.

"Officially, no." Then his tone shifted slightly. "However you two work out the details about information sharing is no concern of mine or the army's. Understood?"

"Understood," I said. Unofficially, I could be as involved as Adam.

"Yes, sir," Adam said. The two men saluted each other and then Adam and I left.

"Where are you staying?" I asked once we reached the outside. It was dark out and a cold wind was blowing off the river.

"At my club. The army's paying for it, since they ordered me here. Let me change clothes and I'll pick you up for dinner."

"Someplace local and reasonably fancy?" I asked.

"I'd take you dancing, but we both have to go to work in the morning." He smiled and held my gaze for a moment before we hurried to flag down a taxi and get out of the wind.

It wasn't until we were in the taxi that we dared hold hands. Apparently, army uniforms and affection don't mix.

Once home, I changed into a long, blue velvet gown with small, puffy sleeves and a square neckline front and back. When Adam arrived in evening dress, looking very handsome and a little thinner, I decided I'd chosen the right dress.

We took a cab to a nice restaurant in a hotel and

spoke of trivial things until we'd been seated and ordered. I glanced around before I murmured, "You've lost weight."

"All we do is study and march. That and get drenched sailing rubber rafts. I'm not much of a sailor." Adam kept his voice pitched so only I could hear him.

"I'm sorry." My hand crept over to his and he gripped my fingers tightly.

"I'm not. It's better to be prepared." He dropped my hand as they brought over and poured our wine.

Left alone again, I said, "Dickie and Rex confirmed everything I reported?"

"Yes. So who is it, Livvy?"

I glanced up to see the waiter coming with our soup and kept silent until he was gone. "It's not Reina. She's dead. It's not Brigette. She's no more than nineteen. And Mimi's daughter, by the way."

Adam nodded and ate his soup. He must have been hungry. He finished his before I was half done.

"Don't they feed you?" I asked.

"Nothing you'd want to eat."

They took away our soup bowls and brought chops with potatoes and greens. Adam polished off half his dinner before he looked up and said, "Now I can hear you over my grumbling stomach. Not Reina, not Brigette."

"That leaves Mimi, close friend of the Duke of Marshburn, and Fleur, whom I know nothing..."

I stopped in mid-sentence, drawing Adam's attention. "What is it?"

CHAPTER TWENTY-THREE

"In a trunk in the basement, there is a collection of vials and bottles filled with different powders and liquids. Reina said Fleur uses them to work the fabric to make it do what she wants when she cuts out the frock."

"And you don't believe her."

"It's not a matter of believing her or not. If we knew what the powders and liquids were, we'd know if Fleur or anyone else had anything to work with to make those exploding cigars."

"Take some samples, you mean. We could get the Yard's forensic lab to analyze them."

I nodded. We'd have an answer, one way or the other.

"Hmmm." Adam was considering something. "This would obviously have nothing to do with the investigation I'm supposed to be on. Scotland Yard won't send over any of the lab boys unless they're brought fully into the picture, which the army won't do."

"Can you get some empty, stoppered glass vials and carry them in your pocket or something?"

"What do you have in mind?" He sounded suspicious.

"I'll get into the salon and go down to the basement and let you in the outside door. Then we'll take some samples from the powders in the trunk and you can leave by the basement door and take them to Scotland Yard to get them analyzed."

"Won't this Fleur be suspicious of us taking samples from her trunk?"

"We're not going to tell her."

"Livvy. That's illegal. And how can we prove who those chemicals belong to?"

I sighed. He was right. "At least we'd be sure whether or not someone in that house was behind the exploding cigar." His stern expression told me we'd get nothing more done that night. "Do you have room for dessert?"

* * *

I arrived at work early the next morning and set right to work, knowing I'd be away from my desk for a while. Miss Westcott looked at me suspiciously but said nothing.

I left my desk in time to meet Adam in front of Mimi's salon at ten-thirty, knowing everyone in the building would be busy then. Telling him to wait, I walked down the concrete steps and tried the door handle. It turned in my hand and the door opened.

Peeking in, I saw the area was empty. This was better luck than I'd hoped for.

I signaled Adam to come down and slipped inside. He was there in an instant and shut the door silently behind him.

With a gesture, I led him across the floor to the trunk that held the glass bottles and vials. He opened it and found what I'd seen, carefully stored glass bottles and vials as well as small boxes.

"It looks like a portable chemical lab," he whispered as he handed me a small glass vial and stopper to collect a specimen.

I was glad the gloves I wore were tight against my skin because my hands were trembling. The first powder I tried to collect didn't want to leave its container and I had to carefully tap it to get a sample into the smaller container. The next wanted to pour out all at once and I spilled more of the gray powder on the floor than into the vial.

No wonder I spilled some. We didn't know which of these chemicals might have caused Churchill's cigar to explode, and the idea of suddenly catching on fire made my hands shake.

I was very careful not to spill any on my clothes. My gloves might be destroyed, but I refused to sacrifice my dark gray suit to this investigation.

Adam collected samples from three different bottles and wrapped them in lamb's wool before tucking them into his pocket. I noticed he didn't seem frightened at all, calmly working with these liquids and powders as if this were an everyday occurrence.

Then he dumped small amounts from a couple of the small boxes into even smaller boxes. I turned away, took a calming breath, and turned back to procure small amounts from two more vials. With the rest of our glass tubes wrapped in thick layers of lamb's wool, Adam's pockets now bulged with the collection.

I put the trunk back the way we found it and closed it while Adam left the basement. The powders I'd spilled weren't too noticeable unless you checked the floor carefully. I hurried to follow him, running on tiptoe so my heels didn't click on the stone floor. In a moment, I was out the door and up the stairs, my hard breathing more from fear than exertion.

Adam had signaled a taxi and we rode to the Scotland Yard laboratory. I leaped out of the taxi behind him, but while his badge gained him admittance, I couldn't enter. Giving me a quick grin, he said, "Go back to work. I'll meet you there for lunch."

"What time?" I asked.

"Wait for my call."

I trudged away, brushing the various powders off my gloves. I wondered if Fleur would notice I'd spilled chemicals on the floor by the trunk, although in the weak light it wasn't too obvious. I wasn't about to risk being caught by returning to the basement and sweeping up the mess. I hoped I hadn't given the game away with my sloppiness.

I caught a bus and rode the short distance to Fleet Street before heading to my desk. Miss Westcott looked at the large clock on the wall before staring at me while holding up some quick-typed copy.

I knew I was in trouble as I strolled up to her desk, trying to look unbothered by her frown.

She held out the copy. "This just came in from a shooting party in Yorkshire. Take a look at the names and see if we should print this."

I raised my eyebrows. Decisions on printing articles wasn't the sort of thing the *Daily Premier* left to me.

"They just phoned this into us," she explained. "I didn't recognize the name of the caller or any of the attendees. It seems odd. See if you can make anything of this." Her tone was dry, hinting at the skepticism in her attitude.

I carried it back to my desk, glancing over it. On the face of it, everything appeared normal. Dreary, unimportant, middle-aged aristocrats met to shoot birds and marry off a daughter. But Miss Westcott was right. There was something odd about it.

I sat down to analyze every word as it was phoned in to us. I had heard of some of the attendees. The name of the family who owned the Georgian mansion was correct. These people were hardly more newsworthy than I was, so I had no idea if this country house was where they'd been spending the previous days.

But then I noticed some errors. Rievaulx Abbey was north of the pretty stone house where they were staying, not south, and the house was near York, miles from the coast and not nearby. I'd met the pinch-faced Norma Bradley-Scott and was certain her name was spelled with an "e," not "Bradly" as the notice spelled it. Her father hadn't been given the order of the crested leopard from George V. There was no such thing. Also, her daughter hadn't come out in society. There was no way they'd be husband hunting for her yet, but the article was written as if this were a weekend in the country with matrimony on the menu along with shooting.

First, I asked my colleague Anne, who'd typed up the notice, if she was sure about the details. I knew she was generally accurate, but I wanted to be clear on this. She told me she'd asked about many of the details and had all the names spelled out to her.

She said the caller, a woman, was insistent that the item go into the paper exactly as she'd dictated it. Anne also said the line was as clear as if it were a local call.

The call seemed odd to Anne and she reported it to Miss Westcott immediately.

"How long ago was this?" I asked.

"Ten or fifteen minutes ago."

After Adam and I had left the basement with our samples. I hurried over to our copy of Burke's Peerage and began to look up the people mentioned.

It didn't take me long before I was back at Miss Westcott's desk. "You were right to question this," I told her. "There are several deliberate errors."

She frowned. "Anne is generally so reliable. I don't understand."

"Anne took this down exactly the way it was given to her. 'The order of the crested leopard' doesn't exist. The house mentioned is near York and isn't north of Rievaulx Abbey. This is far beyond a simple typo."

"But why?" She sounded baffled.

I held her gaze. "It reads like some sort of coded message. I think we need to let Sir Henry know."

"We've always prided ourselves on our accuracy at this newspaper. Even on the women's pages. Why would someone want to use us this way?" She kept her composure, but in her pale eyes, I saw fear.

"Because we are known for accuracy. They wanted to get this into the paper exactly as they'd written it. Otherwise, if it is a code, it wouldn't do anyone any good if it had been mucked about."

I didn't want to admit someone suspected me of being involved in the investigation and wanted to use me for whatever reason this message was to go out.

"Didn't they realize we wouldn't run it without taking a good look at what they sent in? That we might rewrite it? Our reputation is at stake." Miss Westcott's voice had risen and a couple of the girls were watching us. She lowered her voice. "Back to work, ladies."

"We should take this up to Sir Henry," I repeated.

"I'll take it up. Apparently, someone wants you on the telephone." She did not sound happy.

I looked over in the direction Miss Westcott had glanced and saw Anne holding up the receiver toward me. I walked over and took the call. "Hello?"

"Livvy?" It was Adam.

"Ready for lunch?" I had so much I wanted to tell him.

"I'll be over in fifteen minutes."

I looked over to Miss Westcott's desk to find that she had disappeared.

When Adam strode up to the building, I was waiting out front. We walked a few streets to an ABC shop for a quick lunch, talking of sports and the latest movies from Hollywood. At one point, when no one was too close to us on the pavement, he said, "I delivered the samples to the analysts. We may have the answers by dinnertime."

I smiled, inviting myself to dinner with him. "Where are you taking me?"

"I'll bring in fish and chips. Make us a salad. We'll need to have a long and detailed discussion."

There wasn't a chance to say any more since the eatery was crowded. On the way back to the *Daily Premier* building, I took a chance and said, "We were given information on a shooting party that was patently false. Miss Westcott took it to Sir Henry. If you have someone who's good with codes, you might give them a tip to get a copy of this message."

"How did it come in?"

"By telephone."

He shook his head. "That's too bad. A call won't give us any clues." Then he smiled. "But I know just the people who should talk to Sir Henry."

"And it came in after we left the basement with our samples." I looked at Adam and raised my eyebrows.

He nodded.

Adam dropped me off at the building, promising to arrive at my flat at half seven that night with the fish and chips. I had to do some flying around after work, going to the greengrocer's before hurrying home to straighten the flat, make the salad, and brush and repin my hair.

It was worth it when I opened the door and found Adam looking handsome and smiling at me on my landing. "I could get used to this assignment," he said before setting down the fish and chips and a bottle of wine in the dining room. A thrill went up my spine when he gave me the lingering kiss I'd been waiting for all day.

Eventually, he set the table while I brought in a big bowl of salad. "Beautiful," he commented when he saw it. "Can't get anything like that on my regular assignment."

I wanted to ask about his "regular assignment," but

knew he couldn't answer. I also knew how difficult it would soon be to get winter lettuce, much less any other salad greens, until spring. "You must be hungry. Let's eat, and then you can tell me about the chemicals and the strange notice sent to the paper."

We sat across the table from each other, sharing salad and fish and a good wine. Finally, Adam said, "You're not going to want to hear what I have to say."

My mind raced. He was leaving again for places unknown. They'd received word that Hitler planned another attack. My stomach tightened so much it hurt. "What?" came out as a whisper.

"This morning, we took a sample from that trunk that has been confirmed as the chemical used to set fire to Churchill's cigars and almost set fire to Churchill. Both Mimi and Fleur swore it was Reina's trunk. Scotland Yard believes she was murdered for failing to kill Churchill, probably by her handler."

CHAPTER TWENTY-FOUR

I banged down my fork and it clattered against my plate. "That's impossible. Reina was Jewish. The Germans have taken over her village and she couldn't get word from her family."

"That's what she told you," Adam said gently. "We found a letter Reina had received recently from her mother. Fleur said the Nazis force people to be their spies in exchange for protecting their families. Reina wanted nothing more than to protect her family in Germany."

I nodded. That was true. "Where did you find the letter? I searched her room after Scotland Yard had been through there."

"Under a floorboard in a corner. It was hidden well enough to get past Scotland Yard's first search, but they weren't looking for anything more than a routine killing." He took my hand. "Don't be too hard on yourself, Livvy. Reina had to live a double life to be an assassin. She would have kept that part of her life secret from everyone."

"What's happened to the trunk with the chemicals in the basement?"

"Scotland Yard laboratory technicians took it back to headquarters. They want to study the contents further."

"Will they test it for fingerprints?"

"Yes, but several women in the salon admit to

looking in it while searching for fabric or ribbon."

"And they didn't ask any questions?" I would have. Someone in that salon must have been curious. I couldn't picture Mimi keeping quiet about anything in her salon.

"Madame Mareau's rule was for everyone to stick to their own task."

Still, everyone had opinions on colleagues. Mimi couldn't stop her workers from judging each other, if only privately. "What did the seamstresses say who worked with Reina? What did Brigette say?"

I was being demanding, but Adam kept his voice gentle and his tone calm. "None of them believed it. They all said she was a nice, quiet person. Not well-educated or driven. No political views. Of course, they didn't have any evidence to explain the trunk or refute the accusations. And they said she was always the one to go down to the basement."

"Yes, I'd noticed that, too." Something I couldn't explain. Why did she keep going down to the basement? "But I still don't believe it. Reina was terrified of something, and I don't think it was because she was afraid of being found out as a Nazi assassin."

I folded my arms over my chest. "What does Scotland Yard think happened to Elias? General Alford said he was a British spy."

"Reina killed Elias when she met him in the basement."

I couldn't believe that. "She was genuinely upset about his death. They'd grown up together in the same village."

"Of course she'd be upset if she were ordered to kill someone who'd been her childhood friend. Even though they were now working for opposite sides."

I was disgusted. A killer was going to go free. "Have you told Sir Henry this nonsense?"

"I haven't. I don't think anyone has spoken to him."

I rose from the table, my appetite destroyed by bad news. "I'll call him now. Finish your dinner. You look like no one's fed you in days."

I went out to the hall and dialed the familiar number. I was surprised to hear Sir Henry answer.

"Sir Henry? It's Olivia Denis. I just learned Scotland Yard thinks Reina killed Elias and tried to blow up Churchill."

"I've heard the same thing. Balderdash," roared out of the receiver. "Why would they think such a thing? Or how could you have been so wrong about her?"

"Adam and I took samples from a trunk in the basement of Mimi's salon and he had them analyzed by Scotland Yard. One of the chemicals was the explosive in Churchill's cigar. And Mimi and Fleur said the trunk belonged to Reina."

"Reina, who is no longer alive to defend herself." By the time Sir Henry spoke, Adam was next to me, listening to the receiver.

"Sir Henry? Captain Redmond here. If it wasn't Reina, who did the trunk belong to?"

"There aren't too many choices, are there?" Sir Henry said.

"And there is nothing to say the person who

tampered with those cigars also bludgeoned two people over the head," I said so I'd be heard over the telephone line.

"You're army, Redmond, not Scotland Yard. There's no reason you have to follow Scotland Yard's conclusions," Sir Henry responded. "Oh, and while I have you on the phone, Livvy, Nauheim has convinced me to send you to Prague with the Mandels."

"What will I be doing there?" I asked. Adam stared at me with raised eyebrows, looking as surprised as I felt.

"Nauheim wants you to smuggle some things out of Prague. Valuable things."

"When?" The ice in Adam's voice must have carried down the telephone wires.

"She leaves the day after tomorrow and will be back two days later. Well, two days or so later." Sir Henry's tone was unyielding.

"What if she doesn't want to?"

"You can't—"

I was determined to stop this argument right now, or it would follow me for years. "I'm going to do it, Adam."

Both men fell silent.

Finally, Adam asked, "Why?"

"Because I believe in it. Because somebody needs to do something. Because I can help."

Adam made a grumbling noise in his throat and walked away.

I clutched the receiver. "I'll talk to you tomorrow, Sir Henry. Find out more about this trip."

"No need for you to come to the meeting tonight. I'll

fill you in at the office. Good night, Livvy." The line went dead.

Oh, good grief. Adam arrived in town and I forgot about meetings I should attend. I went into the kitchen to find Adam pouring the coffee. "You're angry."

"Not angry. Worried. The Germans' next step is to take over the rest of Czechoslovakia. I don't want you trapped behind enemy lines."

"I think that's why we're going now. So we won't be. The couple I'm going with is Jewish, and we'll be trying to bring monetary support out of Czechoslovakia to get young families to Britain. The Mandels don't want to be captured by the Nazis even more than I don't."

"What will you be smuggling?"

"I don't know. I suppose I'll find out when I get there."

He carried the coffee tray into the dining room. I followed, finding he'd cleaned his plate and mine, too. They must starve the army, since his face seemed thinner, although he seemed to fill out his suit jacket even better than he had before.

I couldn't wait to get that jacket off.

Once we were seated with our coffee, I said, "May I make a suggestion?"

"What?" His voice dripped with suspicion.

"Can you put a watch on Mimi's salon and follow either Mimi or Fleur if they leave? They are the only two possibilities for the explosive chemist."

"Besides Reina."

I held his gaze. "You don't need to follow her

anymore."

He rubbed his hand on my bare forearm. "You liked her and trusted her. I'm sorry she's dead."

I nodded, already considering the other possibilities. "What do we know about Mimi? She has a daughter, Brigette, born just after the war. Father reported to be a married Jewish banker from Stockholm. She currently has a duke for a lover who is rabidly pro-German."

Adam nodded. "What do we know about Fleur?"

I shook my head. "Nothing."

"Nothing?"

"She answers questions with the bare amount of information. Her surname is Bettenard. She's only been with Mimi a few years. I don't know where she was before that. And she doesn't like having her picture taken, but we did get one, a group photo that Jane Seville took."

"Do you have it?"

"Sir Henry has a print, and Jane has the negative in her office."

He smiled. "I'll drop in at the *Daily Premier* in the morning."

"Then you agree one of the two of them has to be the chemist who sent Churchill the exploding cigars." I felt vindicated.

"I think we can't afford to blame Reina and ignore any other possibilities."

"Especially since someone phoned that coded message into the newspaper. Has there been any luck decoding it?"

"None at all. We have no idea if it has anything to do with the French assassin." He slipped his fingers between mine. "Scotland Yard is bringing Reina's cousin to London tomorrow for questioning. She doesn't speak English. Can I have you act as my interpreter?"

"I'll be glad to, although I know you speak some French." I squeezed his hand, excited that I'd have an opportunity to do some questioning of my own.

"I'll arrange it."

We had a pleasant rest of the evening by staying far away from murder and espionage. But after Adam left in the early morning, I got very little sleep. My mind struggled with what I knew about Reina as opposed to what I believed, how little I knew about Fleur, and a question Adam had asked me about our future.

I wore a dark blue dress and jacket to work in the morning under my mac and made sure to carry an umbrella. Our unusually long streak of fine weather had ended during the night.

My first task after shedding my coat, hat, gloves, and umbrella was to phone down to Jane's desk and ask her to print another copy of the photo she'd taken at Mimi's, focusing on Fleur. Then I called Sir Henry's office, and after being connected by his secretary, I told him I would be put to use by Adam and Scotland Yard as a translator for Reina's cousin.

We agreed we'd talk afterward.

At ten I received a call from the lobby that Adam was there. I told Miss Westcott I had a task to perform for Sir Henry, pulled on my outerwear, and hurried down to the lobby.

"Do you have the photograph?" he asked me.

I patted my handbag.

"I received word that Mimi left her fashion house early this morning. We're having her followed."

Despite everything, I didn't want the assassin to be Mimi. I found I was still carrying a rose-tinted picture of Mimi in my mind.

We took a taxi to Scotland Yard and were waved in through the gates. Adam had me placed on some sort of list that the guard consulted, allowing me to enter the maze of red and gray fake-towered buildings. Only the Victorians would build something so unified and yet so incongruous, I thought as Adam led me to one of the entrances.

Two police constables stood along the wall near the door when we entered the conference room. Two men in suits sat on one side of a large table. They rose when we came up to them and introduced themselves as a detective chief inspector and a detective sergeant. Adam introduced us as he shook hands with the men.

On the other side of the table, a thin young man stood as we approached them. He sat again next to a girl of about twenty in what appeared to be a hand-me-down frock.

None of them looked comfortable.

"*Bonjour*," I said, and introduced myself in French, gaining a faint smile from the girl as I pulled up another chair and sat at the end of the table near the girl.

The thin young man introduced himself as René, the

official translator, and we greeted each other.

The girl introduced herself as Deborah Feld, Reina's cousin.

"It isn't Blumfeld, like Reina?" I asked in French.

"You knew Reina?"

"*Oui.*"

She looked down, and finally gave a little nod. "I changed it to make it easier to find work in Paris. Our fathers were brothers."

The men sitting across from her leaned forward and the younger of the two, the sergeant, in his thirties and with a notebook in his hands, demanded, "What are you doing here?"

"I'm Mrs. Denis, sent by the army to translate."

"You're not needed."

"Tell that to General Alford."

The detective chief inspector snorted and leaned back. Obviously, he'd dealt with General Alford before. The younger one asked, "What has she told you so far?"

"Her name, and that Reina was her cousin because their fathers were brothers." The official translator, René, concurred.

The younger one scribbled in his notebook. "Go on."

I turned to Deborah. "Have they told you they suspect Reina of killing Josef Meirsohn and trying to kill Mr. Churchill?"

"What? Why would they think that? Are they crazy?" spilled out in rapid French. "Reina was always a good girl."

"They think she may have done it to keep her family

safe. They found a letter from her mother hidden in her room here in London." I turned to Adam and said in English, "Is the letter from Reina's mother available? May we see it, please?"

"This is highly irregular," the sergeant said while Adam stared at him. The older man handed the letter to Adam, who handed it to me.

I showed it to Deborah.

She read it once quickly and then again more slowly. "Where did you get this?"

"Hidden under the floorboards of Reina's room here in London."

"It wasn't written by Reina's mother," Deborah said. "It's a forgery."

CHAPTER TWENTY-FIVE

Her words were surprising, but her tone of certainty was shocking. "How do you know?"

"What did she say?" the detective sergeant ordered in English.

We both ignored him.

"Reina's mother's pet name for Reina was 'Navah,'" Deborah said. "It was what her older sister called her when they were tiny. She would never address a letter to her as Reina. And Reina had two younger brothers. Her mother wouldn't say 'your younger brother' without saying which one. And the letter is in German. We speak Yiddish." She slapped the letter down on the table and folded her arms.

"What do you think of Reina's mother's claim that their lives were much easier now that Reina was working for the Reich?" I asked her, curious to hear her reaction.

"I know there are those who sell out their friends and neighbors to save their families, but not Reina. She would do whatever she could if it would do any good, but she knew there is nothing that can be done." She gave me a look through eyes dark with anger. "And this is a forgery. Reina wasn't helping them, and our family's lives aren't any better. Why is this the only letter Reina has received from her family in over a year? Why haven't I received a letter?"

"What is the name of her village?"

"Brechelstof. It is my village, too. Why?"

"We wondered exactly where Reina came from. And how hard it would be to reach the village from outside Germany."

"It was close to the Czech border. Before the Sudeten crisis. Now that way is closed, too."

I translated all Deborah had said.

"She's lying," the sergeant murmured to his superior in a voice loud enough for me to hear.

"Based on what?" Adam said. He'd heard the sergeant, too.

"How do you know this woman is reliable?" the sergeant countered.

"I speak enough French to understand part of their conversation. I also know General Alford trusts her. And the official translator hasn't corrected anything she's said." Adam stared at the man for a moment. "Now, why do you think the girl is lying?"

I was proud of Adam for sticking up for me.

At that moment, another uniformed constable came in and handed Adam a note. He looked at the men at the table and said, "Fleur Bettenard has disappeared. She gave our man the slip in the Underground. We need to have everyone looking for her."

"Wanted for murder?"

"Wanted for attempted murder of Mr. Churchill. She's the French assassin we've been looking for," Adam said.

"How can you be sure of that?" the chief inspector

asked.

"By the drugs and chemicals in a trunk she brought to the salon where she worked here in London." Adam looked grim. I suspected he'd been told of the assassin's crimes associated with the various chemicals.

"Fleur and that Madame Mareau she works for both swore it was Reina's. In separate interviews," the sergeant told Adam.

"Do you have a photo of this woman, Fleur?" the chief inspector asked.

I reached into my handbag and passed the photograph over my shoulder to Adam. A photo, trimmed by Jane Seville, showed only Fleur. Adam gave it to the older Scotland Yard man.

"We'll put out an alert. At the very least, this presents more information to follow up on," the man added.

The sergeant grumbled as he stood and walked out of the room with the photograph.

"What has happened?" Deborah asked me in French.

"The trunk that contained the explosives and poisons associated with a French assassin that we were told belonged to Reina actually belonged to a colleague of Reina's called Fleur."

"Reina knew nothing of poisons, of science, of medicine. She hated noise and fire. She hated school. She liked to sew and talk to her friends and watch handsome boys, although she was too shy to flirt with them." Deborah grabbed my hand. "Reina wouldn't assassinate anyone."

I looked at her closely, trying to let her see my

sympathy on my face. "I didn't think she would," I said before I translated Deborah's words for Scotland Yard.

"And she didn't like Fleur," Deborah continued. "She didn't trust her. She was wonderful at cutting fabric, but Reina was afraid of her."

"Why?" I hadn't picked up on Reina being specifically afraid of Fleur. Only that Reina was constantly frightened.

"Fleur told her once she could cut patterns out of human skin. Reina said that was terrible. Fleur answered, 'The master race can do what they want.' With a bright smile on her face."

I shivered at the words. The translator, René, looked ill.

When I repeated the words, in English, for Adam and the older policeman, they both looked distressed. "A Nazi infiltrator," the policeman said.

"I wonder what her name really is," Adam said. "She's probably taken everything incriminating with her."

"I would hope you'll allow Deborah to go home." Then I switched from English to French. "They've sent Reina's possessions in London home to Paris?"

Deborah nodded.

I switched back to English. "We need to go to Mimi Mareau's to ask her for Fleur's Paris address. The Sûreté could check her Paris home for anything that might lead to her identity or where she might be headed."

The Scotland Yard chief inspector thanked Deborah for her help. I assured her that Reina was no longer under suspicion and her name had been cleared. Then one of the constables escorted her and the translator out.

Adam and I traveled with the chief inspector and another constable to Mimi's a few minutes later. Adam spoke to the girl at the desk, who immediately called the designer.

Mimi arrived a minute later in a pale-red knit dress and jacket worn with pearls and black and white two-tone shoes. Next to her, the rest of us looked rumpled and shoddy.

"What do you want? Reina is dead. Fleur has left. You've wiped out my top assistants. I should never have come to London. You English!"

"We'd like Fleur's Paris address," Adam said.

"You'll be too late," Brigette said.

I hadn't noticed Brigette until then. She stood silently near the entrance to the back room, her face a blank mask hiding her feelings concerning all that had occurred.

"Why would they be too late?" I asked.

"Fleur's much cleverer than everyone else. Mother didn't know what she was up to until she left, and she usually knows what's going on under her roof. And Fleur knew you were from the government right from the start," she added, sneering at me.

With that attitude, Brigette would hold her own against the Duke of Marshburn's family. She'd need strength to deal with Lady Patricia, but only if Mimi's affair with the duke survived this disaster.

"I need to go upstairs to get Fleur's address for you," Mimi said and headed up the front staircase. At Adam's nod, I followed.

I discovered Mimi had carved a tiny office for herself out of the dressing area behind the showroom on the first floor. "Why are you following me?" she demanded as she sat down at her desk.

"You'd rather a policeman followed you?" I asked.

She shook her head and pulled out a large notebook full of papers, some attached, some stuffed inside, to set on the desktop. Finding a scrap of paper, she copied an address out and handed it to me.

"I wonder how long I would have stayed in London if you hadn't driven me out."

I looked at her, stunned. "I've done nothing of the sort, Mimi."

"It's 'Madame Mareau' to you. And you've upset everything, with your constant questions, poking your long nose everywhere. That's why I decided not to use your drawing for an advertisement, even though it was good. You've disrupted my salon. And now Reina's death is on your head."

"I didn't kill her. That was someone else's decision. Someone else's sin. I suspect Fleur's."

"No. She swore she didn't do it. I believe her. She was angry about Reina's death. Said it was unhelpful, bringing the constables back to snoop around the basement again."

"Because her trunk was down there."

Mimi gave me a dark look and didn't respond.

I realized what this meant. "You knew about her trunk. You knew she was the French assassin."

"Not until recently. Not until I was told."

"By whom?"

She looked away. "Fleur."

There was something about her voice. Something in the way she wouldn't look at me. "The duke told you. Marshburn told you. Was it Marshburn's idea to bring Fleur to London? Was Marshburn behind the attempt on Churchill?"

"Fleur told me." Then she looked at me, her eyes blazing with anger. She rose from her desk and with her chin up, said, "Tell the police I have work to do."

I knew I'd never get her to tell me the truth.

I went downstairs, gave Adam the address, and told them Mimi admitted to learning from Fleur that she was the French assassin. Disgusted with the woman who'd been my hero, I left to go back to the *Daily Premier.*

Walking into Sir Henry's office, I said, "Fleur Bettenard is the French assassin. She's escaped and they're looking for her. You'd better check with General Alford before you print anything."

"Good work, Livvy." My publisher was all smiles.

I wasn't smiling. "I can't prove it, but I think the Duke of Marshburn is behind the French assassin coming here and attacking Churchill. I think it was his idea for Mimi Mareau to bring her fashion house here and bring Fleur along."

"Can you find a way to prove it?"

"No. Mimi won't give him up." Then it occurred to me. "Unless Marshburn cuts his losses and drops her. Maybe then she will tell us about the French assassin and the duke's role in her attacks."

"It's a good thought, but right now, you need to pack. You're flying to Prague in the morning," Sir Henry told me.

I wanted to continue to be part of the hunt for the French assassin or to search for Elias's killer. However, the terms of my employment said I would travel to the continent or carry out other duties for Sir Henry as required. With a sigh, I asked, "What exactly will I be bringing back from Prague?"

"Riches beyond your wildest imagination. The silver altar pieces from the Old-New Synagogue in Prague."

I felt my heart slam into my lungs. I was sure that instead of hunting for killers, I'd now become the target. "How many people will be trying to kill me to get their hands on all that silver?"

CHAPTER TWENTY-SIX

"No one will be trying to kill you. The leaders of the synagogue want it out before the Germans come across the border. The Czech government doesn't know anything about this shipment. If no one talks, you'll be fine," Sir Henry told me.

"How often have you known people not to talk?" I asked.

He shrugged. "It's a chance we'll have to take."

"We?" It sounded like I was the one taking the chances, and I wasn't happy.

"The Mandels will be going with you. They'll vouch for you in the Jewish community, but if the ornaments are shipped under your name, the Czech government will be less suspicious. If anyone asks, you are there on behalf of a wealthy art collector."

"Who? And am I empowered to drop his name?"

"Anonymous."

Swell. "And why are the Mandels going there? Am I supposed to know them when we are away from the Jewish community?"

"No. We've arranged for them to stay in the same hotel so you can communicate, but you'll arrive on different flights."

"Will I be given bills of sale so no one accuses me of theft?"

Sir Henry nodded. "Fake, of course. No cash will change hands. They'll be held in England as surety for funds to support the emigrants."

"What if the Czech government, or someone else, wants to see evidence of this 'payment'?" I could see so many things going wrong.

"The committee still has the account with the Swedish bank that we set up for Elias. Let me give you the details in case it comes down to a need for proof."

He wrote out all the info and I put the paper in my purse. "When do I leave?"

"Early tomorrow morning." He handed me my tickets, by air through Amsterdam and Berlin on my way in, by train and ferry on my way back. "I suppose you'll leave Sunday, but that is up to your hosts. We've been warned the chances are too great that the silver will be stolen if you fly back."

Wonderful. "What am I supposed to do?"

"If you go by train and ferry, you can watch the crates be loaded and unloaded from the baggage area. That will be the safest way, but it'll take a little longer. If anyone asks, say your employer expects it of you."

Sir Henry didn't often look guilty, but this was one of those times. "How long will it take?"

"Three days. Maybe a little longer."

"What if Adam has to go back to his training before then?" I said with dismay. That was my primary concern. The time we had together was too short as it was.

"You both have careers that take precedence, at least until Herr Hitler goes away." Sir Henry gave an exasperated sigh. "Just marry him, will you?"

"You sound like my father."

"You and Esther are so close and I've known you so long that I feel like your father. Or at least your uncle."

I knew he meant well. "I was married before, to a man with a tame job working with credentials and details at the Foreign Office, and you saw how well that worked out."

"That was unfortunate, but you're not jinxed." Sir Henry gave me a rueful smile.

I sighed, letting out my frustration with my breath. "Please let Miss Westcott know I'll be off tomorrow working for you. I need to go home and pack." And hope Adam called.

He did better than that. I'd just finished packing for the chilly trip to Prague when I heard a tap on the door. I answered the same time I heard his key in the lock. We were in the hallway with the door shut before he greeted me with a kiss that could have lasted all evening.

And might have, if he hadn't spotted my suitcase in the hallway behind me.

"Where are you going?" he asked, trying not to sound disappointed. "Oh. Your trip for Sir Henry. When?"

I really didn't want to tell him. "I go to Prague in the morning. I'll be back sometime next week."

"I have to leave Saturday morning to join the hunt for Fleur in France."

"Oh, I was afraid of that."

"Can't you postpone until Sunday?"

"No. I'm not the one making these arrangements. Can

you?" I knew he couldn't, but my feelings were bruised.

"Tell Sir Henry you can't go until Saturday," his tone demanded as he pulled away from me.

"This time it's not just Sir Henry. I'm involved in helping young Czechs gain entry at the behest of some Londoners who want them here to help fight against Hitler. There's a whole committee making these arrangements."

"And I suppose none of them asked you if this was convenient." He dropped into Reggie's favorite chair in the drawing room and shut his eyes.

He looked exhausted, and I felt guilty leaving him on such short notice for my work. Unfortunately, a lot of lives in Prague depended on me. Was it too much, I wondered, to have assignments for Sir Henry when Adam was out of town with the army?

I followed him. "No, they didn't. Now we can either fight about this or enjoy our last night together until you get back to London."

"Do you care if I come back to London?" He sounded like he was afraid I would break up with him.

"What is this? Of course I do. You have a demanding position, chasing after an assassin and who knows what else. I have a slightly less secretive position helping smuggle people out of the path of the Nazis." And more, which I didn't bother to mention.

"Jews."

"People," I corrected him. "Until Hitler's gone and the world goes back to normal, we're going to have to grab every chance we get to be together. And I'm still thinking about what you asked me. I haven't stopped thinking about it."

He looked down, and after a pause, nodded. Then he glanced back up at me. "Oh, Livvy. I'm crazy about you. The whole time I'm off playing soldier," he grumbled, "I lie in my bunk at night and think of you before I go to sleep. Wondering what you're doing."

"I'm thinking of you. Wondering where you are. Wondering if you're safe."

"Now I'll be wondering if you're safe." He gave me a grin, but it was wistful.

"I will be. I won't be breaking any laws, fighting with anyone, or trying to sail in rubber rafts. Unlike some people I could mention." My smile was equally wistful.

He pulled me down onto his lap. "I'll say it again. Let's get married."

I threw my arms around his neck. "Let's get engaged. I'm not quite ready for marriage yet. I need to get used to the idea first."

His expression turned serious. "Was marriage to Reggie that bad?"

"No. Not at all." I swallowed, trying to find a way to be honest without sounding too frightened. "He was murdered here in London. Seeing him in the morgue, so pale and cold, when I'd just seen him the day before, alive..."

He nibbled on my ear. "I'm going to survive this war, Livvy. We both are. There's no reason to fear the future."

Acting braver than I felt, I said, "Then let's get engaged and do this properly."

"Anything else you want to do properly?" His grin widened.

I climbed off his lap and held out a hand. To my shock, he got down on one knee and asked me to be his wife in the proper and approved manner.

I said yes, and the celebration began.

* * *

The next morning, Adam rode out to Heston Aerodrome with me to see me off on the first leg of my trip to Prague. Once on the aeroplane, I slept most of the journey, tired out from the celebration the night before. I didn't have a ring to show for my new status, but it didn't matter. There was no one I wanted to tell until I returned to London.

I knew most of the population in Prague spoke German from the days of the Austro-Hungarian Empire, but apparently, it was considered patriotic after the decapitation of the Sudetenland not to use German. I found myself apologizing to taxi drivers and hotel clerks in English for not speaking Czech before I began apologizing in German.

I had been given directions to a small hotel in the Old Town by Sir Henry, where I checked in at mid-afternoon. I sneaked a look in the registration book while I had the desk clerk searching for a message from my employer. The Mandels hadn't arrived yet.

I wandered down Charles Street to the Charles Bridge, marveling at the ancient architecture and the determined expressions on the faces around me. Hitler would meet an implacable enemy here. At least that was what the faces around me and the purposeful stride of many feet on the cobblestone streets said.

Would the Jews here stay and fight with their countrymen, or flee to Britain or America? Would they want me to take their goods for safekeeping in Britain or tell me to leave empty-handed?

From what I had learned in London, that debate had pretty much ended, and most of the Jews in Prague wanted our help to get as many of their congregation out as possible. I hoped the losing side of the debate didn't tell the Czech government what I was doing.

As it started to grow dark with nightfall and thickening clouds, I hurried back to my hotel. I came in to find the Mandels heading for the stairs, following a porter carrying their luggage. I went to the desk and asked for my key to room 201 in a loud voice.

By the time I had my key in my hand, they had disappeared up the staircase. I climbed quickly and saw them heading toward the third floor as I reached my landing.

I went to my room and waited. In about fifteen minutes, there was a knock on the door. When I answered, Mrs. Mandel slipped in.

"Is there really a need for secrecy?" I asked her.

"Czechoslovakia has had a long, changeable relationship with its Jews. Now with Hitler and his Aryan views on the doorstep, who knows what the Czechs will do? And it's imperative that the Czechs don't know what you're shipping out or who it will benefit."

I nodded. "When will we do this, and how?"

"No one will be surprised that the entire community is in the synagogues since it will be the Sabbath at sundown. We'll do it then." Mrs. Mandel gave me a smile and added, "You'll have to meet us at the Old-New Synagogue. Do you mind sitting through the service? We'll go to dinner with one of the families afterward, and then start packing up what you will transport."

Start packing? "Will this be heavy?"

"A little. And awkward. We'll need to find a removals company to bring it to the airport on Sunday morning."

"We will?" My voice rose and Mrs. Mandel flinched. "I wish someone had told me before now. I've already been told I have to go by train and ferry to make sure the goods get on and off the baggage car safely."

"Is that what they decided? I'm sorry. That's going to make a long trip for you. But I'm sure our hosts will know who to contact to get you safely onto the train."

I certainly hoped so. And getting valuable goods through foreign customs wasn't a time to start hoping for the best. "Where is this Old-New Synagogue and what time should I be there?"

Mrs. Mandel gave me the information and slipped back into the hall. I looked at the clock. I would need to leave soon to find my way in the street-lighted twilight to the place where this adventure, this madness, would begin.

Looking down on the street a few minutes later, I saw the Mandels cross the narrow road in front of the hotel. Time to go.

I went downstairs and left by the wide front door in

the lobby. Plenty of taxis were out, as were lots of pedestrians hurrying along in the chilly wind. I suspected by later on that night, the air would be icy. I was glad I wore my heavy fur-collared coat, the collar dyed to match the black of the wool, and a wool felt cloche.

My legs inside my opaque stockings were freezing by the time I reached the steep-roofed synagogue. I was quickly directed to the women's section and joined Mrs. Mandel. There I was introduced, in German, to Mrs. Vltiva, the rabbi's wife.

"Do not worry, Mrs. Denis," she said to me. "I have the pots on simmer and the lights turned on. You will not starve or eat in the dark."

I looked to Mrs. Mandel for guidance.

She told me, "The Vltivas, and this congregation, are Orthodox. They do no work on the Sabbath. Cooking or turning on a light is considered work."

"What do they think packing whatever I'm supposed to transport is?" I asked. That had to be work.

Mrs. Mandel's eyes widened as my words sunk in. She obviously had no idea.

"It's already done and moved to the Town Hall," Mrs. Vltiva assured me. "It can sit there out of the way until Sunday morning."

"Is there a packing list spelling out the contents? I'll need that to get through customs, along with a bill of sale."

The service began as I was speaking, and several women shushed me.

It was hauntingly beautiful, the vibrant men's voices

echoing in the high-roofed room, but I didn't understand a word. I sat quietly and let the sound wash over me.

After what seemed like eternity, the service ended and Mrs. Vltiva rose and said, "Come with me." I followed Mrs. Mandel out. "We will answer all your questions at dinner."

Dinner with the Mandels, the Vltivas, and their neighbors the Grenbaums was filling and flavorful, the dumplings with chicken chunks and broth particularly good. While we ate, they told the Mandels and me about the Josefov, the Jewish Quarter. Fortunately, we all spoke German. It was the only language we had in common. Considering it was also the language of the Nazis, it felt odd.

"I noticed a number of Art Nouveau buildings as we walked here after service," I said.

"Most of the quarter was ancient, a slum. At the turn of the century, many of the buildings were torn down and replaced by new blocks of flats," the rabbi told me. "Many of the fronts were embellished with Art Nouveau designs."

"They're lovely," I replied, but my mind was on business. "Please, I need to know about the paperwork to get through customs on Sunday."

"The shipping papers are all ready, plus we want to give you a list of those we most want to get out of Prague. Young people. Young families." They passed me a sheet of paper covered with names.

"There must be a couple of hundred names on this list."

"What is in the crates is worth the support of these people for a hundred years," the rabbi told me.

I had the challenge of transporting this fabulous wealth across several national borders by myself, without having the treasure stolen or me being murdered. I wouldn't breathe deeply again until I was back on English soil.

CHAPTER TWENTY-SEVEN

I put the paper in my handbag. "I also need a bill of sale listing the items mentioned on the customs declaration."

"It's in the Town Hall with the crates. Where will you want them delivered?" The rabbi had a calm, soft voice, reassuring at this perilous moment.

"The train station. I'm going through Warsaw to the coast and then on the ferry to make my way home." I'd studied the train and ferry timetables. I thought I could make all my connections without difficulties.

The rabbi considered for a moment. "You might have better luck on the night train. How do you feel about leaving Prague at ten on Saturday night? That train will get you straight to Warsaw and then you can transfer to another for the Gdansk area. From there you can get a ferry to eastern Sweden on Sunday afternoon."

I hoped Adam would be held up in France chasing after Fleur until I had enough time to cross Europe by train and ferry. I wanted to see him before he had to return to his usual army duties. Under the best of circumstances, I'd be lucky to get to England by Tuesday afternoon.

"We want you to arrive safely with the goods we are sending," the rabbi said. "It will be a long trip, yes, but this should be the safest way. At night, the border guards are not vigilant, and on Sundays I've been told they just wave people on to the ferries."

I felt fear claw at my throat. The danger of theft or arrest from the border guards seemed more real by the moment. "Is there something wrong with the papers?"

"No. We think it is safer if no one notices what we are shipping. It might bring out the greed in the guards or the railroad personnel."

"Will you come to see me off?"

The rabbi shook his head. "Some of my people will be the removals men with the truck. Perhaps the Mandels will go with you to see you off." The rabbi looked at me with kindly eyes.

Now I understood. "The goods I am shipping are not supposed to be coming from the Jewish community."

"You're an agent buying from one collector and delivering the goods to another collector. Nothing could be more simple or commonplace."

We finished dinner in silence. I felt uneasy, and I saw Mr. Mandel curling his hands into fists. Mrs. Mandel bit her lower lip.

After dinner, the women went into the kitchen to talk over coffee while the men stayed in the dining room. Mrs. Grenbaum sat down next to me and said, "Have you heard anything of my husband's niece, Leah Nauheim?"

"I wondered if Leah is related to you. Yes, I've met her. She's very pretty," I said.

"Is she happy?"

I must have looked startled, because Mrs. Grenbaum said, "I'm sorry. I probably sound crazy."

"Not at all. I've just never considered the question." I thought a minute before I answered. "She loves her husband and he is devoted to her, but she seems a little lost. Haunted by the past, maybe? Or maybe she has trouble speaking English."

"Her past is enough to haunt her," Mrs. Grenbaum said.

I looked at her, puzzled, until she said, "Leah was married before, in Germany when she was quite young. Seventeen. The family liked the groom, but I didn't think they would suit. I was right."

I waited, hoping she would say more. When she didn't, I said, "What happened to her?"

"Her husband was a firebrand. It wasn't long before the Nazis threw them both into prison. When she was let go, just skin and bones and shaking, poor lamb, she fled Germany and came to us. She got better, and then she met her current husband and moved to England. Perhaps she'll feel safe there. She was terrified here that the Nazis would come and take her away again."

"It must have been a nightmare for her." I couldn't imagine the horrors of a Nazi prison.

"It was. I'd have killed Josef myself if the Nazis hadn't done it for me." I saw a fire in her eyes that made me believe her.

"Josef? Who's Josef?"

"Her first husband. Josef Meirsohn."

Despite the heat in the flat, I felt cold. Josef Meirsohn, also known as Elias, had been married to Leah Nauheim. She was a bigamist. Or had been, until he was murdered.

I didn't know if that could get her deported back to Nazi Germany, but if I were her, I wouldn't want to take the risk.

And what would David Nauheim think of their illegal marriage?

The murders of Elias and Reina now made sense. The object Elias had wanted his childhood friend to keep for him must have been their marriage certificate. The only proof in existence outside of Germany.

Except for the Grenbaums of Prague.

I couldn't wait to get back to London. Then again, it meant a frightened woman would hang. Three deaths where there had been two. I found I wasn't in such a rush after all.

I needed to know. "Mrs. Grenbaum, please tell me about Leah's life before she came to England."

* * *

I arrived the next night at the railway station in plenty of time and watched the removals van arrive. Two young, burly men loaded the wooden crates on board the baggage carriage while I went through the customs process with an indifferent guard.

When the guard strolled off to check in another shipment, one of the removals men came over to me and said, "Thank you. We're two of the men who'll be making our way to England to fight with your country."

"Wish me luck. And good luck to you." We exchanged nods before he disappeared into the night and I climbed aboard the night train.

I had finally fallen asleep when the border guards

came on the train. They paid little attention to my papers or my customs forms as they grumpily went from one passenger to the next.

I rose then and walked to the door at the end of the corridor and stepped off onto the platform. An official shouted something at me in Polish.

"I came outside for some air," I said in German. None of the guards were near the baggage carriage.

"Let me see your papers," the official said as he came over to me.

My heart raced, making me wide awake. I tried to control my breathing so I didn't appear so frightened.

"You are English," he said in German.

"I don't speak Polish," I told him. "I hoped you spoke German so I could answer you."

"You'd best get back on the train. It is leaving," the official said, handing back my papers.

"*Danke.*" I climbed back on, certain no one had stolen my goods so far. I slept fitfully and rose early in Warsaw to supervise the transfer of the crates to the train bound for Danzig.

I nodded off a few times on the trip to the coast, and then had to use a mix of orders and bribes to get two porters with a hand truck to move my precious cargo from the train downhill the short distance to the ferry dock. There, as I watched, dockworkers shifted my crates on board into the hull. Another customs official, one who liked to flirt, meant I feared I wouldn't get my papers stamped in time. But with a few minutes to go, he stamped them and I rushed on board. I gave a loud sigh when we set sail into the Baltic Sea.

We'd made it out of Poland.

We reached Sweden in the middle of the night. The border guard showed no interest in me or my crates there, holding up a hand to hide his frequent yawns. When it was my turn, I held up my English passport and he waved me through. I wondered if it was a reaction to the hypervigilance along the German border all over Europe.

With a mixture of cajoling, bribery, and pleading, I received help from another porter with a hand truck in moving my crates from the dock onto the train, but I had to assist him with the awkward crates. I just had time to find the telegraph office in the station and send Sir Henry a message letting him know I'd reached Sweden.

It was the next evening, Tuesday, before we reached Esbjerg. The Danish border guards were more efficient as they tried out their English, but they asked few questions. Once again I had enough time to send Sir Henry a telegram before we sailed. I would have liked to send Adam a telegram telling him what was going on, but I had no idea where to send a message.

I was so relieved to finally get onto the ferry to England with my crates that as soon as we left the dock, I went to my cabin, lay down on my bunk, and fell asleep.

I was awakened by the ship rolling in what felt like stormy seas. It was October. I shouldn't have been surprised. I wasn't, but I was frightened. I peeked out of my cabin. No one was in the passageway. I put on my coat and my shoes and went out into the passageway to climb the stairs.

With every step I thought, we can't sink. I was carrying too many valuable things. Priceless articles from the Prague synagogues, and jewels and gold coins from the congregations, meant to support the young people they would send to Britain. And something else. I carried something evil and frightening. The identity of a murderer.

I'd have been happy to throw that burden overboard.

I reached the top level of the ferry by hanging on to the railings. Most of the seats were taken in the restaurant, but I managed to reach a chair at one of the tables. A steward came up to me, balancing carefully. "We can only serve coffee," he said in heavily accented English.

"Coffee would be fine. What time is it?"

"In England? Four in the morning." He must have seen the panic on my face, for he added, "This is the roughest part of the journey. And tonight it is not too bad."

Not too bad? We had eight more hours. I drank the coffee he brought me and looked out the windows. It was black outside, so all I could see was the reflections of the people in the restaurant. Most of them didn't look worried. Only tired or bored.

Going back to my cabin, I tried to get more sleep. I managed to doze off, only to awaken with a jerk. At least the sea didn't feel as rough now. I fixed my hair in the tiny mirror, brushed off my clothes, and went back up to the restaurant to have breakfast.

I was hungry for bacon, eggs, and toast. I'd had too many blah dumplings with tough chicken or salted fish with salty soup on the trains and ferries on this journey. That morning, I was in luck. With all the English customers on this route, they did a reasonably good breakfast.

Energized by some sleep and a hearty breakfast, I was one of the first to disembark when we landed in Harwick. I hadn't been standing in the passenger area long when Sir Henry, the Mandels, and Daniel Nauheim appeared.

"We've been keeping track of your journey by your telegrams," Mrs. Mandel said.

"We've hired a truck to take the goods to London," Sir Henry told me. "And Mr. Nauheim brought me out in his car to give you a ride the rest of the way home."

"Good," I murmured in his ear. "I need to talk to the two of you. In private."

Sir Henry raised his eyebrows, but he didn't ask any questions.

After a great deal of standing around, we finally saw the crates off in the truck, followed closely by the Mandels. Then Sir Henry, Mr. Nauheim, and I climbed into the Nauheims' long, sleek car for the drive to London. The chauffeur sat in the wide front seat, while the two men and I were packed into the back.

"Has Fleur been apprehended?" I asked.

"No. She seems to have gone to ground in France. Captain Redmond and some other army types are still looking for her," Sir Henry told me.

So Adam was still in France. I wished him luck so he could hurry back to London. To me.

"What else did you want to tell us?" Sir Henry asked.

"Mr. Nauheim, did Leah go with you to the meeting where Elias was introduced?"

"Yes, all three of us attended."

I sighed and closed my eyes. This was going to be difficult. When I opened them, I found both men were looking at me. "Leah was married to Elias, when he went by his real name of Josef Meirsohn. They were arrested together by the Nazis because of Elias's work. Leah believed that Josef, or should we call him Elias, died in prison. When she encountered him at the meeting, she realized she was a bigamist."

CHAPTER TWENTY-EIGHT

"What? That's impossible," Mr. Nauheim bellowed.

I took a deep breath. "I'm sorry, but I learned all this while I was in Prague. I will have to tell the police. I wanted to tell you first."

At his glower, I continued. "When Leah was released, she went to Prague to live with her aunt and uncle. Elias was either released or escaped and went on attacking the Nazis."

"Leah was already married when she and David wed? Why didn't she say something when she saw Elias? No." Nauheim shook his head, "It can't be."

"She thought he was dead. Elias was identified by a childhood friend, Reina, the other person murdered in the basement of the fashion salon. They met by accident near Elias's hotel and Elias wanted Reina to keep something safe for him. That was the reason he was in the basement, but Reina was sent on an errand before they could meet. He was found dead before she returned."

"What difference does that make?" Nauheim demanded.

"I think he planned to give Reina their wedding certificate for safekeeping. His pockets were emptied after he was killed. And since Leah was at the meeting, she would have found out not only that her husband was alive and in London, but where he was staying."

"You think they met at the hotel? Then why kill him elsewhere? Why not just work out some sort of agreement?" Nauheim wanted to know.

"I don't know. I also don't know why she killed Reina. Reina might have been able to identify her, having met her years ago in her home village. Did Reina threaten to blackmail her? Tell the rabbi about her bigamy?" I had questions. I hoped Leah would provide the answers.

"Nonsense."

Daniel Nauheim was angry enough that I thought he was going to throw me out of the car and make me walk back to London. His face grew redder as I continued.

"Both victims were struck from behind. They both felt safe turning their backs on their killer. And neither would fear a soft-spoken young woman like Leah."

"I will hear no more of this!"

Sir Henry broke in. "Livvy, are you sure?"

"Yes. Mrs. Grenbaum, Leah's aunt, whom I met in Prague, told me how badly Leah was suffering when she left prison in Germany and arrived in Prague. How happy Leah was when she met your son. How much Mrs. Grenbaum hoped that moving to London would make Leah feel safe." I glanced at Mr. Nauheim. "And Mrs. Grenbaum told me her husband's name was Josef Meirsohn."

"There must be more than one Josef Meirsohn," Mr. Nauheim growled.

"Who was jailed by the Nazis early in their reign? Valerie Mandel noticed that Elias recognized someone at the meeting. Someone he didn't go over and speak to. Did Leah speak with him at any time during that meeting?"

Mr. Nauheim shook his head.

"When we had dinner, your son David teased Leah about not having been able to take her eyes off the handsome Elias. Are you certain they never spoke?"

"Only to say hello. Not more than a minute." Nauheim frowned at me. "I'll question her. I will. And we'll see what she has to say."

"We'll go with you," Sir Henry said.

Mr. Nauheim appeared ready to argue, but then he turned to me. "He called himself Elias. How do you know he was really Josef Meirsohn?"

"From Reina."

"She's dead," he said in a brutal tone.

"Meirsohn, or Elias, whichever you want to call him, was also a British spy. The British general who told me this knew him by both names."

"If he was a British spy, that's all the more reason for the Nazis to assassinate him." Nauheim glared at me.

"If the Nazis assassinated him, there was no need to kill Reina. But if Reina and Leah met up, Reina would have realized the truth. Leah killed her husband to hide the truth of their marriage."

Mr. Nauheim appeared to deflate. After a minute, he rallied and said, "We will ask Leah. We will not judge her until she can speak for herself."

We rode in silence for the rest of the trip to Richmond.

When we arrived at his beautiful, well-proportioned

home, we climbed out of the auto by the walkway to the front door. Since I'd been squished in the middle and was already tired from my journey, I made a stiff, ungraceful exit from the back seat. Fortunately, it was growing dark so I doubted anyone noticed.

We went inside to find David and Leah waiting to invite us into the small parlor for tea. As Leah poured, Mr. Nauheim rose from his chair and poured himself a glass of brandy. It was then I saw Leah's hand shake.

Her husband, David, didn't seem to notice as he asked me about the trip. I told him I'd brought back all that the people of Prague had sent as individuals and as congregations. I was amazed at how little interest the shipment had generated along the journey, and there had been no problems.

I barely had the last words out when Mr. Nauheim said, "Leah, were you married to Josef Meirsohn before you married David?"

"You know I was." Her voice was barely above a whisper.

"And Josef Meirsohn was Elias." Mr. Nauheim sounded brokenhearted as he spoke those words.

"No," came out as a sob.

David rose and said, "What is this?"

I kept my voice calm and quiet as I sat down by her. "You recognized Josef at the meeting where he spoke to the committee. That must have been a shock. You thought he died in a Nazi prison. You thought he was dead."

She looked at me through teary wide eyes and nodded.

David dropped back down into his seat next to his wife.

"But if Josef was still alive, that meant you were still married to him. A strong-willed, dedicated man like Josef would expect you to return to Germany with him. To take up his crusade against Nazi tyranny. You didn't want to return there after what the Nazis did to you." I understood that would have been a nightmare for any woman, particularly one as fragile as Leah.

Again she nodded.

"Did you ask Josef to forget he saw you? To tell no one he was your husband? To go back to Europe and fight his fight alone?"

This time, her nod was accompanied by tears streaming down her face.

"He wouldn't agree to that, would he? He was going to tell."

"He was going to tell David. I had to stop him." Her voice was little more than a whisper.

"You killed him?" David said, peering closely at her face.

"Yes," she sobbed. "I'd rather die than go back there. I'd rather die than leave you. It was easy to find out where Josef was staying. I went there to talk to him, but he was leaving the hotel. I followed him to that basement."

CHAPTER TWENTY-NINE

Leah's whole body shuddered before she continued. "He had our wedding certificate. He said that meant I had to go back to Germany with him. I was his wife." She looked at David. "But I am your wife now. You are my only husband. I will not go back."

"Why did you have a length of pipe with you?"

"I carry one in my purse all the time. I never know when I might get cornered by SS troopers. I won't let them take me. Not again. Never again."

"There are no SS in London," David said in a soft tone.

"They are everywhere," Leah said in a monotone.

"But a length of pipe? Leah, where did you find it?" David asked.

"There are plenty in the basement, left over from a repair, I suppose." She shrugged.

"What did you do with the marriage certificate?" I asked.

"I tore it up and threw everything from his pockets in a dust bin down the road." Her voice was growing calmer. Less hysterical. But she sounded as if she were answering by rote.

I still didn't know the answer to the question I most wanted to learn. "Where did you meet Reina? Why did she have to die?"

"I met her at the synagogue. She recognized me and

said we needed to talk. She still loved Josef. She took me back to that basement, to show me where he died and to tell me she never received whatever he wanted her to keep safe. I think she would have realized what I'd done, so I had to kill her too. I can't go back to Germany. To prison. Don't you see? I can't go back there." Her monotone broke on the last words.

She began to sob then, a piteous sound that wracked her body as it escaped. She swayed as she sobbed, her eyes closed and her mouth open.

Mr. Nauheim rose and walked toward the hall.

"Father? Where are you going?" David asked.

"I'm calling our solicitor. I want him here when the police arrive."

"No!" David shouted, an echo of his father just a short time earlier.

I put out a hand to him. "The only way you can get help for Leah is to be completely honest with your solicitor and the police. I think after what she's been through, she'll go to a mental institution rather than hang."

I turned to Leah. "You'll be safe there. And there you'll have hope for a future. Away from danger. Away from the Nazis."

Sir Henry and I sat in the Nauheims' small parlor with our teacups as we waited until the solicitor came and took Leah and David into another room. Then he returned and held a hasty meeting with the elder Mr. Nauheim.

When he heard my part in her confession, the

solicitor told me to stay. Daniel Nauheim and Sir Henry locked gazes before Sir Henry said, "I'll stay too. I'm as responsible as anyone for Livvy hunting for the killer."

Luckily, I'd had a decent amount of sleep on the ferry from Denmark, or I would have fallen asleep in my comfortable chair. Sir Henry and Daniel passed each other as they paced the room on ancient, thin rugs with faded patterns. Their constant movement began to give me a headache.

A phone rang in the hall and Daniel Nauheim went to answer it. He kept his voice low. When he returned, he told me Mr. and Mrs. Mandel had arrived at the bank in the City of London where the goods I had transferred were now stored in the vault.

I breathed a sigh of relief, but it didn't seem important. Not when I could hear Leah sobbing and moaning in another room.

Shortly afterward, the tall, dry-looking solicitor came out and conferred again with Mr. Nauheim before walking out to the phone in the hall. I heard him ask for a doctor. I suspected a psychoanalyst.

Then he called the police, requesting a specific Scotland Yard detective. I wished it were possible for Adam to arrive with whomever was sent from the Yard.

No such luck. And just seeing the constables in uniform sent Leah into hysterics. Fortunately, the doctor showed up and gave her a shot that not only calmed her down but put her to sleep.

The room fell silent as David scooped up his wife in his arms and carried her up to their room.

The detective, a chief inspector that the solicitor knew, made Daniel promise to bring Leah to Scotland Yard the next morning for a formal interview. The doctor insisted on attending as well.

Then the detective sat across from me and had me tell him the whole story. Sir Henry and I received some skeptical looks when I told him about some of my actions. He didn't appear to be the type who would miss things, so I told him everything he could possibly want to know. Sir Henry verified some of the more outrageous events.

The detective instructed the sergeant taking notes to get in contact with Adam, who had been attached to Scotland Yard's investigation into these murders. I hoped that meant he'd have to come back to London immediately.

I didn't tell him about the hunt for the French assassin or my role in it. I didn't think General Alford would like it if I brought his name into this.

I was told not to leave town and to make myself available for further questioning. That was fine with me. I'd done enough traveling for the present.

Sir Henry had the Nauheim staff call us a taxi and we rode back in the dark. "I hope you'll be at work tomorrow," Sir Henry said while we waited for a traffic light.

"I hope so, too," I answered, looking at the familiar London traffic and buildings and relieved to finally return home. "Are you going to tell Esther who the murderer is, or shall I?"

"I will," he grumbled. "She's going to be angry."

"At me," I added.

"At you," he agreed. "But this was a very successful investigation. We should be able to sell some papers while we build up sympathy for Leah. It might even make getting refugees admitted to England easier."

"Unless people will be afraid they'll be murdered by the refugees," I said.

"No. Not when we finish writing up this story."

He sounded certain. I felt sick. Leah wouldn't want to be at the center of a controversy, read about over London's morning coffee.

Sir Henry dropped me off at my building. I rode up to my flat, lugging my suitcase that seemed to get heavier with every step.

Whether Leah hanged or whether she ended up in an asylum, she'd never forgive me. Her husband and father-in-law would never forgive me. Esther would probably kill me herself for trespassing on our friendship.

Why did I persist in searching for the killer? It didn't bring anyone back to life. It might bring the planet back into balance, but it certainly didn't make me more popular.

As I dropped my suitcase inside the door of my flat and picked up the mail off the hall rug, a little voice inside me said, "Because murder is wrong, catching killers is the right thing to do, and you do it very well. Even your father admits you're good at uncovering secrets."

Even if it hurt sometimes.

CHAPTER THIRTY

I rose early the next morning, looked at the dreary sky leaking on everything in London, and put on a somber dress. The last thing I wanted to do was walk from the Underground to Mimi's salon, getting splashed by passing buses and tangled with other people's umbrellas.

There was no reason for it. Mimi probably wouldn't speak to me. She might not care who killed Reina or know where Fleur had gone. She would probably blame everything on me.

And in a way, it was my fault. I wanted to do a story on someone I idolized as a fashion genius. I saw a chance the day I met Mimi at Lady Patricia's fitting in the Duke of Marshburn's drawing room, and I seized the opportunity with both hands. I didn't realize until too late that I might not like the person who carried that genius inside her.

I walked up the opposite side of Old Burlington Street and gazed up at the building that held the *Maison Mareau*. There was a removals van parked outside the door and in front of the van was a familiar, fast-looking red two-seat tourer with the canvas top up against the weather. I couldn't make out the features of the man sitting in the driver's seat of the smart car.

Pulling out my notebook, I flipped open to the page

where I'd jotted down the license plate number of the Duke of Marshburn's car. I glanced up. That was the auto.

At that moment, a flash caught my eye. A woman in wide, low heels raced out, water splashing up at every step, and jumped into the passenger seat of the high-powered auto. She was perfectly dressed, a big hat covering her hair, without a thread out of place as she dashed. I was surprised Mimi was wearing sensible footwear for the weather.

As soon as the woman was seated and the door shut, the car roared to life and raced down the street with a mixture of speed and authority.

The perfect image of the Duke of Marshburn and Mimi Mareau as they dashed off to Scotland or the Riviera or the wilds of Africa. There was a time when I would have been envious, but that was a time before I'd met them.

I walked up to the open front door and stepped inside to get out of the way of two men carrying a modernistic black bench that had been in the showroom.

"Taking it back to France?" I asked Brigette as she walked up behind me.

"All the furnishings are being moved to a warehouse owned by the duke. He's renting the building to a firm of solicitors."

I turned to look at her. "So Mimi hasn't written off having a London salon in the future?"

"She's lost her lead seamstress and her lead cutter. It will take a long time to rebuild the business. We've sent the seamstresses back to Paris to complete the last few orders from our London couture house." Brigette stood with her arms crossed, glaring at the front door.

"At least she has you. Everyone else can be replaced."

"Until next autumn. Then I'm going to university."

"In France?"

"Of course."

"What are you doing here?" Mimi's shrill voice cut my back to ribbons. "Writing a piece on the end of the French invasion into British fashion?"

My heart skipped and thudded when I realized that hadn't been Mimi in her lover's car. Was the duke driving? "I came to say I'm sorry about how things ended. And to tell you Reina's killer confessed."

When she didn't immediately respond, I swung around to look her in the face. Her expression changed from sad to hard and bitter. "Who was it?" she finally asked.

"The wife of the man who was killed in your basement. Reina had known the man when they were children, and the wife considered Reina a threat to her secret."

Mimi frowned. "We both know Reina couldn't have seen the man killed. She was away from here shopping."

"The woman's secret was she was also married to a British man, making her a bigamist. Her British marriage was invalid. She didn't want to be sent back to Germany any more than Reina did."

"She was Jewish." Mimi nodded and watched more furniture go out through the door. "They complain about Hitler, and then they kill each other. Fools."

She didn't look at me and so missed the glare I gave her. "Who was the woman riding off with the Duke of Marshburn?"

"Oh. Was he here?" Her tone rang with false innocence.

"Yes. Who was she?" And then it hit me. "Fleur. No wonder they couldn't find her in France."

"They won't find her here either." Mimi sounded smug.

"Do you like your chief cutter riding around town with your lover in his fast motorcar? They're both likely to end up in jail."

"Perhaps. Perhaps not. He is a duke, and I've been told that means something in this country."

It meant a great deal. It would make the Duke of Marshburn, and Fleur, practically unstoppable. She would be free to try to attack Churchill again, or the cabinet, or the king. The whole business made me sick.

I wanted to punish Mimi for not being who I wanted her to be. I blurted out, "Reina's killer had the same last name as Brigette's father. She could be Brigette's half-sister."

All the color drained out of Mimi's face.

I walked out into the cool October drizzle. I was angry at not being able to definitely identify Fleur. I was angry at Mimi for protecting a Nazi assassin in her fashion house. I was angry at a British duke helping a Nazi agent.

And I was angry at myself for the cruel taunt I had thrown at Mimi.

My feet were soaked by the time I reached the *Daily Premier* building, but my anger had kept me warm. I left my coat, hat, and umbrella in the cloakroom and hurried into our office. Fortunately, I was only a few minutes late and Miss Westcott, after all my recent disappearances, didn't seem to notice.

I called Sir Henry's office and was put directly through. "I just saw a woman I think was Fleur leaving Mimi's salon in the Duke of Marshburn's auto. And Mimi didn't deny it."

"Are you certain it was her?"

"No. She was wearing a big hat. I couldn't see her face."

"The army is awash with sightings of Fleur. I don't think they'd appreciate another one." At my huff of aggravation, Sir Henry said, "They'll catch her. And it's time for you to get back to doing your normal job."

I did. About eleven o'clock, Miss Westcott called me to her desk as she held the telephone receiver out to one side. "Sir Henry's office," she said.

"Hello?" I said.

"Mrs. Denis? Mrs. Olivia Denis?" a man's voice asked.

"Yes."

He identified himself as a Scotland Yard detective. "We want to speak to you in Sir Henry Benton's office as soon as possible."

"I'll be right up."

I hurried upstairs where Sir Henry's secretary pointed me toward the conference room. I walked in to find two detectives in limp three-piece suits and two constables in pristine uniforms facing Sir Henry. Two men in army uniforms stood nearby.

"When you get done with this lot," Sir Henry said, "come to my office."

"Yes, sir. Esther?" I added.

"Furious."

I was afraid of that. She was fond of Leah.

Sir Henry left and I was invited to sit. As soon as I did, one of the army officers said, "You are not to divulge any information you learned at Mimi Mareau's salon or in Kent."

"Understood."

The detective said, "What is this?"

"Don't worry," I told him. "Everything you want to know has nothing to do with the matter they are protecting. Ask your questions."

They did, mostly about my conversations with Leah, Mrs. Grenbaum in Prague, and Reina. The army men looked relieved when the Scotland Yard men finished with me.

"Is Captain Redmond currently in London?" I asked.

The army men looked as if they'd like to fidget. "Not yet," one of them told me.

I felt the first flash of hope. "Then he'll be here soon?"

"He's been recalled."

I almost asked from where before I stopped myself. That was the kind of question they couldn't answer.

As soon as the Scotland Yard men were out of the room, I told the army men, "I believe I saw Fleur here in London in the Duke of Marshburn's car."

"Were you close enough to see her face?"

"No. She was wearing a big hat. But Mimi Mareau didn't deny it when I asked her."

"Thank you for telling us," one of the officers said. It was obvious from his tone that my information would go no further.

The rest of the day dragged without any word from Adam. As soon as I could, I went straight home and waited for the phone to ring.

About seven, the phone finally rang and I raced to pick up the receiver. "Livvy," Esther's voice came through the line to me, "they've decided Leah isn't fit to stand trial. She's going to a sanitarium where they're going to try to help her. David is standing by her, and Mr. Nauheim has arranged for them to be married again by a rabbi. A very simple ceremony, but one that will be legal."

"I'm glad for them, but I'm sorry I didn't realize how ill she was before Reina was killed," I told her.

"None of us did. We all failed her," Esther said. I was relieved she had calmed down.

"Do you forgive me for telling Mr. Nauheim and your father what I learned in Prague?"

"Of course. You had to uncover all the nasty secrets surrounding the murders, and you had to tell the truth."

"Thank goodness. I don't think I could stand it if you never spoke to me again," I admitted.

"After we sent you there, and after what you did for the Jews in Prague? Livvy, we owe you. I owe you."

I was about to ask exactly what I had done besides being a goods transporter when I heard a knock on my door. "Esther, I've got to run. Someone's at my door."

"Adam?"

"I hope so." I hung up before she had a chance to reply.

When I threw open the door, Adam was standing there with his teasing grin and his gorgeous hazel eyes and his wide shoulders. I leaped into his arms. Between kisses, I said, "I'm so glad you're back."

"I'm glad you're back from Prague. I was worried about you."

Without letting go of each other, we managed to get inside my flat and shut the door. When we came up for air, I asked, "What happened in France?"

"Fleur escaped into Germany. Fleur isn't her real name, but we don't know what it is. We have her photograph at every border crossing, thanks to you."

"I think I saw her in front of Mimi's salon in the Duke of Marshburn's auto. And before you ask, she was wearing a big hat."

"And you didn't see her face. We get a lot of those. Livvy, it could have been anybody. We suspect some of these sightings are arranged to throw us off the trail. We're pretty sure she's in Germany now." He gave me another kiss. "And I heard you caught Elias's killer."

"It was his wife."

"Really?" He chuckled. "Maybe I should forget this getting married idea."

"She was a bigamist, married to an Englishman the second time. She'd thought he died in prison, and she didn't want anyone to force her to go back to Germany.

I'm not married, and I'm not German. So you should be safe."

"In that case…" Adam reached into his suit jacket pocket and pulled something out. When he held it out to me, I saw it was a little box, already opened. And inside was a delicate gold band with a small shining diamond.

I took it out and put it on my finger. By some miracle, it fit perfectly. "It's beautiful."

"Your father had a ring of your mother's he said fit you, so I used that to get the right size. It's all right?"

My jaw dropped before I managed to say, "My father knows we're engaged?"

"Yes." When he saw the look on my face, he cringed.

"The ring fits. We're engaged. And my father knows." I took a deep breath. "Two out of three isn't bad."

Then I smiled and hugged him close. "In fact, it's tremendous. I love you, Adam."

"I love you, Livvy. Now if we can stop running all over for our jobs, maybe we can sit down and talk about a wedding. Please."

I looked at the ring that symbolized his love for me and smiled. "That sounds wonderful. Let's talk."

If you enjoyed Olivia's newest adventure, here is a FREE short story about her first investigation. Sign up for my newsletter list for occasional email messages at https://dl.bookfunnel.com/o38fytkiuq.

Download your FREE short story and read it today!

Author's Notes

I've been fascinated by the clothing styles of the late 1930's for quite some time. So elegant. So sexy. So mysterious. And this led to my interest in Coco Chanel, a leading French fashion designer who reinvented herself at least twice, but whose styles were so timeless they didn't need to be changed. She led an amazing life, including designing for the London stage and the American movies as well as taking a British duke for a lover.

I fictionalized her life and came up with Mimi Mareau. Unlike Coco, Mimi began a London haute couture establishment where the action of this story starts.

I have to admit, pouring over book after book of clothing designs from the 1930's while doing research for this book has been a pleasure. I've given Olivia my love of fashion, but I've also given her the flair to carry off wearing these styles and a talent for sketching them that I lack.

An article found in the British Library newspaper files for 1938 led to the French assassin. The article in the London Sunday Express was about a female German spymaster. No one knew her real name or had a good description of her, allowing her to keep her freedom as she moved from country to country. I was fascinated with the possibilities.

Again, I have to thank Jen Parker, Elizabeth Flynn,

and Jennifer Brown for their help and unfailing support in making Deadly Fashion a better story. Removal of Americanisms was aided by the editing of Les Floyd.

I hope you enjoy Olivia's adventures. If you do, tell someone. Word of mouth is still the best way to discover good new reads. Reviews are also a good way to tell others about books that you've enjoyed.

About the Author

Kate Parker grew up reading her mother's collection of mystery books and her father's library of history and biography books. Now she can't write a story that isn't set in the past with a few decent corpses littered about. It took her years to convince her husband she hadn't poisoned dinner; that funny taste is because she can't cook. Now she can read books on poisons and other lethal means at the dinner table and he doesn't blink.

Their children have grown up to be surprisingly normal, but two of them are developing their own love of creating literary mayhem, so the term "normal" may have to be revised.

Living in a nineteenth century town has further inspired Kate's love of history. But as much as she loves stately architecture and vintage clothing, she has also developed an appreciation of central heating and air conditioning. She's discovered life in coastal Carolina requires her to wear shorts and T-shirts while drinking hot tea and it takes a great deal of imagination to picture cool, misty weather when it's 90 degrees out and sunny.

Follow Kate and her deadly examination of history at www.KateParkerbooks.com
and www.Facebook.com/Author.Kate.Parker/
and www.Bookbub.com/authors/kate-parker

Made in the USA
Las Vegas, NV
18 April 2024